At long last we get to hear Baby Doe's compelling side of the hurtful tale that made her the most hated woman in the West. Donna Baier Stein has captured young Lizzie Doe's agency in her first marriage, as well as older Lizzie Tabor's deep spiritual resilience during her decades of isolation. Through Stein's artistry, Baby Doe's story makes the heart ache.

—Judy Nolte Temple, author of *Baby Doe Tabor: The Madwoman in the Cabin*

Explosive, gripping and romantic, *The Silver Baron's Wife* is a story that exposes not only the scandalous marriage and perplexing life of a woman who starred in the wealthy 19th century social circles while being shunned from them. It also opens a fascinating window into 19th century American social mores and Washington DC's politics.

An absorbing read about a fiercely independent woman who charted her own course only to find herself paying the price.

—Talia Carner, author of *Hotel Moscow*, *Jerusalem Maiden*, *China Doll*, and *Puppet Child*

The Silver Baron's Wife is a beautiful and absorbing novel, rich in history and vivid period detail. In exquisite prose, Donna Baier Stein captures the extraordinary and tumultuous life of Lizzie "Baby Doe" Tabor, with all of its longings, joys, and tragedies. This is a moving and memorable book.

—Ronna Wineberg, author of *Seven Facts That Can Change Your Life*, *On Bittersweet Place*, and *Second Language*

With *The Silver Baron's Wife*, Donna Baier Stein pulls off that most difficult of novelistic feats: breathing fictional life into historic characters and situations. From the dark, unpropitious, and dismal depths of Baby Doe Tabor's biography, she mines a vein of pure silver.

—Peter Selgin, author of *The Inventors, Drowning Lessons,* and *Life Goes To The Movies*

Donna Baier Stein paints a heartfelt, poignant picture filled with loving details of Baby Doe's celebrated life that lingers long after the last page is turned.

—Ann Parker, author of *The Silver Rush Mystery Series*

Donna Baier Stein reveals the deeper levels of Baby Doe Tabor, the fascinating 19th century woman who caught silver mining fever, and whose fortune vacillated again and again between stunning riches and hardscrabble dearth. Having lost children, spouses, and wealth Lizzie is drawn more than ever to the invisible world, yearning to know if the dreams and visitations which have guided her life are real. With sumptuous, tactile prose, rich historical detail, and an evocative recreation of the American West, *The Silver Baron's Wife* excavates the legend of Elizabeth McCourt Tabor to expose a character's humanity and soul.

—Diane Bonavist, author of *Purged by Fire: The Cathar Heresy*

The Silver Baron's Wife

by

Donna Baier Stein

Serving House Books

The Silver Baron's Wife

ISBN: 978-0-9971010-6-5

Serving House Books logo by Barry Lereng Wilmont

Author photo by Denise Winters

Published by Serving House Books, LLC
Copenhagen, Denmark and Florham Park, NJ

www.servinghousebooks.com

Member of the Independant Book Publishers Association

First Serving House Books Edition 2016

Cover design by Allen Mohr of Allen Mohr Creative Services https://www.behance.net/AllenMohr

Map image courtesy of The Philadelphia Print Shop, Ltd., Philadelphia, PA www.philaprintshop.com

Cover photos:
Photo of Baby Doe Tabor in front of mine by Florence Greenleaf, The Denver Public Library, Western History Collection, Call Number Z-14609

Photo of Baby Doe Tabor in ermine coat from the Horace Austin Warner Tabor Collection, Mss.00614 (Scan #10025178), History Colorado, Denver, Colorado

Dedicated to my beloved father, Martin Baier, 1922-2016

*"I also think this: Nostalgia is roused in us
less by the memory of what once actually was
than by the memory of what once was possible in our dreams."*

James McConkey, "Fireflies"
The New Yorker, July 18, 1977

*"Yes: I am a dreamer. For a dreamer is one
who can only find his way by moonlight,
and his punishment is that he sees the dawn
before the rest of the world."*

Oscar Wilde
"The Critic as Artist," 1891

The novel that follows is a work of fiction.
It is by no means intended to be
a completely accurate historical re-creation
of the life of Baby Doe Tabor,
though the dreams shared are her actual writings,
many of which are housed in the Colorado Historical Society.

March 1935
Leadville, Colorado

I know she's here. Even if I can't always see her. It's the warmth I feel at the base of my spine, the sense of a hand almost brushing my shoulder, that tells me Mama's spirit hangs nearby. There, by the bed with its snarl of gray blankets.

I shake snow off my heavy cloak, hang my hat on a rusty nail by the cabin door.

I've been sick all week now, and the steep walk up Fryer Hill has tired me more than usual. Today I had to make my way through high, white drifts of snow. I slipped and fell, at times even had to go down on hands and knees. God bless Mr. Zaitz for driving me and my few groceries at least part way, to our usual getting-off place, the curve at the end of Seventh Street. I'm 81, usually strong, except lately I've felt a terrible weariness I cannot shake. When I lean against the cabin wall to pull off my work boots and the sheets of newspaper stuck inside them for warmth, I stop to catch my breath.

I'm afraid to really look toward my bed and its iron headpiece in the shape of an egg. Afraid I'll see the spirit of my mother and afraid that I won't.

I empty the gunnysack. There's turpentine and lard to clear my chest, stinging nettle to help me breathe, eight new brown eggs, thin slices of salt beef, pale yellow corn meal, and Colorado wheat flour. I put the eggs in a mix of coarse salt and un-slacked limes so they'll keep fresh and sweet.

I know this storm will last a good long while, and outside, in spots, snow has already drifted higher than my small frame.

I asked Mr. Zaitz's boy Teddy, the one whose green eyes narrow in scorn whenever we cross paths in town, to haul up, no later than tomorrow, the remainder of my supplies. The love of my life, one of the wealthiest men in this country, set that boy's grandfather up in business nearly forty years ago. Sometimes, when I see how shamed Mr. Zaitz is by his son's behavior, I want to speak.

Mr. Zaitz whispers, "That's Mrs. Tabor, Teddy. Don't be impolite."

The boy pretends not to hear.

Sometimes I wonder if anyone remembers anymore.

I push aside a jar of green tomato ketchup, knocking over a tall canister. The opened canister releases the smell of sage. I breathe deeply then drop snow into an iron kettle, clean handfuls of the white powder I stuck in my pockets as I neared the cabin. As I bend to stir the fire, I hear, or think I hear, the sigh of the canvas curtain behind my bed.

With one hand tucked in the small of my back for support, I turn.

Two calendars from Zaitz's swing from wood screws on the far wall— one from this year and one from last. A dome-topped trunk stands sentinel at the foot of the bed.

I force myself to stare without expectation. The gray blankets and pale sheets don't stir. But from the corner of my eye, did I catch the rocker moving? So slightly I could not be sure but so vividly I could not doubt?

"Is that you, Mama?" My heart cries out for her to answer.

I turn back to see the water in the kettle begin to bubble. This is the way creation happens. An untouched surface, chaos disrupting, and change. Some primal substance that is different but the same as what was before.

I drop the wrinkled leaves of sage into a china cup I've saved, as best as one can save a memory, a fragile physical thing. A whiskery brown crack runs from its lip to base.

I take the cup in both hands and walk toward the dome-topped trunk. I kneel, set the cup on the floor, finger the brass button nails, leather straps, and lock bearing the raised image of a hawk.

If only the Zaitz boy could see what lies under this hawk's care: the Belgian lace baby caps and English silver tea set, my love's porcelain shaving mug, the ermine collars and cuffs of my opera coat.

To my left, I see the rocker. It does seem to move, almost invisibly but still as though it is something alive, wanting to speak to me. I know they are already here, Mama and others like her, waiting for our eyes to see and ears to hear, waiting for the mind of the world to open.

I've marked their visits on Zaitz's calendars:

> I saw the spirit of Lily Langtry today, gold and pink
> on blue snow.

or

> I saw the younger of my daughters, Silver Dollar,
> astride a big red, gold horse. So big it was, as big as

four or five normal horses.

Leaving the trunk open, I raise myself with difficulty and look to the window behind my bed. The glass ripples within the pane, and beyond, snow still falls.

"If you're in the rocker, Mama, I wish you would show me."

Why should she begrudge me now? When I am so tired, and it is so cold, and I have tried so hard for so long. I sit in the rocker, almost taunting it. There's a Bible underneath its seat slats, and I pull it to my lap then open it to read:

> Out of heaven he made thee to hear his voice,
> that he might instruct thee: and upon earth
> he showed thee his great fire.

I close my eyes and remember.

CHAPTER 1

August 1866
Oshkosh, Wisconsin

For nearly three months there hadn't been rain enough to lay the dust. By August we were choking on it. Even the wind that ruffled the bluestem grasses of the prairies and the slate surface of Lake Winnebago blew hot or not at all. We took to squinting against a fiery sun. Sprinkling wagons drove up and down our streets, but Oshkosh stayed dry and ready for change.

It was the day of my confirmation, the day the Holy Spirit would descend upon me. I stood in front of Mama in the house on Algoma Street, wearing a beautiful white gown, turning slowly before her. All the bedroom's windows were open, but no breeze stirred.

Mama touched my hip and turned me another half circle. "Something more," she said, worrying the straight pins she held in her mouth. "It needs a bit of fancy."

She'd persuaded Papa to give her three yards of white satin and one of white organza from his tailoring shop and sewn me a dress with puffed sleeves and a shimmering white ribbon sash.

I caught a glimpse of us in the tall mirror by hers and Papa's bed. Papa always said I looked like a cherub with my blond curls and violet eyes. But Mama, kneeling before me, still frowned. She pulled the pins from her mouth and stuck them in a cushion the shape of a strawberry. As I watched in the mirror, she stood and walked toward the bed she and Papa had brought to Wisconsin from Ireland. She picked up a magazine that lay on the bed's woven blue-and-white coverlet.

"Look," she said, pointing to a photo of an ornate necklace with five large pear-shaped diamonds surrounded by smaller round diamonds. "The Khedive of Egypt gave this to General Sherman's daughter for her wedding." Her eyes went dreamy, the way they did when she read her books of romance and adventure. "How I would love to see you in such beautiful jewels one day!"

I sighed. I really didn't share my Mama's passion for jewelry. All I wanted that moment was to get to the church so I could feel the one true fact of Jesus enter my life. Truth be told, Mama's desire for expensive things made me nervous. But she had given up so much, she often reminded us, when she married Papa and followed him to America, I felt I owed it to her to share her sharp longings for material things.

"It's all right, sweet Mama," I said, chewing on my lip. "I don't need anything else. My dress is fine just as it is. And the jewels aren't what's most important right now."

She muttered something I couldn't hear then left the room. I remained in front of the mirror, slowly spinning to see how the ribbon sash caught the light from one window. When she returned, three carved mother-of-pearl buttons rolled on her palm.

"These will do," she said. "I'll make a shamrock. Sign of the trinity. I looked for a real one growing in the yard yesterday but found only wood sorrel. So this will have to do."

I recognized the buttons from her wedding dress, another treasure she'd carried across the ocean.

She put a finger to her lip. "Ssshhhh," she said. "This is our secret. Not for Papa's ears, remember. I'll sew them back on tomorrow, but today they are my baby's."

I started to say that after today I would no longer be a baby, not in the eyes of the Church anyway, but thought better of it.

"Thank you, Mama." I stood still while she removed my satin headband and stitched the buttons in a three-petalled shape, adding a thin line of silver embroidery at their base for the stem.

Just as she tucked the headband back in my hair, Papa's voice boomed up from the parlor. "Are you beloveds ready then?" He tapped the newel post at the base of the staircase. "It's stifling in these dress-up clothes, and poor P.D. is about to faint, all stuffed up as he is in that vest you've made him wear."

Mama rubbed a finger over the mother-of-pearl shamrock. "With a prayer for more jewels in your future," she said and quickly kissed my forehead. Then she brought the silver crucifix that always hung around her neck to her lips, closing her eyes in silent prayer. I watched Mama carefully whenever she kneeled in prayer at Mass or made the sign of the cross two dozen times a day at home. I'd had a few of my own short, brilliant moments when I believed that Jesus not only hung in plaster on the wall above the bed I shared with my older sister Cordelia but could also be felt as a Real Presence beside me. I'd tried so hard to feel His hand on my shoulder as I turned the pages of my confirmation lesson, sitting next to our parish priest, or to hear Him whisper in my ear as I bent over the examination I'd so feared.

After I passed the exam, Father Bonduel told me how, twelve years earlier, he'd seen my parents carry me into St. Peter's, or rather into a smaller version of our church, for my baptism. And on my confirmation day, he would ask me to renew the promises made then by Mama and Papa and commit myself anew to following Christ. I assured him I was more than ready.

It was sweltering inside St. Peter's that day, and throughout the congregation women and even some men waved pleated fans of silk and painted paper back and forth. Because my family, the McCourts, had helped build the first small Catholic church and rectory in Oshkosh, we had a pew near the front. I sat there, squeezed between Cordelia and Stephen, with P.D., Barrett, Lucy, Adela, and Colt to our right. Baby Abigail sat on Mama's lap, reaching up to play with the collar of Papa's shirt, which was already gray with sweat.

When my name was called I stood, shaking like a leaf as I left my family in the pew and made my way toward the tall wooden altar. To keep my balance and calm my nerves, I focused my eyes on Father Bonduel's snowy white linen vestments, his three-cornered hat, his high Roman collar. I loved every bit of ceremony in my faith. Every bronze candlestick, every silver bowl, every statue of a saint excited me.

As long as I could remember, we'd come to St. Peter's every Sunday to listen to the Father preach. It was sometimes hard to follow him in prayer despite the fact that the missal showed Latin on one side and English on the other. When I was little, I'd amuse myself by making faces at my brothers and sisters, slide around restlessly on the pew. But as soon as Mama and Papa and Cordelia stood to receive communion, I'd stop fidgeting and pay close attention. More than anything, I wanted to take part in the mysterious ritual I saw unrolling before me.

Father Bonduel touched my shoulder with his hand, startling me. His silver signet ring with a stag's head flashed as his finger traced the sign of the cross on my forehead.

"*Accipe signaculum doni Spiritus Sancti.* May you be sealed with the gift of the Holy Spirit," he whispered into my ear.

I'd already confessed my sins to him the week before: Slipping NECCO wafers into my pocket at Pickering's Grocery. Staying up late to read if the moon was bright. Liking a boy I shouldn't like, simply because the fine lines of his face, his blue-black hair and long lashes, made my stomach flip in somersaults. Harvey Doe was Protestant, and I blushed as I confessed to Father Bonduel how often I snuck glances at this handsome boy in school. Somehow the priest—and I assumed Jesus—forgave me and there I was, kneeling in front of the Father to receive communion, my head tilted back, mouth open and tongue extended. I held my breath and waited, eyes fixed firmly on the large wooden crucifix behind the Father's shoulder.

The Sacred Host landed on my tongue. At my first communion, Mama had told me not to chew it but let it soften. I'd been afraid I might close my mouth too soon, like a snapping turtle, but the Father's fingers with their large rings were gone, and I closed my lips and swallowed, the thin wafer remaining. When it stuck to the roof of my mouth, I pried it loose with my tongue. The congregation continued to whip their fans back and forth behind me. My eyes stayed closed as I tried so hard to feel God's presence—in the tasteless wafer in my mouth, the piney smell of frankincense burning on the altar. I tried so hard to imagine the body of Christ filling up my own insides.

Father Bonduel prayed, "We humbly beseech You, almighty God, to grant that those whom You refresh with Your sacraments, may serve you worthily by a life well pleasing to You. Through our Lord Jesus Christ, Your Son, Who lives and reigns, world without end. Amen."

And then, I felt Him. I felt Jesus inside my bones, and hovering around the boundaries of my skin. I wanted the moment to last forever, but the priest touched my elbow and gestured for me to return to my family. Later I had to stand uncomfortably in the sweltering church hall, munching cookies and drinking punch with the other congregants. I had to smile at their well wishes when all I wanted to do was go home, lie in bed, and wait for my new Beloved Jesus to make His presence forever known to me. I knew that what had just occurred was a marriage to Christ I would never forsake.

After the service, I walked out of St. Peter's as though I were stepping into a new world. Almost immediately, I saw Harvey Doe walk up High Avenue across the way. When he stopped and stared at me in my beautiful white dress, he looked as though he'd seen an angel.

That night in a dream, a voice told me to prepare to meet the husband of my heart. I wanted it to be Jesus, but I also wanted it to be Harvey, though he appeared in the dream only briefly. I saw a fire devouring mannequins like Papa kept in the window of his tailoring shop. I saw swirling snow and long, dark tunnels. The images kept coming, weighted with some mysterious meaning: a man near the Capitol Building in Washington, a tall wooden cross rocking back and forth in a strong wind, a small painted box overflowing with precious gems. Silver wedding bands rolled across a floor like toy hoops.

I knew from Bible stories how often God used dreams and visions, and I wanted to be open to whatever messages they might hold. For my confirmation gift, I had asked Mama to buy me a softcover pocket diary at Pickering's, and the next morning, I wrote down the dream on its first page. I vowed that I would listen to whatever God wanted to tell me in my night-time visions, and I made a secret pocket in my under skirts so I'd always have the diary with me.

Two days after my confirmation, Mama asked me to play with my younger brothers and sisters in the yard. Cordelia was off with her beau Andrew Haben, so I was in charge. Mama sat in a rocker on the porch, cranky from the heat and doing her best to lose herself in a book. I'd gone with her to Mass earlier that morning, mimicked her as she rose and knelt, rose and knelt, marking the sign of the cross on her breast. I tried to make my eyelids flutter the way hers did.

I told the children we would have a pretend wedding in the yard. I found an old, once-white tablecloth and wrapped it around me like a makeshift wedding gown complete with train, then set the confirmation headband on my curls. Mama had already removed the mother-of-pearl shamrock and, I assumed, sewn the fancy buttons back on her wedding gown. I showed Lucy and Adela how to make a necklace out of wire and small beads to match the pattern of the one given to General Sherman's daughter. None of the older boys wanted to stand in as my pretend husband, but seven-year-old Colt finally agreed to put on one of Stephen's outgrown suits, stuffing the overlong pant legs into the tops of his boots.

A black cherry tree grew near the neighbor's wrought iron fence, and I sent my youngest brother P.D., who was four, up to sit on one of its low branches.

"You'll throw these down after I take my vows," I said, giving him a handful of cherry pits and small chunks of red bark.

We'd played versions of this make-believe before, but it held new meaning after my dream, and I wanted everything to be perfect. I positioned Stephen and Michael on either side of me as guests and instructed them to hold a long arched branch over Colt and me. I stood, eyes closed, trying to remember more details from the dream. Mama called out, "Elizabeth!" then, more gently, "Come here, please, Lizzie."

I glanced toward her. Faded pink slippers wilted next to her feet. The family Bible, also brought over from Ireland, rested on the floor beneath her rocker and her new book lay open on her lap. Often when Papa was at work, Mama read—stories of kings and queens, romances between dashing soldiers and young maidens. When she read, I knew I'd lost her to another world, one she fancied was better than the one in which she lived. This new Civil War romance, *The Wearing of the Grey*, had been written by a decorated lieutenant in the Army.

"I'll bet you he's handsome, and so famous now," she'd said with a faraway smile.

I lifted the train of my tablecloth gown, tied it tightly around my waist, and walked to the porch. To my dismay, the children immediately scattered away from the pretend wedding under the tree.

Mama wiped a line of sweat from above her lip. "I could stand a taste of lemonade right now. Would you be a good girl and bring me some? It's so *hot* out here!"

Barrett yelled out that Baby Abigail, who had been crawling around on the grass, was sticking her nose into a clump of clover where there might be bees.

"Shoo, Abigail, shoo!" Mama said then added, "Lots of ice but no sugar."

I went inside to the icebox in the kitchen and filled a tall glass with lemonade. As I stepped back outside and handed the glass to Mama, a woman screamed, "Fire at Morgan's Mill!" A second, then a third scream followed. The bell chime in the steeple of the First Presbyterian Church began to toll, and a man ran past our house, shouting, "Fire! Fire!"

Mama dropped her glass; lemonade spilled across the porch floorboards. She ran out to the yard to pick up Baby Abigail and gather us around her. An awful red glare was starting to spread low across the sky.

The face of our neighbor, the widow Belle Fritsch, appeared between the latticework of the fence that separated our yards. She waved her arms wildly even as she tried to reassure us. "Don't worry. It started way downtown, in Goat Town. It'll take a bit to get up here. There's time for us to get to the lake. Bring me some of those children so I can help."

Goat Town was a part of town I rarely saw, a place where wood shacks jammed together, butted up against stables, pig sties, and henhouses. Though my family was by no means rich, we lived in a part of Oshkosh known as the "Gold Coast." Besides Belle Fritsch, our neighbors included a lumber baron and Wisconsin's attorney general. Even Mayor Doe and his family lived in a large house at the end of our block.

P.D. dropped the cherry pits and bark I'd given him and clutched the folds of Mama's skirt, leaving red stains.

Three pigs scrambled down Algoma Street, and a woman, holding her skirts high, ran after them. A boy pulled a donkey cart with a little girl in it. Then more people came, and more, all rushing past us. I reached for Mama's hand and tried to speak, but the rattle of wheels buried my words. The colored barber who sometimes cut Papa's hair ran behind it, clutching a silver bowl in his arms.

Then Mr. McCutcheon, one of Papa's oldest tailoring customers, rode by on a chestnut horse. He held his young son in his arms and in front of the child, a carved wooden clock, the glass on its round face shattered.

"Joseph!" Mama yelled, "Joseph McCutcheon!"

He reined in his horse. "Fire's out of control!" he shouted. "It's hit the barbershop and the bank, and it's coming this way. Best move your family to the lake now!" Then he spurred the horse and rode on. Others followed behind him, staggering under heavy loads of blankets, clothes, and dishes. A terrible smell like scorched leather filled the air.

Mama turned to me. "Somebody's got to get Papa. He'll want to save everything in the shop, but he's got to get out of there!"

I realized I'd been expecting Papa to show up any minute, to tell us what to do.

But according to Mama, he wasn't going to do that. I would have to go get him, pull him away from the tailoring shop. "You'll make it," she shouted. She was already maneuvering the children over to Belle Fritsch. "We've got to get to the lake. Get Papa and meet us there. I'm sorry, Lizzie. But Papa won't leave that store without a reason. So go! Hurry!"

Baby Abigail wailed in Mama's arms, and Mama pushed me forward. "Meet us at the flat rock near the pier," she yelled. "Go!"

I ran off with the tablecloth still wrapped around me, and as I got closer to town I pulled it over my arms and head for protection from the heat and smoke. A man threw a horseshoe through the front window of Pearsall's Meat Market as I ran past. Mr. Pearsall, still behind the counter, shook his fist as the man lifted a slab of beef from its hook and disappeared with it back into the crowd.

Someone called out to me, "Going in the wrong direction! Turn around!" But I kept pushing against those running away from the fire, towards the safety of the lake. The tablecloth kept the smoke from my eyes, but hundreds of bright sparks and embers fell around me. Horses whinnied in fear as one after another glass storefront shattered and timbers crashed. Finally I saw Cameron & McCourt, the shop my father owned with Jack Cameron. Its front window was intact but the signs there— "Prepared to Supply All Your Tailoring Wants" and "Dealing Fairly and Honorably"—were scorched around their edges and burst into flames as

I made my way toward the front door. Before I reached it, a great piece of burning weatherboarding flew through the air above me.

"Papa!" I cried out.

The weatherboarding landed a few yards from me, crashing into a peddler's cart.

The storefront glass crumpled. A mannequin stood dressed in a frock coat and trousers. Its face was melting, and its beaver skin top hat burst into flames. Only a mechanical sewing machine stayed intact, though its wooden casing collapsed around it.

Someone yelled, "Commerce and Trade's going!"

I turned to see the wooden building across the street fall down then screwed up my courage and ran into the overwhelming heat of the shop.

Papa and Jack Cameron stood in front of a tall safe to the side. Cameron had three cash boxes in his arms and was loading up a fourth.

"Come on, Papa!"

He didn't move, didn't even acknowledge my presence.

I didn't know why he was letting his partner make off with all the money. When Cameron dropped one of the cash boxes, it burst open, spilling out Gold Eagles and silver dollars. I picked up what coins I could and stuffed them in my pockets.

Still clutching the other boxes, Cameron turned and pushed past me into the street.

Just then, a bolt of fabric to my right caught fire and fell to the floor. I kicked the burning piece away and grabbed my father's hand.

"We need to go," I begged. "We've got to get out of here."

His eyes were closed doors. I had never felt so invisible in my life. But finally he spoke. "I can't. It's all I have."

"No, it's not." I tugged on him.

"No," he said again, and I thought he might give up then, sit down and let the flames engulf us both.

I grabbed the lapels of his vest and screamed at him. "No, Papa, no! This isn't all you have!" I was so angry. "Come on now, Mama's waiting for us."

And that's what got him to move. He pushed me ahead of him out to the street. We ran side by side down the middle of the road, away from the buildings and the flammable goods inside them. Harding's Opera House, one of the few structures in town made of brick, still stood, but its windows were broken, and huge flames roared behind them. The coins I'd picked up weighted down my pockets and hit my thighs as I ran.

Finally, we reached the pier. There were hundreds of people there, but somehow we found Mama and Belle Fritsch and the children huddled together on the edge of the largest flat rock. Cordelia and her beau were there, too, and Andrew was busy setting down plaid blankets on a strip of sand. When Cordelia kissed the top of my head, I realized I was still wearing my confirmation headband. I pulled it down and saw that it was covered in soot and burned in several places.

I spotted Father Bonduel walking among the crowds. There was a splotch of ash on his right cheek, and his white robe was filthy and torn. His lips moved as he made the sign of the cross over peoples' heads. Harvey Doe and his mother and sisters sat at a picnic table under a shelter by the pier; his father the mayor stood at a podium giving a speech I couldn't hear. And all across the beach, clocks and clothes and dishes and saddles lay scattered.

By the time the sun dropped below the horizon, we heard news that the fire had been extinguished. But we spent the night there on the beach anyway, afraid of what we might find back on Algoma Street. I curled tightly next to my sister Cordelia, adjusted the lump that was my hidden pocket diary, and the next morning wrote down my second dream in it.

I dreamed Pa and Ma were sitting in a seat of a wagon & I was behind them others were standing around & all over was dark looking & dusky & Ma had on a big dark rich coat of heavy dark fur she looked very large Pa looked so young & bright & gay & had a smart brimmed hat on O so young looking & handsome & he talked gaily to me turning around to me all the time I said to Ma why don't the cook make us some pies & cakes & doughtnuts I am so hungry so hungry so hungry

CHAPTER 2

December 1876
Oshkosh, Wisconsin

My dearest Cordelia,

I hope you and Andrew are well and settling into your new home.
Seventy-five miles is such a long ways away from us, and we all miss you
so much. I can't believe it's been ten years since Andrew proposed to you
that night of the fire.

And now, I have my own exciting proposal to share. My beautiful,
beloved Harvey has asked me to marry him! Last week, after we'd spent
hours ice skating on the lake. He kneeled there right on the snow,
removed my hand from my fur muff, and slipped a pretty ring on my
finger.

No, I have not shared this news with our loyal parents. I wanted you
to be the first to hear. And maybe to give me some advice on how to tell
them.

For you know as well as I how much this news will upset them both.
I pray it does not upset you! I truly believe that God looks kindly on
both Catholics and Protestants, and I cannot imagine he would nurture
such feelings of love in me if He did not want to see them fulfilled. Still,
I feel a volatile mix of joy and apprehension regarding both my parents
and our parish priest! As you can well imagine.

So even though Harvey's kisses make me wild with joy, we have been
very very careful to keep his wooing of me secret.

Here at home, Papa continues to mope about and waste his days. He
drinks far too much whiskey of an evening, and Mama is still forced to
take in sewing work that keeps her up until all hours of the night. None
of us have ever been able to convince Papa to open a new shop, and God
only knows what happened to that thief of a partner he had.

You were lucky to marry Andrew Haben when you did, to move to
your own home. The small place we were forced to move into after the

fire provides cramped quarters indeed for the bunch of us. I know Mama and Papa and all of us still miss that grand old house on Algoma Street!

I've taken on several small jobs—keeping books at a sawmill, working as a secretary at the *Daily Northwestern* newspaper. Wherever I worked, sweet Harvey seemed to show up almost magically come quitting time, offering to walk me home, just as he did when we were in school. Every time I saw him, my stomach flipped over and over, like it was tumbling in the grass. I lay in bed at night, picturing those gorgeous curls of hair on the nape of his neck, the curve of his lips.

I know I am a silly girl!

Still, I was taken by surprise when he proposed. "I haven't asked your father," he warned. It was nearly ten at night. All the other skaters had gone home—brother Petey had been there, and Stephen, too—but we stood by the remains of one small bonfire still lit on the shore. I wore that dark green velvet skating outfit Mama had sewn for me. Harvey reached up to rub the skirt between his fingers. Oh, Corny, I could have died and gone to Heaven right in that moment.

But I kept my wits about me, somehow. "Papa wouldn't agree to our marrying anyway!" I said. "You're Protestant!" I felt reckless, giddy with happiness but also keenly aware that this was not to be.

Do you remember how you told me you'd heard men at Papa's shop tell him I was "The Belle of Oshkosh" on more than one occasion? Well, how terrible is this that of all those young man, none of them made my heart spin the way Harvey did? I knew he wasn't a suitable candidate and knew his father, our Mayor, would disapprove as well! And yet, and yet, I was drawn to him more than any other.

And there he was, sweet Sister, kneeling on the snow in front of me and holding up a small black box. I lifted the lid to see a rose gold buckle ring with ten tiny seed pearls.

"It's beautiful," I said. "But I can't take this, Harvey. You know that. Your father would object to this just as much as mine."

"It's not him I'm asking to marry me," he said. His face was lit by the flames from the bonfire, and maybe it was some fierce magic that made me let him slip the ring on my finger and cover my mouth with kisses before I could object more.

I know our beloved Mama will be heartbroken! But what am I to do? I am in love, Sister. I cannot think that Jesus put this strong love in my heart without expecting me to follow wherever it might lead.

In passion and turmoil,

Lizzie

PS Tell that Andrew Haben to take good care of you and to bring you home for Christmas. I have made a special gift for you and your new home.

CHAPTER 3

As expected, Mama strongly objected to my marrying outside our faith, but Papa saw how beneficial Harvey's and my union could be financially. At our wedding, my new father-in-law William Doe presented us with the gift of a quarter-share in a Colorado mine called the Fourth of July. This gift came with one condition: that Harvey spend three months working there. William said it was high time his son left the comfort of home and became a man on his own. The unexpected gift excited me, and I saw it might well be a way for us to recoup some of what my family had lost in that horrible fire.

"Say your prayers, Mama." We stood on the train platform one week after the wedding. A huge black locomotive rumbled noisily on the tracks before us, and a red-coated porter loaded three travel trunks, including a dome-topped one that held my small trousseau. "Harvey's father said a rich new lode was struck last week. Somewhere near our mine."

"What on earth does a Wisconsin mayor know about mining in Colorado?" Mama asked. "And I'll not waste my prayers on this foolishness. I will pray for you, Daughter, and pray for your return."

Tears trembled on her lower lids. We were surrounded by my brothers and sisters, Harvey's sisters, Papa, and my new in-laws. Mama reached up to unclasp the silver chain she always wore. "You'll need prayers for far more than silver."

"Don't take that off, Mama," I said, but she wrapped my fingers around the crucifix and squeezed my hand tightly.

"Keep it with you. Pray on it every morning."

A conductor shouted, "All aboard!"

I held the crucifix between my fingers, said a silent prayer that my new husband and I would soon return to Oshkosh with riches beyond our dreams, then kissed my family goodbye and followed Harvey and William onto the train.

We planned to spend several nights at the American House Hotel in Denver while my father-in-law finalized the supplies for the second leg of our journey, which would be in a covered wagon. The hotel was elegant and modern, with heavy walnut furniture and metal bathtubs in the room. Our first night there we dined on oyster soup, antelope cutlets, pickled peaches, white perfection cake.

"Let me tell you more about where we're headed." William pointed his fork toward the stunning view of the rolling Rockies out the window. "It's called California Gulch. Near the center of the state, in a valley near Mount Sharma."

We'd heard all this before in long monologues on the train ride, but I was happy to hear it again.

"Ten tons of gold have been mined there in the last seven years. This is prime property we're talking about," he continued.

"I thought you said it was a silver mine," Harvey said. He'd been petulant all day. The train ride had been uncomfortable; our sleeping berth was much too short for his tall frame. And I was quickly learning how anxious Harvey and his father became when they spent too much time together. William was a self-made man, a hard worker who treated his oldest son with disdain, for reasons I didn't yet understand.

"I did say it was a silver mine." William drained the whiskey in his glass and motioned for another. "The Fourth of July should yield a good supply of both silver and lead."

Harvey raised a finger. "Another whiskey here as well," he said.

William put his elbows on the table and began to tell us the story of how the mine had been discovered. "My partner, Benoni Waterman, fell through a hole in the snow last winter. Found a natural tunnel that dropped well below ground. He kept quiet about what he'd found 'til Independence Day, when he made his claim. Hence, the Fourth of July."

Harvey scraped his fork against the gold-rimmed china dessert plate, picking up the remaining crumbs and bits of frosting from his cake.

"Remind me where we'll live? Dogvine? Dog Town?"

"Dogwood," I said quickly, hoping to prevent an argument. They were both tired and both inebriated. And Harvey's doubts about his father's wedding gift had grown the farther we travelled from Oshkosh.

William rocked back on two legs of his chair. "Dogwood. It's a few miles from the mine. I've arranged a cabin for you there."

Harvey reached for my hand under the table and started spinning the buckle wedding ring around my finger. "You've set us up in luxurious living conditions, I'm sure," he said to his father.

William frowned. He was much less attractive than his son, with pocked skin and an overlarge forehead. The men were nothing alike— William comfortable in the bombast of a life-long politician, Harvey sedate and withdrawn. This seemed to annoy William.

"It'll do," he said to Harvey. "It's a miner's cabin, nothing more."

Harvey finished his drink and turned to look for the waiter.

"I think you've had enough," I said.

To my relief, his face softened, and he nodded in agreement. I'd told him how much excessive drinking frightened me and how hard it had been to see my father descend into its perils after the fire.

"Let's go," Harvey said quietly, laying his napkin beside the plate. He stood and pulled my chair out.

"I'm sorry, Mayor Doe," I began.

"Call me William. I've told you that several times now, Elizabeth."

"Yes, I just wanted to apologize for leaving. Harvey and I are both so tired. You must be as well, sir? Perhaps we should call it a night and meet for breakfast in the morning?"

He stood and bowed slightly at the waist.

"Thank you for dinner," I said. I pressed myself against Harvey's side.

William stared at his son. "I suggest you get a good night's rest, young man."

I started to say something else to diffuse the tension, but Harvey bent down to plant a long kiss on my mouth. I pulled away, embarrassed that he chose to display his affection so publicly.

"If you'll excuse us, then, Lizzie and I will take your advice and enjoy our honeymoon here," Harvey said.

We returned to our room. Harvey and I shed our clothes and made passionate love on a four-poster bed with a feather mattress. Mama had given me a new book, *The Relations of the Sexes*, before the wedding, to prepare me for what was to come. The book's author warned about the "seemingly uncontrollable demands of a sexual nature upon men." But

I adored Harvey's passion for me and surrendered to his longings with delight. As usual, I put the pocket diary under my pillow, and wrote in it when I awoke.

> *I dreamed I went to the Episcopal altar & knelt down with Harvey Doe & was married to him by their minister & I said that Pa would be so happy & told Ma that I was now fixed up in our church.*

We left Denver that Wednesday. The driver of the covered wagon was a short, wiry man named John Fox. He wore work pants and an unbleached muslin shirt, just as William and Harvey did. Their normal frock coats, starched dress shirts, and jacquard vests had been packed away in our trunks. I'd taken John Fox's advice to sew small rocks into the hem of one of my dresses to keep it from blowing in the high mountain winds we would encounter. John Fox had also warned us that we would notice a dramatic change in altitude as we travelled toward the Arapahoe Pass and might experience some sickness. The air did grow thinner and drier as the Conestoga carried us west but at least on the first day, I felt no nausea or light-headedness. The ride was extremely bumpy and uncomfortable though. Harvey and I bounced on the bench that ran along one side of the wagon, and William sat on the other. The floor was curved, so it was impossible to move around on foot during the ride. We had a two day trip ahead of us, and my body already ached after the first hour. The two horses pulling us did their best to find footing in the ruts left by wagons that had travelled the route before us, but it was hard to talk because of the constant rolling back and forth, the creaking noise of the wagon wheels, and the banging of pots and pans, milk cans, spoons, and guns hanging from hooks on wooden hoops inside.

Once we reached the foothills, John Fox stopped to set up camp near a small grove of aspen. Harvey, William, and I jumped down to help unload supplies. I was standing to the side of the wagon, unrolling one of the dark green bedrolls, when Harvey cried out. I ran up front to see him standing with a pained expression on his face. One of the horses had planted its large, grayish-black hoof on Harvey's right boot.

"Damn it, Adios!" John Fox said, digging his shoulder into the horse to push him off. The animal refused to budge until whacked on the haunch with the reins. As soon as the hoof lifted, Harvey collapsed on the ground. I bent to pull off his boot. His sock was soaked with blood, and when I removed it, I saw that several toenails had cracked. The flesh on top of his foot was puffed and already turning black and blue.

John Fox disappeared into the wagon and returned holding a narrow, aqua-colored glass vial.

"Godfrey's Cordial," William said. "I recognize that from when my wife took it for headaches. "

John Fox pulled the stopper from its narrow neck. "I got the last few doses from the jug at the pharmacy. Mister Harvey's in luck because the bottom of the barrel is always the most potent."

Harvey tenderly tried to poke his foot with one finger, grimacing at each touch.

"What's in it?" William asked.

"Opium and treacle," John Fox said. "Molasses. Foul stuff, too sweet for me. But those in pain swear by it." He poured a cloudy liquid into a spoon and held it in front of Harvey's nose. "You won't feel a thing once you imbibe. Knock you right out if you drink enough."

"I don't need it." Harvey tried unsuccessfully to stand.

"I'm thinkin' you'll feel different about that in an hour or so, young man," John Fox said. "Either take this now, or we poke a hole in that big nail of yours to ease the pressure."

"I really don't think…" I started to say, but William interrupted me.

"Take it." He took the spoon and forced it into his son's mouth.

William and John Fox helped Harvey climb back up into the wagon then laid him down on one of the interior benches. John Fox found a wool blanket, folded it in quarters, and propped Harvey's swollen foot on it.

I hurried to sit down and lift Harvey's head onto my lap.

He gave me a rueful smile. "Just what we need."

"It's all right. It will heal." I ran my fingers through his beautiful hair until his breathing slowed. "It's fine," I said to William. "You can leave us here in the wagon. Go eat. Sleep." Within half an hour, Harvey was asleep. I leaned my head against one of the curved wooden bows that held up the canvas cover and closed my eyes. The next thing I knew, a hand gripped my shoulder

"You've got to eat." William offered me a tin plate piled high with beans, bacon, and two biscuits

Harvey groaned. He looked up at me, the pupils of his eyes like pinpoints.

"Will you eat something? Are you hungry, darling?" I asked. He groaned again and pressed his face into my stomach.

William started to reach to touch Harvey's head then thought better of it.

"Potent medicine, isn't it?" John Fox peered in the open bonnet of the wagon. Behind him, purple and pink clouds dotted the sky. He'd built a campfire and tied both horses to a nearby tree.

"Come outside with us, Elizabeth," William said. "Eat your dinner and get some sleep. You can't stay in here all night."

"No, I won't leave him."

William set the plate down beside me on the bench then climbed back down out of the wagon. I watched through the open canvas as he spread his bed things on the ground near the campfire.

"Your husband's going to be fine, Mrs. Doe," John Fox called in to me. "Let him sleep it off."

I stayed inside the wagon with Harvey all night, wiping his fevered brow and trying to make him as comfortable as possible. Harvey woke the next morning as soon as John Fox giddy-upped the horses and the wagon began to move. He immediately reached for the vial John Fox had placed on the bench near my hip.

"No." I caught Harvey's hand in my own. "Please don't take any more." I meant to push the vial away from me on the bench, but it fell to the curved floor of the wagon and rolled from side to side.

To my dismay, William picked it up and handed it to Harvey, who swallowed whatever liquid still remained. Within minutes, his eyelids lowered and he fell back asleep. Even the rattling of the pots and milk cans didn't wake him.

I rubbed Mama's crucifix between my fingers, wishing she were here to tell me what to do. I didn't like seeing Harvey so subdued, and I didn't like the way the other men were ignoring my concerns about him. I sat lost in my thoughts until, mid-morning, the wagon crossed over a stone-and-timber bridge that ran across a steep ravine. A short distance from the bridge trees with shiny leaves surrounded a small clearing.

"Cottonwood," William said then shouted up to John Fox, "Stop here, man!"

He stood as soon as the wagon rolled to a stop.

"I want you to see the mine," William said. It was the most excited I'd seen him, but I was too worried about Harvey to want to see anything other than a doctor and a real bed.

"You said we'd reach camp today," I said. "There ought to be a doctor there." I was sore and tired and sick at heart about the trance Godfrey's Cordial had made my husband sink into. "Someone should look at Harvey's foot, make sure he's all right."

William shook his head. "Nope. First we stop at the Fourth of July."

I put my hand on Harvey's still-hot forehead. He shifted uncomfortably in my lap but didn't wake. "Later. Please," I said. I was furious at William for having given the drug to Harvey so nonchalantly. Didn't he see the damage it had done?

William jumped down to the ground and stood up front with hand raised, waiting for me to follow him. "Come on," William said. "Time's wasting. And we're not going to the camp until I show this god-damn mine to at least one of you."

I knew I couldn't persuade him to do otherwise, so I lay my shawl carefully beneath Harvey's head. I bent to kiss him and whispered that I would be right back. He frowned, muttered something I couldn't understand, then turned to face the canvas.

"This really isn't the time," I said to William as I jumped down onto a small field covered in purple flowers. "And I don't understand. If this is your mine—our mine—where is everyone?"

"Probably drinking," William said, "since it's Saturday."

I'd lost track of the days during our long journey from Wisconsin. William started walking ahead of me, and I hurried to catch up. As worried as I was about Harvey back in the wagon, it did feel good to be outside, to stretch, and I breathed in deeply.

"What's that wonderful smell?" I asked.

"Sweet sage and pine," William said just before he disappeared from view.

"What the hell?" John Fox said, coming up behind me. "Where'd he go?"

"Why didn't you stay with Harvey?" I was annoyed at how blind these men were. I was turning to go back to the wagon when I saw a rusted metal sign a few feet beyond where William had suddenly vanished. It read:

Signal Code:

1 Bell — Stop Skip Immediately if in Motion
1 Bell — Hoist Stone to Tipple
2 Bells — Lower Skip to Next Level
3 Bells — Raise Skip to Next Level
5 Bells — ACCIDENT Move Skip by Verbal Order Only

Behind the sign were an overturned wheelbarrow, sticks of used dynamite in torn red paper, and a square hole in the ground, framed with split logs.

Peering down the hole, I called out, "William? Are you all right?"

In response I heard only a scratching noise, which I later realized was a match head against rock. A small flame popped into view. Then a second, and a third. Six flames in all were lit, and William stood in the midst of them, surrounded on all sides by darkness.

"Take the ladder down," he yelled. "Backwards. I'll catch you on the last step."

A rickety ladder made of two tree trunks leaned against the opening.

"I wouldn't recommend it, Mrs. Doe," John Fox said. "A mine's no place for a woman like you."

Something about his tone made me immediately untie my bonnet and hand it to him, remove my under-petticoat and hand it to him as well. John Fox stood speechless.

The ladder dropped maybe 40 feet into the earth. I couldn't tell if it actually touched the ground where my father-in-law stood or not.

Nevertheless, I placed one shoe carefully on the third rung down, swiveling so I could hold on to the side timbers. I was annoyed at John Fox, annoyed at my father-in-law, even annoyed at Harvey for not being the one to do this instead of me.

But I stepped down, one rickety rung after another, staring straight ahead at the wall inches in front of my face. It grew darker and colder the lower down I went. At one point, I looked up but could no longer see John Fox's face in the opening above me.

I couldn't hear any sounds from above ground either; it was eerily, wonderfully, quiet down in the mine. I kept placing one foot after another on the next rung below me. When I felt dizzy, I closed my eyes.

Then suddenly, hands circled my waist. My father-in-law lifted me off the ladder and set me down on the ground. I stumbled, eyes still closed, either too afraid or too stubborn to open them.

"I've got her, John," William yelled. His words ricocheted off the walls.

I was just about ready to complain to William about everything he'd done wrong so far: about the stupid gift he'd given Harvey and me, the risk he'd taken urging Harvey to take that opium-laced medicine, the endless discomfort of the wagon ride. But when I opened my eyes, all the words I'd planned to spew on William were forgotten.

The area where we stood was about ten feet square. It smelled surprisingly sweet and earthy. The walls were shored up by wooden beams, many of them crooked and cracked. Haphazard piles of wooden rail ties were stacked in the corners, and metal rods jutted randomly out of sheer rock walls. The light from the candle flames flickered beautifully on the walls, the beams, my father-in-law's face. It reminded me of candles placed on an altar. It reminded me of something long forgotten. Maybe a story I'd read in the Bible, or something Father Bonduel had told me about the mysteries of the night sky. I felt as though I'd been spun out of life as I'd known it into the heavens, enveloped in God's mystery.

"Bully for you then!" William said, and I could only stare at him in disbelief.

Above ground was one world; down here was another. And I realized that this world below, a world I had never seen before that moment, yet somehow always knew existed, held the key to something I'd long been seeking.

"This is it?" I asked. "This is what you gave us?"

"Yep." William pointed off to the right, grinning like a madman. "Welcome to the Fourth of July. See that tunnel over there? That runs thirty yards south. There's another shaft off to the left of it, going down another hundred feet."

He picked a candle from an iron spike and held it up to the wall behind the ladder I'd just climbed down. A blue-black vein snaked through the rock there.

"That's silver," he said. "That's what's going to make you and Harvey rich."

I gasped, suddenly remembering Harvey back in the wagon. What if he'd woken up and found himself alone?

"We need to go back. Now. Harvey will need us."

"Rubbish. Harvey's a grown man. You can take five minutes and look at what you've been given." He stepped forward, bending his head to enter the tunnel. "Come on. Just a few feet this way."

And so, because I desperately wanted to explore more of this strange world I'd suddenly dropped into, I followed him. I walked carefully between the narrow gauge rails that ran down the middle of the tunnel, stepping over hammers and drills, leather and steel caps that were shaped like the backs of turtles.

The path forked ahead of us. William held the candle, but the blackness swallowed its small light after only a few feet. Something brushed past my hair.

I jumped and grabbed William's free arm. "What was that?"

"Bat."

I shook my hair and pressed on, following the candle, turning this way and that to try to see what lay beyond its faint light.

"Why isn't it all crashing down on our heads?" I asked.

"Careful planning. Attention to structure. My head miner Tommy Birdsall knows what he's doing." William's boot clanged against metal: a rusted bucket filled almost to its brim with sooty black pieces of mottled rock.

"Give me your hand."

I remembered Mama wrapping my fingers around her crucifix at the train station in Oshkosh. What on earth did William have to offer me here?

He bent to pick up a small bit of rock from the bucket and laid it on my palm. It felt like wet glass against my skin, nearly weightless. When I lifted it to my nose, it smelled of ice. The rock was both dark and bright, with irregular edges and bumpy on its sides.

"Silver," William said. "That's raw silver. We've found plenty of it, much bigger nuggets than this one."

The rock in my hand didn't shine like a diamond; it wasn't lustrous like pearl. Still, it felt magical, immensely valuable. My heart raced; maybe Harvey and I really could make our fortune here. "But…" I had so many questions. "How will we know what to do?"

William looked at me kindly. I knew he appreciated my interest in the mine, something Harvey had yet to show. He curled my fingers just like Mama had done only this time, instead of the bars of the crucifix I felt the jagged edges of the silver nugget press into my hand.

"You're afraid," William said. "I understand that. Most men who come out here to prospect feel like you do. But something pulls them forward. And sometimes, God willing, they strike it rich. Their dreams come true."

Another bat flew past our heads, disappearing down the dark tunnel.

"You won't be doing the grunt work," William continued. "All you have to do is help your husband do his job. Tommy Birdsall's the boss down here. You and Harvey can trust him with your lives." He pressed his fingertips together in front of his mouth. "Hell, I'm trusting him with my son's life. And trusting some of Birdsall's gumption will rub off on Harvey."

I knew Harvey would hate working in the mine. I pictured his beautiful hands, his long, slender fingers far more accustomed to playing the keys of a piano than lifting a pick-axe or drill. But we had promised William three months. If we could make a go of it, this would be the best chance we would ever have to set ourselves—and my parents—up for life. Maybe Harvey and I would strike it rich at the Fourth of July, return to Oshkosh with money to spare.

William turned to start making our way back up the tunnel. "Remember how my partner found this mine?" he asked over his shoulder. "Waterman? He fell through a bloody hole. An accident. One small thing that completely changed his life. I don't want you to forget what it feels like to hold that ore, Elizabeth. I don't want you to forget what magic feels like."

I squeezed the nugget in my hand.

"And there's plenty more where that came from," he said. "The ground's full of silver ore all around these parts. Fellow named Horace Tabor just struck another rich lode up in Leadville. That man's making millions from his mine. I think it's called the Matchless." William lifted me onto the lowest rung of the ladder. "Tabor's the biggest toad in the puddle these days. Let's give him a run for his money, shall we?"

CHAPTER 4

Dropping down into the Fourth of July had, like tasting the communion wafer on my tongue, opened me to a new understanding. If I'd felt betrayed after my confirmation, when Jesus let the fire take everything my family and I owned, a new confidence came over me after my descent into the mine. I was more than ready to believe there were treasures we couldn't see that were ready to be shared.

Harvey was awake and cranky when we returned to the wagon. His foot didn't look any better, but he managed to eat a cold meal of coffee, beans, and bacon—the first food he'd had since the accident. He didn't appear to be in any mood to hear about the mine, so I kept quiet about my adventure below ground. We reached Dogwood, in the shadow of Arapahoe Peak, just before sunset.

I peered out the canvas as the wagon pulled in. There were a dozen small cabins set atop a cleared area of cracked red clay, what looked to be a smokehouse, and a small building with a sign that read "Assayer." The sign was riddled with bullet holes.

My stomach dropped, and all the optimism and excitement I'd felt in the mine vanished.

"Head the wagon to the far end over there," William shouted up to John Fox. We pulled up to one of the low cabins which leaned improbably to the left. A mangy dog ran out its open door.

Harvey sat up on the bench and rubbed his forehead furiously. "What on earth were you thinking, Father? Surely you don't expect Lizzie and me to live here!"

William tugged at one ear. "Neither miners nor bosses live in fancy houses," he said. "I've given you the gift of a lifetime, son. Your wife understands that now and one day, you will too. Appreciate it. Make do with the challenges."

Harvey stood shakily, keeping his weight on one leg. "I won't live here," Harvey said. "I won't have this be Lizzie's first home."

I blinked, my mind working frantically. Mama had slipped some money into my purse before I boarded the train. I'd hidden it inside my corset. If I could just get inside the cabin to retrieve it, I could pay John Fox to take us back to Denver. But the horses were already untied, and William had jumped down from the foot board.

"Hurry up," he shouted. "It's going to be dark soon, and we've got to get your things unloaded. John's leaving us first thing in the morning."

Harvey was a foot taller than me, but somehow I managed to help him climb down, using the brake handle for support. The filthy dog immediately came up to sniff at my skirts.

"Shoo," I said.

"Probably has rabies," Harvey said. He held his bare foot up a few inches above the dirt. Each time he put it down gingerly to take a step, he grimaced.

William stood in the doorway of the cabin, motioning us inside. On either side of him, flattened tin cans and down batting filled chinks between the logs.

"Don't worry about this place," he said, coming down the broken step to help support Harvey. "You'll fix it up. I've put money in the bank in Central City for you, enough to buy you furniture. Whatever you need."

Harvey stooped to enter the low door then hobbled into the center of the room.

"I can't believe what you've done here, Father," he said. "My guess is that Mother had no idea."

William shrugged. "Your mother has coddled you your whole life, Harvey Doe. And believe me, what I'm offering you is better than working in a shingle factory, which is what I was doing at your age."

"Where is everyone?" I asked, suddenly realizing that I hadn't seen a single person since we'd driven into camp.

John Fox entered carrying one of our trunks, which he set down against a side wall. "Most likely at the Teller House bar," he said.

I looked out the doorway at another cabin across the way. A dark red curtain in one of its front windows was pulled back, and a hand waved quickly before the curtain closed.

John Fox brought in another trunk to stack atop the first.

"Wait," I said, but no one paid attention.

I could feel tears ready to spill over as I looked around at the cabin's meager furnishings: a table covered in blue-and-white checked oilcloth, four wooden stools, a ladderback rocking chair, a stand with an enamel washbasin, a low three-drawer cabinet. In the tiny kitchen space, there was a coffee pot with a long spout and a black iron skillet, four tin bowls and mugs on a narrow shelf, a dishpan, and a dish towel made from a Honey Maid flour sack. Strips of cheesecloth peeled off the walls, and grease coated the cook stove.

"What do you think?" William spread his arms as though he'd just finished a triumphant speech at the Oshkosh Town Hall.

Harvey sat himself down on one of the wobbly stools in the center of the room. "You've outdone yourself with your generosity. Always a catch, isn't there, Father?"

I walked over to pat his shoulder. I couldn't stand to see the two men get into another argument. Not now.

"It's not forever," William said. "Three months at most. Just until the first snow falls and the mines close. Then you're out of here, hopefully with enough riches in your pockets to buy your own grand house anywhere you like."

The dog had come inside.

"Get that mutt out of here!" Harvey yelled, and John Fox took a broken board from the floor and flung it at the animal, who ran off yelping.

I surveyed the room again. Every piece of furniture tilted crazily on the warped floorboards, like props in a bad fairy tale. A ladder leaned against the back wall, heading up to a loft. When Harvey saw where I was looking, he shook his head. "Not me."

So I climbed up alone to see the small space that would be our bedroom. Prairie grass poked through a thin tick mattress on the floor. Two pillows still held shiny indentations where other heads had lain. I was surprised to realize another woman had slept there: an empty sewing basket stood on a rickety nightstand.

I remembered Mama sewing the mother-of-pearl shamrock on my confirmation headband, remembered hers and Papa's grand bed that had burned in the fire. Harvey and I had to make a go of this. I wiped away a tear and climbed back down the ladder. "First thing tomorrow morning, I want to order a real bedstead." I knew if I didn't keep talking, I'd burst into sobs. "And I want someone to prop up the porch."

Harvey put his head in his hands. William ignored him and walked over to me, standing as close as he had when we were below ground in the Fourth of July. I reached inside the pocket of my skirt; the silver nugget he'd given me was still there.

"Believe me, I know it's a shock." William cleared his throat.

"It's like throwing a non-swimmer into Lake Winnebago, isn't it?" Harvey asked. "I remember that trick of yours, too."

A strange man walked up to stare into our cabin. He had a long gray braid and wore odd trousers that stopped at his knee.

"Chinaman," William said. "There are lots of them here. They're hard workers."

He helped Harvey stand and started walking him toward the door. The Chinaman ran off, his braid flapping behind him. "We've got to get to Central City before the sun goes down. You'll have another good night in a fancy hotel. It's the nicest hotel in town, and I booked you the nicest room. Hopefully that foot of yours will be better by morning. And you'll meet Tommy Birdsall tomorrow. Good strong Kansan, fought against Quantrill's Raiders. He'll meet us for breakfast at the Teller House then help you settle in here."

None of us said a word on the ride into town. I clutched Mama's crucifix with one hand and the silver nugget in my pocket with the other, repeating to myself a prayer I'd learned as a child, "Dear Jesus, please help us find the way."

Central City was a loud and busy circus with braying mule teams and whinnying horses, shiny carriages and wagon drivers cracking their whips, hundreds of men wearing everything from chaps to top hats, plus a handful of gaudily dressed women twirling feather boas and carrying shiny parasols. The main street was so crowded it was nearly impossible to travel down it, and John Fox shouted at people to clear the way as he maneuvered our wagon toward the hotel.

Buildings of brick and stone stood next to makeshift tents, and I noticed several saloons on every block. Loud strains of out-of-tune piano music poured from beyond swinging doors.

Finally we reached the hotel, which rose four stories and towered above the low buildings to either side. It was built of brick, with TELLER HOUSE painted in large black letters at the top. The sidewalk outside its doors was, astonishingly, paved with silver bricks.

"That's real silver on that sidewalk," William said. "Grant visited here a few years ago, and Henry Teller was a long-time friend of his. Before the President got to town, Teller asked some miners to make a path of silver bricks so the great man wouldn't have to get his boots dirty. But Grant got mad and wouldn't walk on them. Said he wasn't going to favor silver over gold."

"What do you mean?" I asked.

"Gold or silver—whichever backs the dollar," Harvey said. "Miners want silver. Banks want gold. And never the twain shall meet."

William pushed open the door to the lobby. A grand staircase with carved spindles rose in front of us, and a piano-forte stood to the right. Cabinet shelves filled with pieces of silver ore lined one wall. I couldn't wait to take a bath and climb into a comfortable bed. Maybe somehow overnight all the rough horrors of Dogwood would disappear in the magic of dreams and prayers.

We checked in at the mahogany reception desk, and William told a porter to take two overnight bags up to our rooms.

"Good night then, John," he said. "I'll meet you here in the morning so we can start the trip back to Denver."

Then, without asking, he led us into the hotel restaurant. Briefly forgetting how tired and filthy I was, I devoured every bit of food set before me: tomato bouillon, lamb with a paper frill on each leg, dinner rolls with sweet cream butter. I was relieved to see Harvey eating as well.

I was just finishing the last bite of dessert—a Nesselrode pudding stuffed with chestnuts and maraschino cherries—when William said, "I suggest you two head up to sleep. Big day tomorrow."

"I think Lizzie and I will go up later," Harvey said. "But you're welcome to call it a night now."

William raised his eyebrows but didn't object. We said good night in the lobby then Harvey led me toward the hotel bar.

"No," I said. "Harvey, I'm so tired and just want to go upstairs."

"One drink," he said. So I followed him, feeling so tired and so alone; I didn't have the strength to argue. I wished I was at home with my Mama and wondered why on earth I'd followed Harvey and his father to this strange town. I was frightened by what lay ahead, by the petulance I'd seen in Harvey's interactions with his father. Perhaps I didn't know the man I'd married as well as I thought.

A dozen men stood shoulder to shoulder at the dark wood bar. Some wore work pants tucked into rubber boots and had revolvers hanging from their belts; others stood in frock coats and derby hats. I counted five women, all dressed in low-cut gowns. Behind the bar someone had painted large murals of naked women.

I reached for Harvey's hand. "I don't want to be here."

"One drink," he repeated and pulled me behind him toward the bar.

A man in a white apron and black string bow tie was wiping up a spill.

"Whiskey," Harvey said.

"New to town?" the bartender asked.

"Yep. For better or worse." Harvey positioned his bad foot on the brass rail and gestured for me to stand beside him.

I could feel men staring at me.

"Name's Billy Parker." The bartender reached across to shake Harvey's hand and nodded toward me. "You have beautiful eyes, ma'am. Violet, are they?"

I looked down at the shiny surface of the bar.

"Beautiful women are few and far between out this way," he said then added, "I'd keep an eye on her if I were you, Mr. ..."

"Doe. Harvey Doe." Harvey lifted the shot glass and emptied it. "And this is my wife, Elizabeth Doe." He emptied the glass quickly and ordered a second before I could object. "We're new owners of the Fourth of July. Won't be here long though."

I thought I might faint. I was exhausted, and the room was noisy and filled with smoke. "Harvey, I want to go upstairs. Now."

"Oh, don't leave when you just got here, ma'am," Billy said. He scanned the colored glass bottles lined up behind the bar: amber, emerald green, black. "How about a blackberry liquor? It'll help you sleep through the night."

Harvey looked at me, suddenly seeming to realize how truly uncomfortable I was.

"What do I owe you?" he asked Billy.

"It's on the house, Harvey Doe. To welcome you and the Mrs. to town."

As we walked out, we passed a woman in a tight red bodice leaning against a piano. She started to sing:

> *Oh, do you remember Sweet Betsey from Pike*
> *Who crossed the wide prairie with her lover Ike?*
> *With two yoke of oxen, a big yellow dog,*
> *A tall Shanghai rooster, and one spotted hog.*
> *Hoodle dang, fol-de-dye do,*
> *hoodle dang, fol-de day.*

As soon as we reached our room Harvey pulled me close to his chest and began to cover my face with kisses. "I'm sorry, I'm sorry, I'm sorry," he said. The smell of whiskey rolled off his breath in waves. "I shouldn't have brought you here."

He dropped to his knees before me, just as he'd done when he proposed. "Tell me you still love me," he said.

I bit my lip but ran my fingers through his hair.

He reached up under my petticoat and unfastened my stockings. I wanted him to stop. I was flustered by the new behavior I'd seen in him. But I couldn't resist his touch. I unbuttoned my outer skirt myself and let it fall to the carpet. Harvey buried his head in my petticoat then untied the drawstring at the back so it too lay in a ruffled heap at our feet. I stood in front of him wearing only my corset, chemise, and drawers.

"You're beautiful," he murmured into my skin. He ran his hand up my leg.

"The bed," I said, but his fingers were already playing with the cotton of my bloomers and before I knew it, he had reached through their opening and touched me.

He murmured something then stood to lift the chemise over my head. His hands circled my waist, and he unlaced the back of my corset. He moved his mouth to my breast, pushing me onto the bed in the center of the room. His eyes locked on mine, he reached again to stroke me with one hand, using the other to unbutton his pants. I undid the tie-string of his drawers, wrapped my legs around him, and he entered me swiftly, his face pressed hard between my breasts.

Later, when he slept, curled tightly against me, I moved carefully so as not to wake him and got out of bed. Quietly, I poured water into a basin and washed the grime from our journey off as best I could.

CHAPTER 5

The next morning, I put on a clean dress from the overnight bag and went downstairs with Harvey, who apologized again for any rudeness he'd shown me. William was already at a table in the restaurant talking animatedly to another man seated across from him. Both men stood when we approached, and William pulled out a chair for me.

"Elizabeth, this is Tommy Birdsall, the man I've been telling you about. Tommy, my son Harvey and new daughter-in-law Elizabeth."

"Good to meet you, ma'am," Tommy said. The cuffs of his shirt hung too far below the sleeves of a shiny, ill-fitting suit. I guessed that these were dress-up clothes he rarely wore. He had several days' stubble on his chin and eyes the color of smoke. "And you, Mr. Doe," he added.

"Too confusing," William said. "Call him Harvey."

"Yes, sir."

While we waited for coffee, I looked around the dining room I'd been too tired to appreciate the night before. The walls were papered with a chrysanthemum pattern, and bronze pendant chandeliers hung from the ceiling. A dozen tables had been set up with white linen cloths, fancy china, and silverware. I could happily stay in fancy hotels the rest of my life, I thought.

I ordered the new Quaker oatmeal I'd only heard about back home, and the men chose poached eggs and cold joints of meat.

As soon as the waiter left our table, William got down to business. "Tommy, I told these two that my goal is to get one more shaft sunk by winter-time, before all the hill rats go home. Think that's feasible?"

"We'll give it a good shot, sir," Tommy said. "Men'll be mighty happy to see a new miner join the crew."

"I'm afraid I won't be working any time soon with this foot." Harvey pointed to his boot, still untied to accommodate the swelling. "Horse stepped on it."

"Balderdash," William said. "You can't let a thing like that stop you. You don't have a day to spare, son."

Tommy pursed his lips, sizing up the situation between father and son. I was grateful when he deftly steered the conversation in a new direction.

"Your father's given you a mighty generous gift," he said. I guessed he was the same age as Harvey and me, but he seemed much tougher and more mature. "Men are making fortunes the likes of which I've never seen. Tabor, Brimson, others—they're bringing money in hand over fist. I'm hopin' we can do the same at the Fourth of July."

He fingered the linen tablecloth. His hands were big and calloused; a puckered scar ran down the side of one thumb. "I'd say the sooner you join us the better."

I looked to William. "But we need to move into the cabin. You said Tommy would help us today, and we need a new bed, curtains. Surely Harvey can wait a few days?"

Just then a waitress brought our breakfast plates, and William was saved from having to answer.

Tommy cleared his plate faster than I'd ever seen anyone eat. Wiping up the last bits of egg yolk with a biscuit, he said, more to William than Harvey and me, "The placer deposit is pay dirt. And the first shaft had a fair yield. But my bet is we've tapped out the last of the ore there and need to blast further in."

William nodded. "Whatever you think needs to be done, do it."

"We'll start by pushing the current shaft out." Tommy turned to Harvey. "All we need is one good strike."

"More coffee?" The waitress held out a pewter pot with gooseneck spout.

"No," William said. "Just add this to the bill. Tommy, how many men have we got working this week?"

"There's eight of us now. Matt Plunkett, Meecham, Nutshell Jack— they're our best men. They—we—can show Harvey the ropes whenever he's ready to start."

Harvey pushed his chair back and stood.

"If you two strike it rich," William said, smiling up at him, "you can stay at all the fancy hotels you like."

"And if we'd preferred to stay in Oshkosh?" Harvey asked.

"Enough of this nonsense." William spoke so loudly a man in a red-and-green paisley waistcoat at the table next to us turned to stare. "There's no choice in the matter. You knew that when you got on the train to come here."

"Whatever our situation," Harvey said, putting his hand on my shoulder, "my first priority is getting my wife settled into our new home. No matter how shabby that home might be."

Tommy's cheeks reddened.

William stood and slapped his napkin on the table. "Then we'll say good-bye for now. I've asked John Fox to drive me to Black Hawk where I'll catch the train to Denver. I've left money for you in the bank down the street and will wire more if you need it once I'm home. In the meantime, Tommy can answer whatever questions you have."

He bent down to kiss my cheek.

"I don't want to say goodbye like this," I said. I'd felt quite close to him when we were down in the mine together. But my loyalty had to lie with my husband. And the men were obviously still at loggerheads.

William handed me an envelope. "You've got the room at the hotel until 4. There's cash here for your shopping trip. Stock up on food, the basics." He reached to clasp his son's shoulders, but Harvey stepped back.

"Godspeed to both of you," William said.

Tommy cleared his throat. "General Store's right down the way, ma'am."

I stood on tip-toe to kiss my father-in-law's cheek and whispered "Thank you" before following Tommy and Harvey, my heart in my throat. Once outside the Teller House, we turned right past a white church with a red door and an Express Office where Tommy said we'd be able to pick up mail from home. A sign in the window announced a fundraising drive to build a new Opera House in town. The date 1874 had been etched above its door.

"A lot of the buildings in town have that date," Tommy said.

"Why? Surely Central City's been here longer than that."

"Big fire in town that year," he answered. "Everything had to be rebuilt."

If I'd needed strengthening of my resolve, Tommy had just provided it. His words shot me back to that horrible day when I'd run to find Papa. It had been my job to save him; Mama had said so.

"Are you all right?" Harvey asked, taking my elbow.

I shook the painful reverie from my head. "Yes, yes, I'm sorry." I looked across the street. "That looks like where we need to go." I pointed toward a hand-painted sign that read McCauley's General Store.

The store was dark inside and stuffed with barrels, boxes, and crates. Dusty footprints covered nearly every square inch of the floor. Tommy picked up an empty box and began to fill it with flour, dried beef, coffee, baking powder, beans, eggs, a cooked ham. At the back, I found bolts of fabric and picked out a dotted muslin for curtains. Harvey found two lanterns.

"Where do we get a bed?" I asked "There's only a terrible mattress on the floor at the cabin."

"Come with me." Tommy led us to the back of the store. A man smoking a cigar sat at a wood and cast iron drafting table. When Tommy approached, he pushed a Marksman cigar box and cutter aside and said, "Already heard you'd be coming in, Tommy. Mr. Doe had me draw up a bedstead, and I'll have it ready for you in a week."

"Thanks, Samuel. This here's Mr. Doe Senior's son Harvey Doe and his wife."

"Nice to meet you both," Samuel said. "Welcome to Central City. I hear you're staying out at the camp at Dogwood, that right?"

"Yes," Harvey said. "Know a better place?"

A head of ash had developed on the tip of the cigar. Samuel nodded at it and said to Tommy, "Sign of a good stogie." He paused before answering Harvey's question. "No, no, don't know that I do, young man. Most of the miners who come out don't bring lady folk with them. So there's not much attention paid to niceties like bedsteads and the like."

He put the cigar in his mouth and started puffing.

"Don't let that head get too long now, Samuel. We'll be back next Saturday to pick up the bed," Tommy said. "Time we get to camp, folks. You don't want to be bumping into things in the dark in a new place."

Back at the cabin, he unloaded our supplies, insisting Harvey sit inside to rest his foot. "I'll come next morning to see how you're faring. Hope you'll be ready to work by then."

I stood on the porch watching him climb back into the carriage and flick a whip on the flank of its horse. He drove past the assay office and out of the camp.

"Almost sunset," Harvey called to me from inside. "Better fill some of these lamps with kerosene."

I did that then opened the dome-topped trunk Mama had packed and pulled out a cotton sheet. I spread this carefully across the mattress in the loft. The whitework pillowcases Mama had sewn for us were gigantic for the dirty flat pillows so I left them on the nightstand.

"It's dirty. It's uncomfortable. And I'm going to figure out a way to get us out of here fast," Harvey said. Still sitting on a ladderback chair, he removed his boots and socks. His right foot was still twice its normal size, and still discolored with purple splotches. I kneeled before him to rub his ankle for a bit then we undressed and lay down on the terrible mattress, Harvey's arm flung across my breast.

CHAPTER 6

"I want to go with you," I said. The hem of my white nightgown was already dotted with dust balls from the floor.

Harvey stood at the front door in work clothes, the ties on his right boot still loose. Tommy sat on a horse just beyond the porch, the reins of a second horse in his hands.

"I can work just as well as you," I said. I was more than willing to do whatever work in the mines was required. I would much rather do that than be left behind to clean the cabin.

"I'm going into a world I have no clue about," Harvey said. "But one thing I do know is that I don't want my wife working alongside me."

Tommy waved at me through the open door. "Mornin', Mrs. Doe. I'll bring your man back before sundown."

"But what am I supposed to do here all by myself?" I asked. "What if I have questions or need help?"

Tommy ran his big fingers around the brim of his hat. Harvey didn't even try to answer, but his boots tromped across the crooked porch floorboards, and he somehow managed to hoist himself onto the saddle of the second horse.

"Wait a minute." I ran outside with the lunch box I'd packed. There were two slices of cold ham, a capped mug of cold beans. He tucked it in a scratched leather saddlebag and bent down to kiss me. A fly buzzed above the horse's mane, and Harvey waved it off. I grabbed his hand. "Please let me come. I don't want to stay here."

"We've got to take off," Tommy said. His gray eyes met mine. "You'll be safe here, ma'am. All the men are already off at the mines." He pointed toward the cabin across the way. "And my guess is you'll have some neighborly help real soon."

The curtains I'd seen pulled back the night before were now firmly closed.

"Lizzie," Harvey said softly, "we're both going to do what we can today. Father threw us in the creek far as I'm concerned. We'll know soon enough if we can swim or not. Just clean up the place as best you can today. Don't lift anything heavy, and I'll help when I get home."

I watched the men ride off then stepped back up on the porch. I was still barefoot, and a splinter pierced my foot. I sat down on one of the two chairs, wet my finger, and wiped off the drop of blood. I didn't know where to begin, but our moving trunks waited in the room behind me. When I'd finished the dregs of the coffee, I opened the dome-topped trunk and lifted each piece of carefully folded clothing and linens as though it were a treasure. Mama had wrapped everything in old copies of the *Oshkosh Daily News*. It wasn't long before the newsprint ran with my tears. Some things—the lace tablecloth, a crocheted antimacassar, a small glass vase, two china tea cups—I simply left in the trunk; those fancy things had no place in Dogwood.

I laid one of Mama's quilts, a leaf pattern in turkey red and green, on the horrid mattress in the loft then took off my nightgown and dressed in the clothes I'd worn the day before. I reached in a pocket with my left hand to find the silver nugget and grabbbed Mama's crucifix around my neck with my right then said a prayer to both.

I found an old broom made of rye grass and swept the floors upstairs and down. Whoever lived in the cabin before us had tacked cotton sheets to the ceiling, probably to keep dirt from falling; two dried out hornets' nests hung behind them. I knocked these down and shook the sheets out fiercely from the front porch. A woman with a long gray braid flipped over one shoulder exited the cabin across the way and began to walk towards me.

"Should have been over to greet you at dawn, I suspect!" She wiped her hands on a yellow-checked apron. "What a sweet thing you are!" she said when she reached the porch.

Before I could answer, she continued, "Where *are* my manners? Here I go, surprising you like this. I'm Arvilla Bunn, Doc Bunn's wife." She stuck out a hand and shook mine vigorously, giving it an extra squeeze before letting go. She was about my height—just a little over five feet.

"I'm Lizzie," I said. "Lizzie Doe." I realized I'd never said my married name outloud before and found myself smiling as I said it, despite the strange circumstances.

"That's my cabin over there," she said, pointing. "Just kitty-corner to yours." She peered over my shoulder into the cabin.

"Would you like to come in?" I asked.

"Yes, yes, I would. Little lady who lived here before was a real mouse, didn't last long at all."

She followed me in and stood with hands on hips, assessing the place. "Well, we've got our work cut out, don't we? I say we start with a cup of tea at my place then I'll come back and help you tackle this mess."

While the Bunns' cabin appeared as run-down as mine on the outside, inside it was lovingly and comfortably furnished. Rag rugs dotted the floors, potted aloe plants stood in the windows, and a real upholstered couch beckoned any tired visitor. I was even more delighted to see a book propped open on its seat, *Eight Cousins, or the Aunt-Hill*.

"Louisa May Alcott!" I said. "I haven't read that one, but I loved *Little Women*. I've already regretted not bringing books with me." I was flustered. I had no idea what was expected of me in this mining camp, or even whether the social niceties that Mama had taught me would be of use.

"Reading's a damn fine way to pass the time out here," the woman said, motioning me to sit at a table set with a printed cloth. Four stems of yellow columbine stood in water in a jelly glass jar. She lifted the gilt handle of a floral decorated teapot and began to pour into two matching cups. "Brought this pot with me from Philadelphia," she said. "Belonged to my mother. And the tea is oolong, from one of the Chinamen here in camp." She offered a cube of sugar wrapped in blue paper then turned to a pie safe made of tin and packing crates and pulled out a Bundt cake.

"'Course there's no library in town," she continued, setting the cake on the table and slicing a thick wedge. "But a man comes through here once a month with a lending wagon. I give him my books and take someone else's for a spell. He knows how important it is he stop here whenever he's in the Gulch."

I felt so comfortable with this woman, and I quickly realized how much I had longed for another woman to talk to. Arvilla and I sat in her home for nearly an hour, chatting and drinking our tea and eating cake. I learned how she and her husband Merrow had moved west from

Philadelphia and travelled through all the mining camps, staying at each as long as a mine was open. They'd settled in Dogwood because it was close to Central City.

"We've been here in Colorado going on three years now," she said. "I hated this place as much as I imagine you do first off. Stuck my nose up mighty high at the squalor. Worse yet, I'd usually be the only woman in a camp other than the prostitutes who'd come out from town. But I set my foot down, figured out how to make the best of it. It was Doc's dream to come out here, and my job was to help him. He's handled everything from dysentery to syphilis."

I told her that Harvey and I had come to Dogwood because of a surprise wedding gift and that our stay would be a short one, just three months until we'd go back to Oshkosh, hopefully with money to start our lives there.

"Just 'til you make your fortune?" She laughed then added, "It's not that I haven't heard those words before! Still, I wish you and your mister all the luck in the world. Sometimes lightning does strike. The Doc and I have seen a few folks strike it rich out here. 'Course they don't linger long at camp afterwards so I don't know what happens to them after that first flush!"

When we'd emptied the teapot, I helped her clean the table.

"Now let's get to work on your place," she said. "I already pulled out my broom and rags first thing this morning."

Arvilla brought a bucket of water waiting on her porch and showed me how to clean out the soot from inside the wood stove and a better way to scrub it off the walls with vinegar. She stacked paper and kindling in the stove, adjusted the flue, and lit a low fire that she said I'd need come dinner-time. We wiped out the insides of lamp chimneys and cleaned the small sink with lye. Then we used hard soap to wash the frying pan, tin pots, a griddle, and cooking utensils hanging from nails in the wall. She threw the dirty water off a small step at the back of the cabin. Joining her there, I saw some of the columbine that had graced her table, mixed in with other wildflowers in a clump of grass.

"You picked a good time of year to move in," Arvilla said. "It's a short growing season up this high."

Then she told me to pick up two buckets we'd found in a back closet and walked home to get two more of her own.

"Don't imagine you're used to much of this, coming from the city."

Carrying the buckets, I followed her to the far edge of the camp, past tents where she said the Cornish miners and Chinamen lived, and into a clearing of trees. The fresh scent of pine was overpowered by a terrible smell.

"Yes ma'am," she said. "This is where you'll bring your chamber pot and slop bucket. Best you do that a couple times a day."

We continued down a steep slope to a clear stream that ran over stones and broken branches. Tall grasses lined the bank, but someone had cleared an area about six feet square and built a bench made of a piece of lumber set on two flat-topped stones. Arvilla picked up two empty brown bottles and stuffed them in the pocket of her apron.

"This is where you'll get your fresh water and do your laundry. I must walk down here eight times a day. Ever wash clothes in a stream before?"

"No." I was feeling overwhelmed by all the work ahead of me and annoyed at the men for just leaving me here without instructions. I was no more used to this rough living than Harvey was used to working in a mine. I don't know what I would have done if Arvilla hadn't been there to help.

"Well, it's harder work than one of those fancy wash basins with a wringer you've probably got back home. But you'll get the hang of it." She'd already filled three of the four buckets.

"Only problem is this stream's going to be no more than a trickle in a few weeks. Once winter comes, it'll fill up again. But I do a lot less laundry come fall."

She handed me two of the filled buckets. They were so heavy, I panted as we climbed back up to the cabin.

I took off the blue bandana I'd tied around my hair and leaned against a wall to catch my breath. When my curls tumbled out, Arvilla frowned. "Men around here don't bother me because I'm a heavy-set, old lady. But you'll want to watch out for yourself, sweetheart. I don't imagine this place is much like back home in Wisconsin. The rules are different. Or there aren't any rules. You tell your Mister not to let you out of his sight come Friday and Saturday nights. It gets wild here in camp, to say nothing of the commotion in Central City."

The sun had fallen to just above the horizon. Harvey would be home soon. Inside the cabin, everything sparkled.

"One more thing," Arvilla said and left to run across to her cabin. She returned with a pot of sausages and onions. "I made this last night. Figured you could use a little something as you're settling in. And this—" She reached in her pocket and handed me a bar of Pears soap. It was transparent and smelled like flowers.

By the time I heard Harvey's boots on the front porch, I had managed to take a sponge bath. I'd found an oblong tin tub behind a sheet but didn't want to waste the water I'd carried up the hill. I'd heated up Arvilla's homemade dinner on the woodstove and lit two beeswax candles on the table.

But all Harvey said when he walked inside was, "You'll tell me tomorrow how you managed all this." Then he limped toward the ladder to the loft, climbed it. I could hear him swearing as he removed his clothes and fell onto the uncomfortable mattress.

Later that night, I went to the porch and sat by myself in a rocker I'd pulled out there. I rocked back and forth, hearing the yip-yowl of a distant coyote and staring up at the sky which held more stars than I'd ever seen in Wisconsin. I wondered if Mama and Papa were seeing them, too. I missed them terribly.

I must have fallen asleep when I felt a hand on my shoulder.

"You don't want to spend all night out here," Arvilla said quietly. "We do, on occasion, see a pack of coyotes runnin' through camp. Mostly they don't bother us, but there's no reason to ask for trouble."

I had to bite my tongue when I listened to Harvey's complaints about working in the mine the next morning. The men were uncouth; the work was drudgery, the conditions brutal.

"It's truly a hell hole," he said.

I didn't know how he could be talking about the same place I had found so fascinating.

"There's constant noise. Somebody's either drilling or pounding the walls with sledgehammers and picks. And I think the other miners are giving me the worst work when Tommy isn't around."

At night, I'd rub liniment on his sore muscles and wrap my arms around his body until he fell asleep. The next morning I'd wake before he did, make a breakfast of coffee, sowbelly bread with syrup or fried apples, eggs and potatoes. I'd pack a lunch with brown bread and bacon, pork and beans, corn dodgers or beef jerky and see him off to work. Then before I'd start the endless round of daily chores, I'd go over to Arvilla's for tea.

She loved to gossip, so I heard about some of the men who'd lived at the camp: Bill Crickenberg who'd been run out of Denver after robbing a bank. Jacob Frye, who'd lost his hand in a drunken brawl at one of the saloons in Central City. And Amanda Zimmer, the wife of a judge who'd ridden into the camp at Dogwood, taken one look at the place, and told their wagon driver to turn around and take her right back to Cincinnati.

"Her shoes didn't even touch the ground!" Arvilla laughed. "And we had to wait two months for another judge to bless us with his presence."

She told me about her own husband, about the three-story brick row house they'd owned in Society Hill, which they'd sold before following the doctor's wish to go west.

"I'm one for adventure," Arvilla said. "Always have been. There isn't anything or anyone that can intimidate me. So I was ready when he asked.

"It was Merrow getting tired of all the rules and regulations at the hospital where he worked in the city that led him to move us out here to Colorado. He wanted to work where medical men were needed. He knew he could build a good practice because the camps were doubling in population every month."

She stood and walked to the sink, the tip of her braid almost reaching her hips.

"You were brave," I said.

"I trusted him."

Mostly she talked, and I listened. She told me how she hadn't had any doubts about following her husband west and how much she still loved, as

I did, the smell of the pines, the sight of the soaring Rockies. It was those things, she said, that made any complaints about her living arrangements seem minor. I silently admonished myself for my own unhappiness with the cabin. I was about to tell Arvilla how much I wanted to go with Harvey to work at the mine when she said, "Only one thing gave me pause. And that was what I'd heard about the women who lived out here. Most of 'em prostitutes. Soiled doves. I don't think we realized how big a part of his practice they would be. Or how many there were."

Whenever we went into Central City, I'd see the women wearing burgundy, purple, and bright red dresses with low-cut bodices and high white mounds of bosom showing. They wore patterned hose and short skirts that stopped above their ankles.

"Every chance I got when we first arrived," Arvilla said, "I'd tell the mister not to have anything to do with them. Because they're crawling with disease. Skin sores on the mouth, a rash on their palms. He said he couldn't in good conscience leave them without treatment, so he offered what he could. Mercury ointments, arsenic, some patent medicine from a Dr. Ayer though my doc doesn't put much faith in that. He says those fancy bottles are mostly alcohol and opium. I finally gave up badgering him and let him do what he felt called to do. And I thanked the Lord I'd married a good-hearted man."

About a month after we'd arrived, Arvilla and I rode into Central City to the post office. The postmaster, a man with thick mutton chops and wire-rimmed glasses, handed me an envelope. It was the first mail I'd received since coming to Colorado, and I tore it open eagerly, certain it would be from my beloved Mama. But the note inside was from my father-in-law.

> *Angry not to have heard from Harvey by now. The only news I get comes from Tommy, and it's not good. Am wiring extra money so you can hire more men. Make sure you do it fast.*

I was shocked. Harvey had reassured me that even though they had yet to strike a new vein of silver, things were going well enough at the Fourth of July. There was a small but steady output of ore, and he was putting our earnings in a special account at the bank.

But when I went to the bank, the only account I found in our name was nearly empty. Arvilla helped me make the wire transfer William had sent, and that evening I waited on the porch so I could show Harvey his father's letter as soon as he got home.

But Dr. Bunn rode into camp before Harvey. He stopped his horse in front of me.

"You settling in all right?" he asked.

I hadn't seen much of Arvilla's husband since he was often travelling. He was as tall and thin as she was short and stout. A large black medicine bag swung from his saddle. Unlike the other men I'd noticed in camp, Doc Bunn always dressed like a gentleman, as Mama would say, in vest and pants, boiled white shirt, black string tie.

I rose from the rocker "Mrs. Bunn has been such a help to me."

"Well, she does have that way about her!" Despite his enthusiastic words, he was looking at me with concern.

The sun had slid down behind the trees, and the camp had a purplish hue. I realized with a start that Harvey should have been home a long time ago.

"Where is everyone?" I asked, realizing the camp seemed quieter than usual. It was a Tuesday, a week night, not a time the men would normally have been off drinking in Central City.

"I heard a number of them are celebrating an early pay day," he said. "The new train from Denver came into Central City today, and most of the miners rode in to meet it." He squinted as though deciding how much he wanted to say. "You'll hear a ruckus when they come in."

I stayed awake all night and heard the drunk men stumbling back to their cabins. But there was no sign of Harvey.

Arvilla showed up earlier than usual the next morning. "So you didn't get to tell him about the money?" she asked. A bag hung from a strap on her wrist.

I shook my head.

"Then I'm going to give you some advice you may or may not want." She opened the bag and pulled out an octagonal black box with a knobbed lid. "This is for your pocket money," she said. "You're going to take some of that money your father-in-law sent," and, seeing my face, added, "Just a small bit of it—and stash it in this can."

"Why would I do that?" I took a step back from her.

But she grabbed me by the elbow. "Just a few dollars, in case of an emergency. You're going to hide the tin somewhere your husband won't find it."

I shook my head.

"Listen to me," she said. "If your Harvey Doe has decided to join the other fellows in their all-night drinking at the saloons, you're going to have a problem on your hands. First, you don't want him spending all your money on drink. And second, there's no telling what other trouble he could get into."

CHAPTER 7

Harvey apologized when he came home that night. He looked exhausted, with dark half-moons under his eyes. But he said he'd spent the night with one of the miners and gone to work earlier than usual that morning. He made love to me three times after dinner.

But when I told him about his father's letter, he got angry and reached for a bottle of whiskey he kept atop the small nightstand. He said he'd tell Tommy Birdsall to hire more men but complained that William had put us in this mess, and it wasn't our fault if the mine wasn't yielding the riches he'd promised.

"I work like hell," he said, pouring a second shot. "What I want to do is go home. Until I can do that, I'm going to drink when I please."

I touched the hair at the nape of his neck. I longed to be able to ease the burden of his work. And I was more than eager to go back down into the mysteries of the mine myself. But every time I raised the possibility, he refused. So I did my work at the cabin, and like him, I was always tired at the end of the day from lugging buckets of water up from the stream, emptying the slop buckets, cleaning the always dirty floors and windows. I did the work because I knew our time in Colorado would be short and because I still dreamed there might be a rich pay-off before we returned to Oshkosh.

Mama's letters, the first of which had arrived the week after William's, repeated her own constant prayers for our quick return. She recommended books for me to read and told me she'd just finished *Rose in Bloom*, and that the heroine of that story reminded her of me—pretty and ambitious.

I *was* ambitious. I longed for us to strike it rich and ached to do the very work Harvey kept complaining about.

One night, Tommy Birdsall came to the cabin for dinner. He told us new silver deposits had been discovered in Leadville—at the Iron, Carbonate, and Fryer mines. Hundreds of ounces of silver were being found. He explained that the silver around Leadville was easier to access;

in fact, they'd found traces of high grade ore at just sixteen feet down.

Two days later, a new telegram arrived from William.

> URGENT. WATERMAN SET TO PULL OUT.
> MUST SPEED UP WORK. IGNORE WEATHER.
> CONTINUE THRU WINTER.

When I showed Harvey the telegram that evening, he tore it into shreds. Then he went to the cabinet and pulled out a bottle of Sazerac rye whiskey. "That's easy for him to say, isn't it? We're doing the best we can down there. What more does the old man want from me anyway?"

I turned away from him, and we didn't speak the rest of that night. And when we were in bed, and he pushed his hand between my legs, he encountered the cotton rags I had placed there, even though my menstrual period was still a week away.

The next day about noon, I saw Doc Bunn and Harvey ride up on their horses. Harvey's right arm was in a sling.

Doc Bunn dismounted then helped Harvey inside the cabin. "Bad news," he said. "Birdsall told me your husband was heating three sticks of Giant powder in a stove when the dynamite exploded. He broke his arm and damaged his wrist and hand pretty bad as well. Bad burns on that side of his body. But it could have been worse. There was a tragedy at the Printer's Boy just last week—killed four men."

We helped Harvey up the ladder to the loft and carefully positioned him on the bed.

"Just get me out of this damn place," he mumbled. "I want to go home."

I pulled the coverlet up to his neck. The doctor placed Harvey's bad arm on top of it, and I brushed the ends of his fingers, the only part of his hand not covered in bandages.

"As I say," Doc Bunn continued once we were back downstairs, "it could have been worse. Your Mister is lucky. It's his forearm that got broke so I was able to set it right there without trouble. But he's going to need time to heal. Two, three weeks I'd wager."

"I don't know what we'll do." I twisted my hands together, remembering the telegram from William.

"Now, now," Doc Bunn said, patting my arm. "First job is for you to take care of your husband. You'll want to change his bandages every day. And dust flour over the burns. Make a thick coating of it, then add cotton batting in layers." He pulled a stack of white pads from his bag. "I'll leave these for you; they'll help keep the dressing in place.

"In a week, Harvey can get out of bed, not before. You're going to have your hands full feeding and caring for him. I'll make sure Arvilla gets over here to help."

For six days I did what I was told. I cleaned Harvey's wounds and changed his bandages, in addition to all the other chores. I cooked his favorite foods like fat pork and flippers, creamed root vegetables, white pot, molasses pie, biscuits and gravy. I doled out the morphine tablets Doctor Bunn had left. But no matter how tenderly I cared for my husband, he complained and got angry at me. He was upset about the constant pain he was feeling, about the lack of progress at the mine, about his father's unrealistic demands.

That Saturday, Tommy Birdsall showed up on our doorstep. After visiting Harvey privately in the loft, Tommy asked if I had a moment to speak with him as well.

"Of course," I said. I poured two cups of coffee, and we went to sit on the front porch.

"Temperatures droppin' pretty fast," he said then finished his coffee in two swallows, setting the cup down next to his worn boot.

"I'd thought we'd be heading home by now," I said.

He nodded. "That was the plan."

I wondered what communication there'd been between Tommy and my father-in-law.

"The thing is, Mrs. Doe," Tommy continued. "It's rough with Mr. Doe out of commission." He pulled leaves from a pouch and lit a pipe. The tobacco smelled sweet and warm. "The men's spirits are low. Even after we dug out the new drift, there's been no sign of silver."

"Did William tell you that Waterman wants to pull out?"

He nodded.

"Is there any money left to hire more men?" A swirl of smoke coiled above his head. "Do *you* think we can find more silver, or is the mine a lost cause?"

"Oh, there's always a chance. I'm not giving up on the Fourth of July yet. And Mr. Doe has given me enough to bring on one more man. But after Harvey's accident, that still leaves me short."

A bucket of potatoes sat on the floor by my rocker. I'd planned to peel them for that night's dinner.

"Let me help," I said.

Grateful he didn't laugh, I pressed on.

"I went down in the mine with William when we first got here," I said. "I was surprised how exciting it was, how unafraid I felt. I felt drawn to something." I hesitated, not sure if I could tell him how mystical it had seemed, how other-worldly. "I'm not afraid to work. I've wanted to go down into that mine ever since we got here. But Harvey wouldn't let me."

At this he finally laughed. "No, don't imagine he would! I wouldn't have either, Mrs. Doe. No offense meant. But women and mines don't mix."

"What do you mean?" I asked. "I may not be as tall or strong as the men, but I'm sure there are things I could do."

"That's not what I mean, ma'am. It just ain't right. Ain't done."

I stood and put my hand on the sleeve of his flannel shirt. I had to convince him. If Harvey and I had to stay in Colorado while he healed, I had no desire to be stuck in the cabin. I'd help Harvey as much as I could the next few days then once he could manage a bit on his own, ask Arvilla to check in on him during the day while I was gone.

"Just for two weeks, Tommy. Let me try."

He shook his head. "Ain't gonna work, ma'am. The miners, they wouldn't take kindly to you being there."

"Why not?"

"It's bad luck, Mrs. Doe!" he said. "I've lived in camps where the women won't even step outside to do their housework until the men are all underground. Superstition is that if a woman crosses a miner's path on his way to the mine, he'll die in a roof fall or explosion that very day."

"But you just said, that's superstition."

"There's plenty more stories like that, ma'am, and whether they're true or not, my miners believe 'em. A mine's no place for a woman."

I couldn't convince Tommy. After he left, I peeled potatoes and cooked a dinner Harvey barely touched.

"There's nothing romantic about it," Harvey said.

He sat at the table finishing breakfast. Three days had passed since my talk with Tommy. Harvey's arm was still in a sling, but he was finally able to sit upright to eat.

Instead of a dress, I'd put on a denim shirt and a pair of Harvey's work pants, their hems rolled up and the top bunched together by a rope wrapped twice around my waist.

"I won't allow it," he said. "I won't have my wife doing hard labor. Besides, there's no fortune to be made here. Don't you know that by now? My father tricked us."

"I've already talked to Tommy." I didn't tell him that we'd lost yet another man to an accident the day before, and how when Tommy came to tell me, I'd finally been able to convince him to give me a chance.

"You don't know what it's like down there," he said. "It's dark. It stinks. It's dangerous." His pupils were pin-pricks, and his eyes heavy-lidded.

"You know as well as I do we don't have any time to waste," I said slowly. "You know I'm a hard worker. And you know Tommy will take good care of me." I licked my lips, readying a lie. "Tommy said I'd mostly work above ground, helping the men up top. But if I don't get out there now, we'll lose Waterman's money. We'll lose the mine."

No matter how much he objected, there was nothing that he could do to stop me. I tucked him back in bed, made sure that Arvilla would take him lunch, and set off for the Fourth of July. When I got there, half a dozen men squatted on the ground or sat on logs, drinking coffee from tin cups and smoking cigars. Three Chinamen sat in a separate small group to the right, black braids cascading down the backs of their gray shirts. I tied my horse to a railing and lifted the lunch pail from the saddle.

"Something mighty strange here, ain't it, Meecham?"

This loud stage whisper came from behind me.

"Must be lost," another voice answered.

I turned to see who was talking, but no one would meet my gaze.

Tommy stood by the entrance down into the mine. As I walked toward him, I heard, again from behind me, "This ain't no place for berry-picking."

A man suddenly stepped in front of me. A dirty hat slouched on his head, and the grip of a pistol poked up from the top of his boot.

"If you're fixing to take the place of your husband, Mrs. Doe, forget it. Mr. Doe's been no help around here, and your presence won't be no help either."

Tommy joined us. "I told y'all, Mrs. Doe is going to help us out. Just for a few days until I can bring in a replacement. We need all the extra hands we can get, you know that well as I do."

Crude laughter.

"No woman her size can hold a drill."

"You're right, Charlie Jack," Tommy said. "There'll be no lifting a heavy Burleigh for Mrs. Doe. But there's other things she can do. Fill the ore wagons, clean the sluice, you name it, there's plenty of jobs to be done. And goddamn it, you know how short-handed we are." He frowned and shook his head. "Believe me, we won't find anybody, man or woman, with a bigger desire to work here."

The man Tommy called Charlie Jack spit into the dirt as though marking his territory like a dog.

Tommy pressed on. "So that clears that. Meecham, I'm sending Mrs. Doe off with Leonard this morning to work the sluice."

Meecham stood up from the rock he'd been sitting on. "That sounds right to me, boss. Young man could use another mother in the worst way." He hitched up his Levis and tipped his hat at me.

Tommy grabbed my elbow and started leading me away.

"Wait a minute," I said. "You told me I could work in the mine. Where are we going?"

"You're on sluice duty today. Let's give the men time to get used to seeing you around."

We came to a stream. A young man lifted shovel loads of dirt and gravel into a large bucket on the bank.

"Leonard Will, this here's Mrs. Doe," Tommy said. "She's going to help you this morning."

The boy blinked rapidly. "That's—that's fine with me, s-s-sir."

Tommy was putting me to work with his newest, and youngest, recruit, someone least likely to object to working alongside a woman.

"First, you're going to classify the materials," Tommy said while Leonard went back to shoveling, stirring the clear water into a muddy soup. He pointed to a thin wire mesh covering the bucket. "This netting makes sure that all the rocks and dirt that end up in the sluice will be the same size."

A wooden contraption, about six feet long, had been stuck into the stream bed. This box sloped down about four inches, and strips of wood about a foot apart ran across its width.

"That there's the sluice box. Leonard will do the heavy work with the shovel. When that bucket's half full, take what's inside and drop it into the sluice. Go slow. One handful at a time."

Leonard, without stopping his shoveling, said, "Those, those are called riffles, m-m-ma'am. They'll catch whatever silver runs through."

I realized gratefully that Tommy had known Leonard would share whatever knowledge he'd acquired with me.

"We've only got one sluice box because most of the ore's deep in the ground. And we've only got this one stream. Still, there're nuggets here that will fetch a good price at the assayer's. Enough to make it worthwhile," Tommy said.

I heard the low-pitched twitter of swallows and turned to see a large flock of them rise up from the trees.

"Then one more step," Tommy continued. "Cleaning. Leonard will help you lift the box."

"The big-big-bigger nuggets'll be at the t-t-top," Leonard added.

A shout came from behind us. "Tommy, get back here! Problem with the cage."

Tommy frowned. "Think you've got it?"

"Yes," I said, struggling not to show my disappointment. "For now."

"Then I'll leave you to it." Tommy quickly turned away, shouting as he ran, "On my way, Callum!"

Leonard and I worked together all morning. He was very polite to me, showing me how to find silver flakes by panning the black sands and how to tell the difference between silver and mica.

At lunchtime we joined the other miners. I'd brought Harvey's lunch pail and ate beef stew in silence. Looking around, I realized I'd been sending a finer lunch with Harvey than the other miners brought; most had canned pork and beans, or a simple sandwich with strips of salt pork between two pieces of hardtack.

No one made any effort to include me in conversation.

"Heard tell Tabor and Meyers are incorporating Leadville," Charlie Jack said.

"Some folks did that with Fairplay in '72."

"Yep," Charlie said, wolfing down his food. "Oughta head up there come spring."

"Site has better pickins', I hear."

"First gold, then silver." This from the man Tommy had called Meecham. "Weren't just hard work that made those two rich, you know. Had to be a hell of a lot of luck as well."

"No other explanation for it." Charlie Jack wiped his mouth with his sleeve, leaving a greasy streak. "We work hard as hell. Harder than Waterman and the Mayor who drops by then skedaddles back east."

I felt my face warm.

A man with an Irish accent spoke up. "In any case, both Tabor and Meyers have a reputation for being hard workers. Tabor started out like one of us, remember. Just a placer miner sweating over a shovel here in the Gulch."

"I'm sure as hell heading to Leadville first sign of warm weather," Charlie Jack said. "Get my own claim in before some other fool does. Time's a wastin' on this dead-end here."

After lunch, when Leonard and I were back at the sluice, he said, "I'm so-sorry, Mrs. D-d-doe. They don't mean nothin'. Besides, it's mostly red-haired women they don't want here. And you're blond."

He lifted another shovel into the bucket.

"What difference does that make?" I asked.

Leonard thought for a bit then answered, "See, usually wo-wo-women only come here to look for somebody's who's hurt or d-d-dead. And red-haired women, well, they say they're omens of d-d-death. So, you're lucky. With the color of your hair, I m-m-mean." He grinned as though he'd suddenly found an answer to a terrible problem. "They'll come around," he assured me, without a single stutter.

I didn't care whether the other miners came around or not. I was there to work. The more I could concentrate on that goal, the better. I was there to go back down into the mine, feel the excitement and promise I'd felt that afternoon standing with William. So I worked until 5 o'clock then told Leonard and Tommy goodbye and mounted my horse to ride back to the cabin.

When I got there, Harvey was nowhere to be seen.

CHAPTER 8

Doc Bunn brought him home around ten, carrying him like a sack of potatoes up onto the porch.

"I found him over yonder." He motioned with his head toward the far end of camp. "Passed out cold. My guess is he'd paid a visit to Po Li's. Smelled the sweet smoke all over him."

It was true. Harvey's clothes smelled like they'd been doused in one of my Mama's floral perfumes.

The doctor set Harvey down on his feet. Harvey wobbled but remained standing.

"I told you I wouldn't have you working." His voice was surprisingly clear.

"You've got to get yourself up that ladder, young man," Doc Bunn said, pushing Harvey forward.

I watched as the doctor followed Harvey up into the loft, listened from below as clothes were removed and Harvey's body tumbled onto the bed. Only then did I shout my answer up to him.

"We don't have a choice."

The next morning I ran over to Arvilla's and asked her if she would stay with Harvey during the day. I couldn't risk him sneaking off again to smoke opium. I'm sure the doctor told her what had happened, but she didn't ask any questions, just nodded and patted my shoulder.

Tommy kept me working above ground again that day and the next. I was bone tired—taking care of Harvey and doing most of the cooking and cleaning after I got home in the evening. I cut corners, not cleaning the windows daily like I usually did, reusing water so I didn't have to make so many trips down to the stream. Arvilla helped by doubling what she cooked for herself and the doctor. I was grateful that, unlike the men, she didn't seem to be bothered by my working at the mine.

On my fourth day, still restricted to the sluice above ground, I heard an explosion mid-morning. Leonard and I ran over to the log frame that stood above the hole into the mine. A fancy hoisting apparatus had been built, and instead of climbing down a ladder like I had, the men now rode down in a metal cage.

I saw Meecham desperately trying to slow a rope that was quickly unrolling.

Someone yelled, "Windlass broke! Get us down from here before somebody gets hurt!"

"I'm lowering her smooth as I can," Meecham yelled back.

Then a crash and moans.

"Damn it to hell!"

I looked around for Tommy, but he was nowhere to be seen.

Then I heard his voice coming up from down below. "Get somebody down here, fast. Bring gauze, wood for splints."

Leonard sprinted over to a barrel resting on its side, ripped off its top, then ran back with pieces of green wood he dumped on the ground. He left again, returning with gauze that he handed to Meecham. "Can't be me," Meecham said. "And I need you to help me hold this thing."

"I'll go," I said quickly.

Meecham shook his head but lifted me in one quick swoop into the bucket that hung from the second windlass that was still working.

I held on tight to the hoisting cable to keep my balance. Meecham dropped the gauze and splints into the bucket on top of bits of slag and broken drill bits. Leonard handed me a hat. It was cloth, with a metal plate with a hole in it where a candle could be stuck.

I stuffed my hair up then grabbed the greasy sides of the bucket with both hands.

It pitched and rocked wildly as I descended into darkness, far below where I'd ventured with William. Once again, I felt claustrophobic as the dark wet walls of the narrow shaft closed in around me.

Below me I could see maybe a dozen lanterns and lit candles stuck in bent spikes that had been poked into beams and cracks in the walls. The men standing at the bottom cast eerie shadows, and when the bucket came to a halt, I could see two men lying on the floor of the cage that had fallen. Both writhed in pain. Tommy knelt beside them. He frowned when he saw me but said, "Get over here. Now."

White bone stuck out of Charlie Jack's left leg. He screamed as

Tommy straightened the bone and positioned a makeshift splint. The other man had a fierce cut running the length of his leg. It was clear neither would be working for a while.

I helped Tommy with bandages and, once the men were taken care of as well as we could manage, I followed the other miners up above ground. It was already dusk.

Tommy said, "Don't you *ever* do that again without asking me. You hear me, Mrs. Doe?"

"Give her a break, Tommy." It was Meecham, sweat pouring down his face from the weight of the loads he'd just pulled up.

My heart beat fast. I'd gone underground again; I'd felt that live current of excitement. Yes, the accident and the men's injuries were terrible, and I worried about them. But there was also a part of me hoping that maybe, now that Tommy had seen me down inside the mine, he'd let me drop into the Fourth of July again. Only this time, to look for silver.

That night, when I finally got home, I found Harvey and Arvilla and Doc Bunn at the kitchen table, eating sourdough biscuits and steak. Arvilla filled a plate and set it before me.

"We heard what happened," she said. "You all right?"

I nodded.

Harvey pursed his lips and refused to look at me, then ate the rest of his dinner without speaking.

If the head man at the Fourth of July had been anyone other than Tommy Birdsall, I'm sure I wouldn't have been allowed to do what I started doing the next day after the cage accident. But the loss of those two men put us in an even worse bind than we were already in, so that next morning Tommy took me down into the mine with him and taught me how to use a pick-axe and small drill.

I don't know why I wasn't afraid, especially after what I'd just witnessed. But I felt like I had that first day when William put the silver nugget in my hand: that the mine was safe, a place where work yielded reward. As I rode down with Tommy, I realized, too, how each breath became more precious as we descended.

The tunnel I'd seen that day with William still operated on Level 1. But the main digging was now three hundred feet below. Each level we passed on the way down was lit in a yellow glow. On the levels where dynamite had just broken into a wall, rock dust hung in the air.

I wore the hat Leonard had handed me the day before, this time with a candle stuck in its metal plate. Tommy lit its wick as soon as we left the cage then walked me over to where a small pick-axe leaned against a wall. It had an axe at one end and a spike at the other. The handle was made of hickory and probably about three feet long. "This weighs about five pounds," Tommy said. "Think you can handle it?"

I lifted it in my hands. The handle was strong and sturdy.

"You'll want to flex your knees a little, so the weight's less likely to knock you over." He took the tool from me and swung it overhead, extending his arms as he brought the axe forward and down. "If you swing too high, you'll lose control."

He swung again, bringing the axe point directly into the wall. Chips of dirt and rock flew out. "Once you hit, raise the handle up. This will help loosen the dirt." He looked at me. "Ready for a few practice swings?"

I nodded.

"Always make sure no one's behind you before you swing. Don't swing side to side."

I stared straight at the area I wanted to hit.

"Stand closer. You don't want it coming down on your leg or foot."

I moved to about a foot from the wall, gripped the handle tightly, and lifted the axe shoulder-high. Then, using all my weight, I pushed it forward into the wall. The pick axe bounced off, and I stumbled backwards.

I lifted the axe again, moving my feet to steady myself. Again I brought the axe down. This time, slivers of dirt and small rocks shot off. I rested the tool on the ground in front of me, adjusted the cap on my head and got ready to try again.

I lifted the axe and brought it down. This time its point went into the dirt an inch or more. Without resting, I hoisted the axe and swung, again and again and again. The tool felt heavy, but I would not stop.

I heard footsteps behind me but didn't turn. The hole was widening and deepening, and I kept pitching the axe forward, throwing it with all my weight. I would break through this seemingly impenetrable surface if it killed me. I would find whatever treasure might be hidden there.

Again and again, I brought that axe down, until the muscles in my arms burned. On the last swing, I let it fall to the ground. I bent over, heaving in great gasps of damp air. Sweat rolled down my face.

From behind me, I heard the sound of hands clapping. I turned and saw Tommy, Meecham, and Charlie Jack standing there, their faces solemn, their hands clapping against each other slowly and rhythmically.

Tommy stepped forward and pointed to some dark streaks in the wall. "This is what you're looking for," he said. "Lead-silver carbonate."

"You've got a hell of a will for somebody so tiny," Meecham said that day when we broke for lunch. "You're like a toy ... like a baby doll."

And from that day on, the miners called me Baby Doe.

CHAPTER 9

"Mrs. Doe?"

It had been a long time since anyone addressed me so formally. Even in Central City, word spread quickly that I was working at the Fourth of July. I'd decided that I wasn't going to sit around camp fetching water, scrubbing floors with vinegar, and baking bread while I watched our only chance to strike it rich slip through my fingers. Enough new ore had been found to keep the mine open, and William wired money to keep us afloat whenever we needed extra help.

I finished pulling on gray work gloves and turned to see an unfamiliar face. I squinted through the rock dust hanging in the air to see a stranger, looking comically out of place in the underground tunnel. He wore a tan overcoat with bottle-green vest and starched white shirt front.

"Mrs. Doe?" he said again.

A few feet from us the revolving drum of a jaw crusher rumbled.

"Eugene Cafferty, ma'am." The man had to shout to be heard over the noise.

I shook my head fiercely; I had no time for chit-chat. I knew full well that every moment in the mine carried danger. Every miner had to stay focused, move carefully, and look sharply. Despite the danger, I loved the fact that whatever worries I had—about Harvey, about the merits of trying so hard to find a fortune—vanished as soon as I'd sunk below ground level. It was another world down there, magically distant from daily woes. If the work underground came with danger, it only made my time in the mine more precious.

So I turned away from the unwelcome visitor and began to tamp black powder into a hole.

Suddenly the noise of the jaw crusher stopped.

The man said, "I'm editor of the weekly paper in Central City. *Town Talk.*"

I knew of it. I bought a copy every time Arvilla and I went in for supplies. Its pages were filled with ads for medicated vapor baths and stabling horses, business cards for surveyors and undertakers, announcements of worship services I didn't have time to attend. There were notices for meetings of the Independent Order of Odd Fellows and Sons of Malta; announcements of "hug socials" where you could pay ten cents to hug anyone under 20 years old, a dollar to hug another man's wife. The price of gold and silver stocks, which I read avidly. Just that week, I'd read news about the continuing good fortune of Horace Tabor in Leadville, who'd struck "the richest body of ore ever found on Fryer Hill." The ore from his Chrysolite and Matchless mines was already bringing in $100,000 a month.

"I know you're busy," Cafferty said.

"I am," I said.

"You'll need more mud in there than that." This from Tommy, who'd appeared at my side.

"What *is* that foul smell?" Cafferty asked.

Without answering, Tommy bent to pull rags from the turned-down tops of his tall boots. "You'll need these for your ears," he said, handing them to me and Cafferty. Then staring directly at Cafferty, he added, "I told you it wasn't a good idea to come down here but once you're here, you play by our rules."

"If you'll just give me a minute…" The man was oblivious to what was about to happen. "I wrote about this mine when Waterman started panning here. But you've got a real operation now. How many shafts—three, four?"

I finished setting the last powder, and Tommy picked up a flat iron sheet to cover the drill holes.

"How much are you bringing in now?" Cafferty asked.

"Thousand ninety-one dollars last week," Tommy said. "But we're set to blast any minute. You best find a place to rest your head and cover your ears, Mr. Cafferty."

If we'd set the charges right, we could push forward as much as two feet. Enough to find another vein worth tapping.

Tommy motioned us to leave through a crawlway where we joined five other miners, already bent low with hands over their caps.

"I'm on a tour of mines," Cafferty said as he stepped over an oil-flecked puddle of water. "Mostly hard rock mines right here in the gulch. The Printer, American Flag, Five and Twenty." His brogans slipped on the wet floor.

"Shut up," Matt Plunkett said.

Then Tommy's voice echoed, low and steady. "Fire in the hole!" He ran into the crawlway where we waited and pushed Cafferty down to the ground. "Ten. Nine. Eight. Seven," Tommy bellowed. "Fire in the hole! Four. Three. Two. One."

Hot, dusty air rushed into my lungs as the ground shook beneath us. I reached my hand out for support, but it was too dark to see through the huge cloud of dust that pressed toward us. *I am so far beneath this earth, I am part of the earth*, I thought. Ghostly shapes floated against the rock. The men had told me stories about the Tommy Knockers, the spirits of dead miners that could sometimes haunt a shaft. The good ones would be heard knocking on walls to point out profitable veins; the bad ones would trick miners into dead ends and avalanches.

My hat slipped, and Tommy reached to put it back in position. A second loud explosion rang out.

The first words I heard when I pulled the rags from my ears were, "What the hell!"

Cafferty stood, angrily shaking down his knickerbockers. "Why didn't you send me back up? I'm a civilian, remember?"

"But you insisted on talking to the owner, Mr. Cafferty." Tommy was as impatient with this intruder as I was.

"Look, I have a job to do. And I'm going to do it then get out of here." He pulled a pad of paper and pencil from his back pocket, brushing a thick layer of dust off both.

"Where's *Mr.* Doe?" he asked quickly. "Who's really in charge here?"

"He's down on level 3," Tommy lied. Harvey had disappeared after lunch; his absences were becoming more frequent. "We've dug another 70, 80 feet there."

Cafferty scribbled on his pad. "Most folks round here think it's bad luck for a woman to work in a mine."

I removed my hat and shook out my hair. When Cafferty's eyes widened, I remembered how it felt to be beautiful, something I hadn't thought about for months.

"Haven't seen many women like you in my mine tours."

"I'm sure you haven't." I wiped my eyes with the back of my sleeve.

We walked toward the cage that would carry us above ground. Tommy stepped between Cafferty and the thick rope rising above us. He untied the small pouch that hung from his belt, next to his revolver, and opened it in front of Cafferty's nose. "You know this tobacco I got here, Mr.—uh—Cafferty, is it? It's mighty special stuff."

Cafferty tried to push past Tommy. The wheel suspended from the A-frame above us creaked; the two ropes hanging from it shimmied.

But Tommy still blocked the visitor's way. "It comes from willow bark. With sumac, tobacco, and sage mixed in. Plus some buffalo bone marrow."

Cafferty kept his eyes on the cage lurching down toward us, and I saw the mule inside it, its legs slung so it wouldn't kick. The poor animal wouldn't be untied for hours, until it was used to its dark new environment. Later it would help pull ore cars to clear out the two tons of muck just unlodged by the explosion, and it would never see the light of day again. I couldn't bear to look the sweet thing in the eyes.

"See," Tommy said slowly. "I never once heard of this particular tobacco 'til I left Kansas."

The cage and mule were just a few feet above us now; the mule brayed frantically.

"So you see, mister," Tommy continued, "things that seem strange at first—like who works where, for instance, and what they look like and all—might be nothin' more than just somethin' you never heard of before."

Cafferty sputtered as Matt Plunkett and Meecham pulled the mule out and led him down the tunnel we'd just exited.

As soon as the cage was empty, Cafferty rushed in, catching the tail of his overcoat on a strip of rusted metal. The fabric ripped. "Damn it, get me out of here!" he yelled and yanked on the rope. Tommy and

I climbed in behind him then slowly, lifted by unseen hands, the cage began to rise.

Four days later, Arvilla brought me the new issue of *Town Talk*. For some unknown reason, Eugene Cafferty had forgotten his fear and anger and written a generally favorable account of his visit to the mine:

> *I next reached the Fourth of July Lode, a mine which has not been worked for several years, but started up last year under the personal supervision of the owner, Mr. W. H. Doe and his wife. The young lady manages one half of the property while her liege lord manages the other. I found both at their separate shafts managing a number of workmen, Mr. Doe at his, which is 70 feet, and his wife, who is full of ambition, in her new enterprise, at hers which is sunk 60 feet. This is the first instance where a lady, and such she is, has managed a mining property. The mine is doing very well and produces some rich ore.*
>
> *Central City Town Talk*—Oct. 14, 1878

Tommy's lie about Harvey had made it into the newspaper. It wasn't the first time Harvey had left early to drink at the Teller House Bar, and I knew it wouldn't be the last. But I had news to tell him that I hoped might turn him off drink for good.

I was pregnant.

> *I had strong Vision to-day I saw a beautiful little white fat Baby with beautiful round big eyes looking up into my eyes the Baby was close up to my face on my left breast up on my heart close to my face the Baby was all in rich white with a fluffy white baby cap on & white cloak & I saw the Vision for a long time & I said "O you lovely dear little Baby" I love you it kept looking up at me all the time for a long time before the Vision passed.*

CHAPTER 10

Dear Cordelia,

I write with horrible news. I gave birth to a baby boy one week past. Stillborn, just five months old. I prayed to Jesus many times to save him, but Jesus took my baby home to Himself instead. I also prayed that Jesus would bring you and Mama to me, to stand beside my bed, to hold my hand and Heart. And you did appear to me in dreams and visions, both of you holding me and my boy in love.

My Harvey is heartbroken, even more than he was before. He hates it here in Colorado, hates the mine, and now I fear hates me. I do not know my husband anymore, Cordelia, and wonder how marriage goes with you and Andrew. I know I was not to expect more from my husband than I receive from the Lord, but still, the loneliness I feel here is sometimes unbearable, and I fear that my grievances will now be worse. The only friend I have is a neighbor woman. Without her, I would not make it through my days. Harvey rarely speaks to me anymore, and when he does, he is usually drunk on whiskey or tired and incoherent on morphine. He says he needs the medicine for his arm, which, as I last wrote you, was broken in an accident, but I believe he has grown addicted to the horrible stuff. I often find yellow pills and aqua vials in his pockets. The doctor has refused to give him more medicine, but Harvey finds ways to get these addictive substances from others who live here at camp. And he spends hours drinking at the Teller House Bar in Central City. He says he goes to play the piano there, but I know for a fact that he goes to drink. I have begged God to take away the burden of whatever pain Harvey is feeling, but now with the loss of our baby, I fear my husband, who I have tried to love so dearly through all this trial, will slip further and further away from me.

Your grieving sister,

Lizzie

CHAPTER 11

One Saturday in September, Arvilla asked me to go with her into Central City to eat dinner at Cochran's. Harvey had slept until noon that day then ridden into town shortly after he woke, so I welcomed the chance to be with Arvilla rather than sit home alone worrying about his whereabouts and what time and in what state he might return.

It was dusk by the time we reached town and tied up our horses. But instead of heading directly into the restaurant as I expected, Arvilla grabbed my arm, pulling me in close to her as three very inebriated men stumbled past us.

She frowned, but I sensed it wasn't the drunken men that bothered her. "There's something you and I have got to do." Her serious tone surprised me.

"What's wrong, Arvilla?"

"Nothing the good Lord can't fix," she said. "With a little helping hand from us flawed folks down here."

The restaurant door opened, and a well-dressed couple stepped out arm-in-arm.

"Look at me," Arvilla said. "This is going to be almost as hard on me as it will be on you. But there's no by-passing difficulties some days. And since your own Mama's not here to protect you, it's fallen to me to lift the veil that hangs before your eyes."

My jaw tightened. I'd been keeping my feelings under control for months now. Mostly, I went through the motions of keeping a home and working at the mine, downplaying the worries I had about Harvey's drinking and drug-taking, the sorrow I had at the loss of my baby. When I wrote letters home, I assured Mama that we were fine, that Harvey was healthy and a wonderful husband. I hadn't breathed a word of my fears to Arvilla either, but suddenly felt that the strong façade I'd worked so hard to build was about to crumble.

A scent of jasmine and tuberose wafted from the woman who'd just exited the restaurant. She wore a satin dinner dress in taupe and ivory. A terrible arrow of jealousy shot through me. She looked so happy, so well cared for on the arm of a man I assumed was her husband. That's what I had wanted too, I thought.

Arvilla leaned her face closer to mine. "I believe there are certain rules that must be followed," she said. "And keeping the sanctity of the marriage vow is one of them."

"What do you mean?" I spoke so loudly the well-dressed couple turned to stare at us. The man placed a gloved hand under his wife's elbow and led her away. I blinked rapidly. "If you're insinuating that Harvey has broken our wedding vows, you are wrong, Arvilla Bunn." I'd never spoken so harshly to her; she was the only friend I had in Colorado. But I knew that if I didn't put up a fight against her words, the flimsy structure of my life might collapse completely.

I saw in her face that my angry tone had hurt her feelings, and I tried to sound calmer. "I know Harvey has problems," I said. "I know the demons he faces. Your own husband has talked to him about his dependence on morphine."

"That's not what I'm talking about, Lizzie."

People kept pushing past us, and one man wearing a bandana around his throat gave me a lewd wink.

I lowered my voice, almost whispering into Arvilla's ear. "Harvey's ardor for me has never once lapsed," I said. "And I have no reason to imagine he would need to be unfaithful."

I wanted to feel angry; I wanted to feel anything other than this sinking despair.

"In fact," I said, "I am planning to telegram William next week. It is time for us to go home to Wisconsin. Harvey can get the help he needs there to wean him off the medication, and we can settle into a normal life."

"Where's your man now?" Arvilla asked.

The door to the restaurant opened, and a gale of laughter blew out from a table of diners.

"Probably the Teller House," I said. "Billy lets him play the piano there." At last here was something solid I could do to show her she was wrong. "Let's go; I'll show you."

Arvilla shook her head back and forth, her long gray braid swinging from side to side. "Nope," she said. "My bet is he's not there. And here's why: Merrow told me he saw Harvey at the Bon Ton last week."

I stepped backwards off the sidewalk, grabbing the railing where we'd tied the horses.

"In case you don't know, that's one of the brothels over on State Street. Merrow was there to check out the girls," she said.

The tail of the horse brushed against me, and I stepped back up on the sidewalk.

"In order to leave him, you must make a good legal case," Arvilla said. "And you need evidence for that."

"I don't know what on earth you are talking about, Arvilla Bunn. Come on, let's go inside and have a nice dinner." I tried to lead her toward the door, but she wrestled from my grasp. "I won't do whatever it is you want me to do, Arvilla," I said. "I won't."

"You've got to. And much as it hurts my heart, I'm the one who's going to make you do it." She wrapped her fingers tightly around my blue sleeve. "We're going to Sheeny Pearl's."

I felt dizzy, as though all the fight had left me, and I let her drag me like a stuffed doll down the street. I lost all sense of the commotion around us on the sidewalk and kept my eyes glued to Arvilla's gray cotton skirt and the marks her lace-up leather boots left in the dust. I looked up only when she came to a stop. We stood in front of a pink house guarded by four tall spruce trees. A gas light with a red shade hung above its door.

A man stepped out from behind one of the trees. A six-pointed gold badge twinkled on his navy blue shirt.

"Deputy Hanrahan, ma'am," he said, taking off his Stetson. "Andy. The Doc asked me to meet you two here."

I ripped Arvilla's fingers from my arm and yelled, "No! I won't do this!"

"Come on, Lizzie," she said. "We're trying to save your life."

"I brought the bar key," the deputy said. "That'll get us in if Sheeny Pearl decides to give us any trouble."

The door opened, and a large black-skinned woman wearing a red satin dress stood there, hands on her hips. A puckered scar snaked down between her ample breasts.

"Making a house call tonight, are we, Deputy Hanrahan?" Her voice was deep and husky.

The deputy waved a piece of paper in front of her, and she stepped aside.

Arvilla was behind me, pushing me forward. My eyes stung from the smoke hanging in the room. A flocked red wallpaper covered the walls, and colored paper flowers framed a large gilt mirror. I blinked, trying to take in everything at once: men sitting in overstuffed chairs and half-naked women draped over medallion-backed sofas. A group huddled around a small table, passing a long-stemmed pipe over an oil lamp. It felt like a nightmare had come to life, and all I wanted to do was wake before it devoured me.

"We're here for Harvey Doe," the deputy said, and it took a minute for me to realize that the moan I heard came from my own mouth.

Sheeny Pearl ran a finger down her scar, eyeing Arvilla and me. "You two hens do-gooders?" she asked.

Andy swung the baton hanging from his belt to point at me. "This one's Mrs. Doe."

Sheeny Pearl grinned; three gold teeth gleamed in her mouth. She nodded toward a staircase at the back of the room. "Room 8," she said. "But you listen here, little man Deputy Han-ra-han. I don't want my girls thinkin' this is a full-blown raid."

"No, ma'am," the deputy said then turned to the stairs, putting his hat back on his head. Arvilla pushed my back to make me follow him. When I turned to see if I could make a run for the door, I saw Sheeny Pearl blocking it, her arms crossed and those gold teeth shining.

So, as if in one of my own dreams, I followed the deputy up carpeted stairs and down a long hall. I kept my arms tight around my waist, counting the numbers marked in brass on doors with peeling paint. We passed #1, #2, #3, and I steadied myself by putting my fingers against one of the doors. I took a deep breath, then another, and closed my eyes. I could walk this way, sensing the deputy's slim form before me and Arvilla's heavier one behind. If I kept my eyes closed, I might wake up back in the cabin, in bed in the loft, with Harvey lying beside me.

I bumped into the Deputy when he stopped and opened my eyes. There was another white door on which a brass #8 tilted jauntily to the right.

Arvilla's hands pressed hard into my lower back.

The deputy unhooked a key ring from his pocket and removed one of its smaller keys. From down the hall came the sound of breaking glass.

For some reason, that sound jarred me awake at last. "Do it," I said. "Open the door." The muscles in my legs tightened, ready to run if I had to.

The key turned in the lock; the door swung open. I had to stand on tiptoe to look over the deputy's shoulder. And there was my Harvey, his familiar body naked and white on a too-narrow bed, his beautiful long legs entwined with the paler legs of a young girl, who was also naked and had red hair, even on the tiny triangle between her legs. On a dresser to the side stood a bottle of bourbon, a hairbrush, a syringe.

Harvey stumbled up from the cot, pulling the sheets around him, leaving the girl exposed. Her breasts were those of a child, and her skin was slick with sweat. Every detail burned itself on my mind.

Harvey's hand reached out toward me. "Lizzie," he said, and finally, I saw how the man I had married, the man I had loved, was no more, was lost to me. Without a word, I turned and ran down the hall past all those numbered doors and down the stairs, ignoring Harvey's insistent shouts behind me. I ran past the lounging women and the pipe-smoking men, and somehow made my way out to the street, where I sucked in great gulps of cold air before leaning over and vomiting into the dirt.

I was kneeling down by the bed praying—and all at once I heard down outside of my window as if low down—and all was so still not anything stirring I heard a loud piercing heart-rendering shrieking cry so sad and awful, then in a few seconds about a minute it gave out the very same loud terrible cry so sharp so agonizing piercing the night & so mournful only twice It cried I got to the open window before the 2nd cry was finished O it was unearthly like the Banchee-Cry.

CHAPTER 12

The next morning I rode back into Central City and sent telegrams to my parents and father-in-law saying that Harvey needed to be sent home and placed under a doctor's care, and I would be filing for a divorce. I spent the next two weeks in bed at Arvilla's cabin, burning with fever and plagued with nightmares. There were dark, menacing figures in these dreams. Rail-thin figures in black. Striped snakes coiled in hieroglyphs. I even saw a yellow-eyed Devil in one, wearing a top hat and grinning.

As I expected, Mama sent a return wire begging me to return home as well. But I felt too much shame. I was drowning in it. I had embarrassed my family, been too blind to see how much Harvey had betrayed me. I simply couldn't face returning home as a divorcée. I knew that a divorce would lead to ex-communication from my church, though I could not, in my heart, understand why. Why would Jesus want me to stay with a man who betrayed me? Why should I be punished for a sin someone else committed?

One afternoon I sat in bed at Arvilla's, writing in my dream diary, when I heard the soft clomp of horses' hooves on the snow outside.

I had a grand dream of my Harvey Doe. He was with us in our home—my Mother was with us, dear Harvey sat at the piano, as he always did and all at once he sang a grand rich operatic great song his beautiful voice was strong full and Rich and swelled out in great volume it was glorious we listened & he sang a long time he was so happy handsome and grand he was so so happy & we were all with him.

Arvilla brought Tommy Birdsall into my room. "We've missed you," he said.

I wanted to hug him.

"The shaft we blasted in October looks like it'll yield," he said. He stood a few feet from the bed, spinning the brim of his hat in his hands. "Next spring we'll see a profit on the books. But for now, we've got to close down." He cleared his throat. "I persuaded Waterman to keep his investment in until next year. That satisfied your… Mr. Doe…." He pursed his lips, uncertain how to continue.

I couldn't believe what I'd just heard. "Waterman's not pulling out?"

"Nope. We'll have another year. Come spring…"

I felt light-headed with relief. "So we're not losing the mine?"

"No, ma'am." He stuffed his hands, still red from the cold, into the patch pockets on his duster.

"Thank you." I touched my fingers to my heart. "Thank you."

Tommy cleared his throat, twice. Finally, he said, "I'm sorry about what's happened, ma'am."

But I didn't want to think about that awful night at the Bon Ton. I wanted to get back to work. "Can't we keep the mine open?"

Snow from his boots had already melted into a puddle on one of Arvilla's rag rugs.

"Well, now," he said, smiling. "It's nice to know you're ready to work again, Mrs… Lizzie…." He dug the square toe of one boot into the rug. "But it'll be a spell before we can go down into the mine again. Site's covered in snow and ice. Too dangerous—for all of us."

My chest tightened. I had to get back down into the mine; without work, I had nothing.

"Now hold on," he said kindly. "I've heard Horace Tabor is keeping one of his Leadville properties open this winter. He's had a contraption built to keep the shafts warm."

"Will you work there?"

"No, ma'am. I've found a job in Central City. Tabor's not looking for a crew manager. He needs workers. And you're a good one."

"Do you think he would hire me, Tommy?" I held my breath.

"I don't know," he said then added, "It's a long shot. But from what I hear, Tabor's a progressive man. I know the manager at the Matchless, and I've already put in a good word for you. That'll count for something."

I tipped my head back and closed my eyes, wondering how I would ever repay him.

"I ought to be on my way then," he said softly.

"Will I see you back at the Fourth of July come spring, Tommy?"

A smile spread across his face. "I reckon so."

From that moment onward, my health began to improve. In another week, I was well enough to ride into town with Arvilla. I closed out the bank account William had set up for us, pocketing the funds William had wired to say were mine to keep.

I promised myself that if I couldn't find work in another mine by the time the $250 in bank notes, plus the money I'd squirreled away at Arvilla's urging, had run out, I'd go home. I hid enough money to buy a train ticket home in a secret lining in my dome-topped trunk. That trunk—with my clothes, my letters from Mama, my Bible—would be all I would take with me to find Mr. Horace Tabor in Leadville and persuade him to give me a job at the Matchless Mine. I wanted desperately to return to the mysteries and possible fortune to be made underground. I knew from William's telegram that Harvey was safely back in Oshkosh and under a doctor's care, but I couldn't face going home until I had accomplished what he and I had come to Colorado to do.

The next Saturday, just after dawn, Arvilla and Doc Bunn drove me to the coach depot in Central City. A group of travellers already waited on the boardwalk: two musicians carrying instrument cases, a man in a snuff-colored overcoat, a woman I took to be his wife, and an elderly gentleman.

"Argentine Pass is treacherous right now," Arvilla said. "Sit with your back to the horses, and you'll have a less bumpy ride."

"All right." I carried a small cowhide bag in which I'd packed two changes of clothing. My dome-topped trunk sat on the snowy ground beside us.

Arvilla lifted its worn leather handle. "I don't know how you'll be able to handle this yourself."

"She'll have no trouble finding a man to help her," Doc Bunn said.

A bald head appeared behind the bars of the ticketing window. "Selling tickets now for Leadville! Spotswood and McClelland's

Line—first in the area! Two trips each way every day!"

A line formed quickly, and when I reached its head, I slid a ten dollar bill under the bars. The man's eyebrows were reddish, a surprising dash of color on his otherwise spotless head. They rose imperiously when he realized I was travelling alone.

"Going to Leadville, miss?"

"Yes."

"Just one?"

"Yes."

Those startling brows met in the middle of his forehead. But I simply waited for him to hand me a ticket. When I rejoined Arvilla and Doc on the platform, Arvilla handed me a sheet of newsprint. "For your scrapbook."

It was the clipping from the *Central City News*

"To remind you what you are capable of. Remember," she added. "You're like a daughter to us. Isn't that right, Merrow?"

Her husband nodded. "Anytime you need anything, you call on us, you hear?"

I blinked away tears.

"And as soon as you arrive, call on Mrs. Tennant," Arvilla said. "I've written to tell her to expect you and to give you her best price on a room."

Four draft horses appeared, pulling a coach mounted on runners. Green scrollwork decorated its shiny black doors.

Arvilla grinned. "There's your booby hut."

The other travelers pressed forward, ready to toss their bags into the hold.

"Wait now!" the ticket man yelled. Then, in a friendlier tone to the driver, "Aye, Charlie!"

"Aye?"

"The mail!"

The driver jumped down from his box and ran into the station, returning with two leather mail pouches with brass locks. He threw these up behind a screen at the front of the coach then turned to us. "Let's see your way-bills then."

I watched the driver hoist my trunk up into the hold then climbed into the coach. I was lucky to get a window seat and leaned out to blow a kiss to Arvilla and Doc, who stood arm-in-arm on the platform.

"We'll see you come spring," Arvilla shouted.

The coach jerked forward, and I grabbed the strap above my head.

"Going to be a rough ride," the violinist said. "Thirty-six hours of this." He patted his instrument case as though it were a dog.

The men talked about the war in Afghanistan and the recent eruption of Mt. Etna in Italy. I'd hoped the other woman on the trip might want a conversation as well, but she pulled out a large cross-stitch canvas and worked in silence. So I unpacked a book Arvilla had pushed into my satchel and read whenever the ride was smooth enough. There were stretches of mountain passes where we were tossed around like loose potatoes in a wheelbarrow. And once, on a narrow curve, we had to dismount while the driver steered the coach around an approaching team. I found it impossible to sleep, and despite the freezing temperatures outside, felt terribly uncomfortable in the layers of heavy clothing I'd worn: two chemises, a wool underskirt, knee-length stockings, fur-topped boots, and hooded cape.

But finally, after two days of travel, we reached Leadville.

CHAPTER 13

When I climbed down from the carriage, it was dusk. But the town was noisy with the sounds of horses and racing sleigh runners, catcalls, and cries from hawking street vendors. I yelled at the driver to point me toward the boarding house Arvilla had suggested. But he shook his head and continued unloading the hold. My fellow passengers hurried off to their destinations as I watched the carriage pull away. I was so tired and sore I could barely stand.

Just then a boy wearing a straw hat appeared, pulling a small cart behind him.

"Will you help me take my trunk to Harrison Street?" I asked. "Mrs. Tennant's boarding house."

The boy removed his hat and held it upside-down in front of him. His hair had been bowl-cut, long on top and close-cropped below.

"Do you expect me to pay you first then?" I asked.

He swiped at his nose with his sleeve and jiggled the hat up and down. "No other way."

Too tired to object, I rifled through my bag for pennies, which he scooped into his pocket.

He lifted my trunk onto his cart, grunting. "It's a heavy one. But Harrison Street it is, ma'am."

He started walking quickly in front of me, pulling the cart over dirty, packed-down snow. I could barely keep up with him. The buildings we passed were lit from inside, but it was hard to make out the faces of the people on the street. When we reached a side alley lined with shacks and lean-tos, the boy abruptly stopped in front of a peddler.

"What'll you buy now, miss? I can smell a pretty new lady in town." The peddler's greasy black hair spilled over his collar. Even in the dark, I could see that his fur overcoat was riddled with holes where moths had chewed. His eyes were open but expressionless. I couldn't tell if he was blind or only pretending to be. His hands flailed in front of him but finally found mine. While I struggled to pull away, the boy ran off, leaving my trunk in the middle of the street.

"Wait a minute!" I cried out. "Where are you going?"

He turned to shout over his shoulder without stopping. "You're on Harrison, ma'am!"

"But you can't just leave my things here! Come back!"

I lifted my skirts and started to run after him, slipping and sliding on the snow. I finally found him pulling the pennies I'd given him from his pocket and placing them on a table set up on the side of the street for a faro game.

"Don't know no Mrs. Tennant," he said when I tapped his shoulder. "Get off my boot!"

I reached to turn him around to face me but was quickly pushed aside by another man trying to place a bet in the game. Across the street, a curtained carriage rolled past then stopped in front of a tall brick building. The sign above its door read "Clarendon Hotel." A doorman in top hat and red livery opened the carriage door, and a tall man emerged with two leather valises.

"Wait!" I waved at the doorman to get his attention; both men turned to look at me. "I'm trying to find the boarding house run by Mrs. Tennant. Is it nearby? And would you help me take my trunk there, please?"

"Tennants closed that boarding house last month," the doorman said. "Not enough business this time of year." He turned to open the glass-panelled door into the hotel.

I caught a glimpse of red velvet couches and a roaring fire inside the hotel's lobby and remembered my excitement when William first took Harvey and me into the fancy American House in Denver. "But..." My voice cracked. "I don't know what to do."

The doorman shrugged.

"Wait!" I had moved closer to them. "How much is a room here?"

The two men exchanged glances. The doorman raised his brows but said, "Four-fifty a night, miss."

Nearly double the price of a room at the Teller House, but I had no choice. "I'll take it. Can you please help me?" I pointed to where my trunk still stood on the snow in the street.

The doorman whistled at two boys throwing snowballs. They ran to him, got their instructions, and were sent for the trunk.

Once inside the blessedly warm lobby, I waited for the man who'd exited the carriage to check in then stepped to the tall reception desk.

"Just yourself, miss?" The desk clerk's monkey-jacket had a standing collar that reached above his ear lobes.

I nodded.

He dipped his pen into a bottle of black ink. "Room 228." The pen scratched across the paper then he pushed the form toward me. "Sign here."

I had to stand on tiptoe to sign: Elizabeth McCourt Doe.

"Well then, Mrs.—Miss?—Doe, here's your key."

A porter was pushing a wheeled brass cart that held my trunk toward the back of the lobby.

"Where's he taking that?" I asked.

"Storage. I assume you have what you need in your satchel?" the clerk said, nodding to the bag I still clutched tightly in one hand.

When the porter returned, I followed him up a wide carpeted staircase. He used a silver key to open the door to the room. Relief flooded over me at the sight of a huge canopied bed and off to the side in a bathroom, a footed tub.

I muttered a quick thank you and closed the door, realizing too late that I'd forgotten to give the man a tip. I quickly unbuttoned my cape and pulled my boots from aching feet then stripped off my stockings, dress, underskirt and chemises, letting everything fall to the floor. Rummaging in the pocket of my cape, I found two balls of sweetened dough I'd bought at a rest stop and ate them hungrily. Then I pulled back the heavy quilted coverlet on the bed, tumbled on the mattress, and within minutes, slept. It must have been two or three hours later when I was wakened by a shout. I hurried to a tall window to see if I could find its source.

A brightly lit catwalk ran between my hotel and another brick building across the alleyway. Maybe a dozen people were pouring out the side door of the building. I glimpsed satin ball gowns and velvet cloaks, a sparkling tiara, ivory top hats on men in tail coats and trousers.

I squinted to make out the lettering on a marquee that hung near the door: "World Class Metropolitan Opera Star Mademoiselle Moracchi."

Leaning my forehead against the cold window, I burst into tears. There'd be no fancy dress clothes, no opera performances for me. I was in a strange town, far from home, with neither husband, family, nor friend to save me.

CHAPTER 14

My Dearest, Most Pined for Mama and Papa,

By now you will have received my telegram explaining that I would spend the rest of the winter in Leadville. I know this will have come as a shock to you, but it is something I must do. I do not want to bring more shame upon you by returning both divorced and empty-handed.

The town I have travelled to, Leadville, is called Cloud City and sometimes Magic City. It IS a magical place, so high up here in the mountains it feels like a way-stop between Heaven and Earth.

I am staying in a lovely hotel temporarily while I look for work. There is no need for you to spend a moment in worry for me.

Please pray though that Leadville will bring its magic to me, and thus to you my beloved family.

Your Loving Daughter,
Lizzie

CHAPTER 15

I wasted no time asking for directions to the Matchless Mine. The doorman told me to take Harrison north to Seventh Street, turn left, walk seven blocks out of town, then up Fryer Hill. He said there would be arrows tacked to trees pointing the way.

I wore some of the clothes I had packed in my satchel: two clean camisoles, bloomers, a white blouse that buttoned up the back, my rose skirt, and again my wool cape and bonnet. I made my way over the snow-covered streets then turned onto a narrow road, where I carefully kept to the tracks made by wagon wheels. When I looked down on the town in the basin below me, I saw a neat grid of 20 or 30 blocks laid out in straight lines. Finally, rounding a sharp turn, I came upon the familiar landmarks of a mine: an A-frame and windlass, upturned ore carts, a sluice in a stream bed, its icy surface cracked.

Leaving the road, I ventured toward the first of two shacks with slant roofs, my boots crunching on icy gravel.

A man appeared in the open doorway. "Who's that?" His hand had rested on the gun in his holster, but he removed it once he saw me.

"Tommy Birdsall sent me," I said. "Are you the manager here? Did you get Tommy's letter?"

He snorted. "Aye, I got Tommy's letter. And had a good laugh when I read he was planning on sending a woman to work." He ran his hand over his hair. "God's witness, though, I had no idea he'd be sending a woman pretty as you."

"He said the mine was operating now," I said, ignoring his attempt to sidetrack our conversation. "He said you might need help."

He took a step toward me. "Yep. Lost three men last week when they up and left town without telling me."

"I'm a hard worker. Tommy knows what all I can do."

"You sure are a pretty one."

"I need a job," I said.

He rubbed his chin with oil-stained fingers. "The mine's only half open. We've got a small crew. Working two, three days a week, no more."

"You can pay me half what you pay the men."

"Pay don't matter. Mr. Tabor's a wealthy man. And generous with all our wages. But a woman…" He shook his head. "I don't see it."

My fingers were numb with cold inside my gloves. "What about the other mines around here? Are any of them open?"

"Nope. The Little Chief, the Chrysolite—all closed. They wouldn't hire you anyway."

He stood quite close now and brushed my cheek with a rough hand. "Don't do that," I said.

"Don't get riled now. I don't mean no harm." He pulled a bandana from a pocket and wiped his brow. "Try Joe Mooney at the assay office. That'd be a sight better place for somebody like you to work. He let go his regular workers come winter so he and his sons aren't up to handling everything Mr. Tabor needs now."

Back at my hotel, I scrubbed the feel of the man's hand from my cheek.

"What are you planning to do for yourself, then? Leadville can be a difficult place for a pretty woman like you."

It was my third day in town, a Monday, and I left the hotel early to look for Mooney's assay office or any business that would hire me.

The man speaking to me stood by a brightly painted dog cart. A flyer was nailed to the side of his cart: Job Available.

"I can manage."

"So do we all, young lady! So do we all!" He wore a red cloth jacket with epaulets and sealskin edging. "So let's see then, dear. Is there any possibility you can copy a likeness freehand? Direct from life?"

"No." I'd never felt comfortable drawing though Mama had said it was a skill all young women should learn.

"Well then." He tapped a black lace-up boot on the snow. "You see," he said, his breaths condensing in the cold air, "I offer drawings in black on white. Or the reverse if patrons so choose. Something stark to make the truth stand out. One should never whitewash, even one's customers."

He bowed then stood tall again. "I am the renowned Elliot Landes Penamaker. Forgive my rudeness."

He stepped to the side to study my profile. "Even if I cannot offer you employment, I would enjoy cutting a paper shadow portrait of you. For you see, I also do silhouettes and am, in fact, a favored student of Étienne de Silhouette. These portraits are à la mode in high society now."

He gestured behind him as though a ballroom filled with elegantly dressed men and women might suddenly appear. But all I saw was an empty dance hall with scraped floorboards and a shanty with a hand-painted sign reading "Lundry."

Penamaker pressed on. "Goethe has a collection of silhouettes. And I made Otis Skinner's likeness when he came to the Opera House here last year. Rose Melville's as well—she is a true beauty like you! Why, I even cut Doc John Henry Holliday when he dealt cards in the Monarch Saloon." His eyes opened wide. "Profile tells all," he said in a lowered voice.

I was impatient to go. If he had no job, there was no reason to stand talking to this strange man, but he had blocked my way.

"I can draw the outline of a shadow cast by sunlight, as well as by candle or lamp. And I *never* use a physionotrace."

"Please stop staring at me like that," I said. Ever since I'd turned twelve, I had sensed an interest from men that I sometimes enjoyed and sometimes regretted. Often, I found their interest held a lustful hunger I did not always welcome since it had less to do with me than my appearance.

"Oh, but dear, when one has a face like yours, one must offer it for the world's enjoyment. Your eyes are especially striking. Violet, are they? Of course that wonderful and strange color won't appear in your silhouette. Still…"

"I can't afford a silhouette." I tried again to push past him, but he caught my arm.

"Please wait! I'm sorry I'm not able to hire you; I should enjoy spending time in your presence each day. But without drawing or cutting skills, there is nothing I can offer except… perhaps… training…"

"No."

His fingers twisted together like small snakes. "At least let me cut your portrait. My gift to you. It will only take a few minutes, then you can be on your way."

So I sat on a stool he pulled from behind his cart. He pushed up my chin, told me where to point my gaze, and flicked a curl of hair behind my ear. A velvet-lined box held a set of drawing knives, and as he'd promised, he cut a perfect likeness of me within minutes. He cut two likenesses, actually, because he had stacked two pieces of paper together before he cut. He handed the top silhouette to me then performed another bow.

"I will keep this one," he said. "I know a gentleman who will appreciate your profile's fine lines as much as I do. And even the well-known Eliot Landes Penamaker must make a spot of money now and then."

I took the silhouette to my hotel room then went back outside to find the assay office. The cross streets in town were numbered 1st to 17th Avenues. As I walked, I was struck by how different the town looked than it had from up on Fryer Hill. From above, Leadville appeared to be the result of a carefully laid-out plan. But at street-level, the town was chaotic. Tents tilted against brick buildings. A log cabin stood in the middle of the street just a few blocks from my hotel. Each merchant had built the strip of sidewalk at the front of his own store so there was no consistency in height or materials. I walked carefully, sometimes stepping down ten or twelve inches, then back up again a few short steps later.

I passed a man sitting on an upturned keg getting his shoe repaired by a cobbler, a salesman peddling a new hair tonic, and many saloons and gaming houses. By the time I reached 17th Avenue, I'd seen two assay offices, neither of them Joe Mooney's. I turned to retrace my steps down the other side of the street. The sun had disappeared behind a cloud, and I was ready to give up and go back to the hotel. Perhaps the man at the Matchless had led me on a wild goose chase. Perhaps, like Mrs. Tennant, Joe Mooney & Sons had left town.

Then for some reason, I decided to turn down a narrow side street.

At first, the buildings looked similar to those on Harrison Avenue, but within a block the atmosphere changed. There were saloons, of course, but also dirty curtains hanging limp in the windows of tiny houses. Hand-painted letters spelled out names like Tar Baby Brown, Diamond Tooth Leona, Mina Rose. Prostitutes' cribs.

As I turned to go back to the hotel, I spotted a one-story frame building tucked between a bottling works and a shoeing shop; its sign read Joseph A. Mooney & Sons, Safe and Sane Assaying. I crossed the street and, cupping my hands, peered through the streaked front window of the shop. I could just make out the shadow of a man standing behind a long counter and behind him, flames in an open furnace. I knocked on the window.

Without turning, the man raised his arm to wave me away. I knocked again, and he came to the door. "I'm sorry, miss. We aren't open."

His hair was red, streaked with gold, and he wore oval wire-rimmed glasses. When I didn't budge, he stepped aside to let me in and closed the door to the cold.

"Is there something I can do for you, miss?" he asked. "Are you lost?"

"I need work," I said quickly.

I was grateful he didn't laugh and that his eyes were kind.

He pushed a pie tin filled with black ore off to the side of the metal countertop and motioned for me to sit on a stool. "It's mighty unusual for someone like you to be knocking on a door like mine looking for work."

"I know." I prayed he wouldn't ask for further explanation. "My name's Elizabeth. Lizzie. I'll work for free for a week so you can see how much help I can be. Please. I need a job."

There was a commotion as two young men, mirror images of each other with their red hair and pale faces, stepped out of a back room.

"My sons, Bertram and Cornell. And I'm Joe Mooney."

Something was odd about the twins, their gaze too child-like for their size.

Mr. Mooney held the pie tin out to them. "Here," he said. "Go weigh this." When they'd disappeared, he continued. "Mrs. Mooney and I made eight children between us. Six of them died. Bertram and

Cornell are God's last gift to us. We say they got the leftovers from all that Light before them."

"I can help you," I said. "I know how to keep books. I can clean. I've worked in a mine. I can learn anything you want to teach me."

He pushed his glasses up his nose. "It's not that I couldn't use the help. Even though Tabor and a fellow down in Spottswood are the only two still working their mines in this weather, I've taken in side work. Turns out I'm good with lab instruments. The kind docs and dentists use. I had one fellow drive up all the way from Littleton to have me fix a piece of equipment for him."

Bertram and Cornell reappeared, simultaneously untying their black aprons.

"We'll be heading home for lunch now, Miss..."

"Doe. Lizzie Doe."

He removed two matching coats from hooks on the wall and handed them to his sons. "Why don't you come back tomorrow morning, Miss Doe? Let me talk with Missus Mooney overnight, and I'll see what I can come up with. We might just be the answer to each other's prayers."

CHAPTER 16

I started work the following Monday. Mr. Mooney insisted on paying me. He gave me keys to the shop so I could arrive early each morning, make coffee and sweep the floors, a task I had to do several times a day since any customer who came in brought snow or red clay on their boots. I dusted, too, since whenever the machinery ran, a fine black powder coated every surface.

Neither Bertram nor Cornell knew how to write or do numbers, so I was in charge of posting the New York rates for silver at the beginning of each week. Pure silver was bringing in about $1.08 an ounce, minus penalties for zinc and other metals. Even if the Matchless was the only mine operating in the area that winter, Mr. Mooney insisted that the miners there be kept informed of what profit their strikes might yield. He also showed me how to use bone ash to absorb lead from nuggets of ore the men sometimes brought in, so that only pure silver would be left behind.

The Sunday after my first week of work, I was invited to dinner, where Mrs. Mooney, with her sweet frizz of brown hair and plump arms, made chicken stew and apple dumplings and brought out a signed picture of Tom Thumb Jr., whom she had once seen in a travelling exhibition.

Bertram was the first to try to kiss me, but that didn't happen until several months after I'd started. It was almost closing time and had been raining all day. Mr. Mooney had gone to the cooper's to pick up a barrel. It was the twins' birthday, but Cornell had gone home earlier that afternoon, sick with fever.

Neither Bertram nor Cornell ever spoke much, to me or anyone else. So I was surprised to hear Bertram say, "Cornell will have to take the bitters. Three spoonfuls."

He sat at a high sawbuck table staring out at the rain, his stockinged feet swinging an inch or two off the floor. "Hostetter's Celebrated Stomach Bitters."

I wiped my hands on my apron, "That should help him feel better soon," I said as I carried two glass jars to a basin on the side wall.

I was washing the jars when I felt him behind me. Surprised, I turned so quickly that I splashed soapy water over his face and dark shirt. He flinched as though I had slapped him.

"Bertram. I'm sorry." I reached to gently wipe the water from his child-like face.

I was wedged between him and the sink. I heard laughter and turned to see three dance hall girls run through the rain, arm in arm, their heads bent together under wet newspapers.

"Do you want to tell me more about Cornell?" I asked, trying to slide away from the sink.

He blinked, his pale eyelashes flashing.

"Maybe we could sit down, and I'll make us a cup of tea."

He leaned toward me, lips pursed together.

I put my hands on his chest, trying to push him away gently. "Cornell will be all right," I said. "I've taken Hostetter's myself several times."

I stood on tiptoe to kiss Bertram's forehead then said, "You are a good friend to me, Bertram. That is the best thing to be."

He walked back to the countertop and began to wipe it vigorously with his sleeve. "Pa might be counting on it, you know," he said quietly. "Unless you want Cornell. When he's feeling better."

Before I could answer, the front door opened. I turned, hugely relieved by the interruption, to see a woman, twenty or thirty years older than me, plain-faced and thick-waisted but elegantly dressed. Gold lozenge-shaped pince-nez rested on her nose.

"Horace is in Denver," she said without explanation, "and there's been a new strike at the mine." She looked around the room. "Where's Mr. Mooney?"

"At the cooper's," I said.

"Horace is in Denver," she repeated, "so I've brought the ore in myself. I want it tested. Now." She was tall and intimidating.

"We can have it for you tomorrow morning," I said as it dawned on me that this must be the legendary Horace Tabor's wife.

She wouldn't hear of it. "We have an emergency," she said. "A potentially happy emergency but an emergency nonetheless. The manager from the Matchless came to my home just thirty minutes ago to tell me. He gave me this sample. I know what my husband would do. He would have it tested immediately, no matter the hour."

To my relief, Mr. Mooney came through the still open door, tipping his wet hat to greet Mrs. Tabor. "Good evening, ma'am."

"I believe the men have found a wonderful new strike at the Matchless. All the other assay offices are closed, so you, Mr. Mooney, have the honor."

He took the black rock from her hand, feeling its weight.

Mrs. Tabor pressed her lips together in what she probably thought was a smile. "How quickly can you do this?"

"Tomorrow morning," Mr. Mooney answered.

I nodded, glad that my earlier suggestion had been confirmed.

"That won't do. Horace needs to know *now*. I plan on wiring him as soon as you tell me what's in that rock."

"I understand, Mrs. Tabor. And I would like to help. But it's Friday evening. And my sons' birthday. Mrs. Mooney has killed a turkey, one she has fed specially with sherry and walnuts every day for nearly a month now." He scratched his jaw then tossed the ore once more in his hand. "I'll come in special tomorrow morning for you."

Mrs. Tabor glared.

I wanted to tell him not to give in to this arrogant woman. But I also knew it would be foolish for him to turn away the wealthiest woman in town and his best customer.

"I have a son, too, Mr. Mooney, as you may know," she said. "Maxcy is twelve years old. I know how important birthdays are. But surely your boys—who are really grown men, aren't they?—won't be inconvenienced by a little delay."

Mr. Mooney sighed. "If you insist. I will tell you what I find out as soon as I can. I'll come to your house later this evening."

After she'd left, Mr. Mooney stoked the furnace. Bertram pulled crackers from his shirt pocket and began to eat them.

"Lizzie, go tell Mrs. Mooney," he said, "with my sincerest apology, that Bertram and I will be late tonight. Explain why and ask Mrs.

Mooney to please expect us no later than 9 p.m. for the birthday dinner. I know the turkey will be delicious. Add that, please."

I ran the few blocks to their house in the rain then returned to the shop, reporting back that Mrs. Mooney would keep the food warm and ready. Then I offered to help.

Mr. Mooney began to pulverize the rock, scooping fine black powder into a bowl.

"So you've met the grand Augusta Tabor. What do you think?"

"I don't like her!" I said. "She's arrogant and rude."

"I can see why you'd say that. But that's a fine, strong woman that just stormed in here. Who's seen her share of troubles like all of us. She didn't start out as such a grande dame. Came from regular stock, just like Horace, back in Vermont. Her father hired Horace as a journeyman stonecutter."

"I didn't know the Tabors were from back East."

"Pretty much everybody out here came from somewhere else!" he laughed. "After he married Augusta, he took her to homestead in Kansas. Caught the political bug there and within a year he was elected to the legislature. Then they came to Colorado when he heard about the gold being found on Pike's Peak. Now I swear that man has silver in his veins. Never seen a man get so rich so fast."

He scratched his jaw. "Some folks like Mrs. Tabor; most don't. She's a very different person than her husband. Horace is a friendly man, rich as he is. But she was with him from the beginning, when they lived like regular folk. And poorer."

"They built the Opera House by the hotel, yes?" I asked.

"Yep. Tabor's been mighty generous to this town and to lots of folks in the area, even when he didn't have much to be generous with. I knew him back when he and Augusta—though I'd hesitate to call her by her first name now—ran the general store in Oro City. He'd slip pieces of salt pork or a few extra eggs into your order if you were on hard times. He put up the money for old man Zaitz to open the first grocery store here in town. Never said a word about it."

He opened the furnace door and set the bowl of pulverized ore on a shelf.

"Some folks think Augusta never really wanted to be rich. But Mr. Tabor is fierce ambitious." He joined Bertram at the work table and ran his hand through his son's hair. "When the Tabors moved to Leadville, Augusta busied herself with their boy and left Horace to his mining. I think it's a real shame, after all those early years working side by side. Family's more important than being rich, that's what the missus and I believe."

One Sunday shortly after Mrs. Tabor's visit, I decided to walk up Fryer Hill. Columbine and yellow lady's slipper peeked up from the grass, and there were other signs of new life as well: gingham curtains fluttered in the open window of a cabin. A dog sniffed the bulky behind of a baby in the yard, and someone had draped laundry over a rock. There were makeshift tents and board shanties and another small cabin with a flower pot for a chimney.

When I reached the Matchless, I saw that, since my last visit, someone had nailed a "No Trespassing" sign to the trunk of a tree. I ignored it and hoisted my skirts to step forward, my taupe ankle boots already spotted with mud. My heart quickened as I neared the A-frame above the main shaft. And just as I had on my first visit, I saw a man standing in the opening to the lean-to.

But it was a different man. One with arched black brows and a thick walrus mustache. An elegant man, wearing a well-cut suit.

"Turn your head to the side," he said.

I was ready to apologize for trespassing and leave, but before I could speak, he repeated his words, "Turn to the side. Please."

I turned my profile to him then looked to see him smile as if he'd found a long-lost friend.

"It's you," he said, stepping out of the lean-to. "But I'm forgetting my manners. I'm Horace Tabor."

I panicked. I'd been curious about this man I'd heard so much about, but now face-to-face with him, I was speechless.

He walked over and stood so close to me that I could see the gray scattered through his hair and the tight bat's wing that knotted his tie. I took a step back but the hem of my dress caught on something. I looked down, embarrassed to see the fabric had ripped, revealing a strip of red underskirt.

"I thought you might be a French courtesan our friend had met on his travels. Or so-called travels." Then, to my amazement, he reached to hold my chin. "It *is* you," he said.

I remembered the silhouette-maker's words: *"I know a gentleman who will appreciate your profile's fine lines as much as I do."*

"Why on earth would you come up here?" he asked.

"I want a job. I want to work in your mine." I don't know how I found the courage to speak.

"What?" He tilted his head to the side, pursing his lips.

But I couldn't stop now. "I work with Joseph Mooney," I said. "At the assayer's office. Your wife came in recently. But before that, I worked at the Fourth of July. In Dogwood. With Tommy Birdsall. He wrote a letter to your manager. I tried once before—"

"Slow down!" He scratched his cheek, still staring at me. "You what?"

"I want to work here at the Matchless. I know you'll need more help now because that ore Mrs. Tabor brought in means you're going to be digging out a new vein. It's incredibly high grade silver."

His eyes held mine. "You know more than I expected," he said. "I was just getting ready to go down into the mine now. Would you like to join me?"

Before I could answer, he gestured for me to follow him back to the lean-to. "I'm guessing you aren't from here originally," he shouted over his shoulder. "Somewhere north, I'd say."

I hurried to keep up with him, afraid he'd change his mind. "Oshkosh, Wisconsin," I said, breathless. "My parents still live there. And my brothers and sisters."

He swiveled to stare at me again, and I stopped short.

"Your parents," he said quietly. "You're someone's child still. It has been a long time since I had that comfort."

I realized he must be nearly Papa's age.

"Are you quite sure you want to do this?" he asked.

"Most definitely."

"Then come on." He stepped into the lean-to then returned, holding a large pile of black rubber. He shook out heavy black tubes that I saw formed two arms and two legs.

"Underground suit," he explained. "I'm afraid it will be too big for you—." His eyes passed up and down my figure. "But it will protect your dress. Oscar Wilde wore it when he accompanied me down into the mine after his performance at the Opera House. We drank a good bit of absinthe that night! Since I wager you never worked in a mine wearing a dress like that, I'd suggest you use it as well."

He sent me into the lean-to for privacy. I bunched up my skirts and, pushing them into the baggy legs, kept up a steady chatter about the Fourth of July.

"I agree, there's something mysterious and vital about these mines," he said as I stepped out, encased in rubber. "Something that has nothing to do with silver or gold."

He lifted me into the large bucket that hung below the A-frame then hopped in behind me. With a shift of the windlass, we began to descend, deeper than I'd ever gone in the Fourth of July. When the bucket finally stopped moving, he climbed out first then lit a lantern before lifting me out. I loved the feel of his firm hands on my waist. When he removed them, I breathed in deeply, realizing I hadn't felt this calm or happy in a very long time.

"I like to come down when no one else is here."

"I understand," I said. "I think it's the potential that hangs in the air. The sense that magic lies just beyond what we see before us."

He pointed the lantern toward a narrow drift to the right. We walked for about ten minutes, mostly in silence though he occasionally spoke to tell me about the mine.

"I bought the Matchless from a brokerage company here in Leadville. It was named before I bought it, after the chewing tobacco from Lorillard's. None of the previous owners found anything here, even though two other high-producing claims are right over the ridge there."

"They didn't go down far enough," I said, and he turned to look at me.

"That's right. Anything worth finding requires a great descent."

I had no idea why I felt so comfortable with him but I said,

"Sometimes at the Fourth of July I heard things. Things I shouldn't really have been hearing. Something alive. As though the silver were molten and running through the veins of the earth."

We reached a pick-axe propped against a wall, next to a pile of hacked-out muck.

"Is this where the ore came from?" I asked. "The piece Mrs. Tabor brought in?"

A shadow flashed across his face; I didn't know what to make of it. "Yes."

"You and your wife must feel very fortunate." I swallowed.

"Why would you say that?" he asked. "I doubt that fortunate's the word." He rubbed his shirt, at a spot over his heart. "Come on. It's time to go."

Back above ground, I removed the India rubber suit and met him outside the lean-to. "Thank you so much, Mr. Tabor. I can't tell you how much this has meant to me. I…"

"It's me who should thank you," he said. "And perhaps apologize, too."

"Why?"

"I've been quite forward, taking you with me like that. But you brightened a lonely morning." He took a deep breath. "Will I see you again?"

"Oh! I don't know…" I bit my lip, uncertain how to answer.

"This Friday night," he said. "Be my guest at the Opera House. Meet me there at 8." He nodded toward a second small cabin to our right. "For now I must get back to my paperwork." He bowed slightly then turned and walked away. I felt terribly overheated and dizzy but somehow made my way back down Fryer Hill to the privacy of my hotel room.

CHAPTER 17

I changed my mind a hundred times that week. Horace Tabor's invitation wasn't necessarily improper, but it might be. I liked him very much. I liked his forthrightness, the strength of his presence, the sound of his deep voice. I liked that he saw mining as something more than just a way to make money. Still, I reminded myself repeatedly, he was married and at least thirty years my senior.

I went to bed Thursday night intending to write a note declining his invitation. I would leave it at the Opera House office on my way to work. But Friday morning, I looked out my hotel window at the tiled roof of the building across the alley. The Opera House. I had wanted to see a performance there since my first arrival in town, and this would surely be my only chance. And if I became friends with the owner of the Matchless, I might stand a better chance of getting work there at the mine. So I decided to meet Mr. Tabor for that night's performance. Surely he intended nothing immoral.

The day passed more slowly than usual, and I was absent-minded. I measured things incorrectly and had to throw out two batches of flux. Mr. Mooney said I looked pale and sent me home an hour before closing.

I lay down to nap in my hotel room but couldn't sleep. I got out of bed and pulled two dresses from my closet, the only ones I had that weren't in the trunk I'd stored downstairs. The choice dismayed me so I turned my attention to my make-up, being careful to use just a hint of *cendre de roses brune* powder and a clear lip salve. I wanted to look pretty but not be accused of being overly flirtatious! I picked the blue dress with black velvet trim and threw a black shawl over my shoulders.

When I left the room at 7:30, opera-goers already mingled in the street—the men in evening dress and capes; the women bustled, bonneted, and bejeweled.

Clutching my reticule, I made my way through the crowd and up the stairs into the lobby. Crimson paint shimmered on the walls, and a thick crimson carpet muffled footsteps. Two huge brass chandeliers hung from the ceiling. A sign on the ticket office read: $1.50 for parquet seats, $1.25 for the balcony, and 75 cents for gallery seats.

"Picking up, miss?" The young man inside the office wore a blue uniform.

A man behind me in line tried to press forward. I leaned toward the gold filigree screen and whispered, "I—Mr. Tabor—asked me…"

To my relief, no alarms sounded. The young man simply swiveled his chair around and reached into a cubbyhole for a white envelope.

There was no name on it, but he handed it to me, and I quickly left the line and headed toward the broad stairway. A chime rang three times. I hurried up the steps, opening the envelope to find a single ticket.

For one performance of "The Silver Slipper"
with George Macke and Samuel Collins.
Doors close at 8 p.m.

I noticed a second, smaller staircase which I assumed led to private boxes. I was confused. Had Mr. Tabor meant for me to watch the opera alone while he sat in his box?

The auditorium was filled with red velvet seats; dozens of gaslight jets flickered on mirrored walls. There were crystal chandeliers with milky glass shades, and a trio of painted pink-bottomed cherubs looked down from the ceiling.

I found my seat two-thirds of the way back from the stage, near the middle of a row. I was ashamed to realize I'd been hoping for something grander. But just as I took my seat, a boy walked onto the stage carrying a torch. Despite hoots from the audience, he bent stoically to light the footlights. The musicians seated below him were dressed in red and gold. I heard clarinets, a piano, and then a single blast from a trumpet.

The lamps on the red walls were extinguished, and after glancing once up toward a cream-colored box bowing out over the side aisle, I settled in for the performance. The drop curtain—which showed a mountain, a castle ringed by a stream, and a road leading to a distant canyon—rose. Just before it disappeared, I saw that the oval portrait painted above the scene was of Horace Tabor.

A bearded actor stepped out on stage holding a telescope. I tried to focus on the first act—it involved a silver slipper falling from the Planet Venus—but most of my interest kept being drawn to the private box above me. Why hadn't Mr. Tabor arranged to meet me personally? Had I misunderstood his invitation?

As soon as the opera ended, even before the applause died down, I hurried to the rear of the theatre and left the building as quickly as I could. I was relieved to see the doorman at the Clarendon was nowhere to be seen. I pushed the heavy door open myself and crossed the lobby, trying to avoid catching the attention of the night clerk. I was already behind one week in my payments.

Once safely inside my room, I threw myself down on the bed. I had been a fool thinking a man like Horace Tabor would have any interest in spending time with a woman like me.

I slept in my dress, and it was only the next morning, when I went to change clothes, that I realized my bag was missing from the closet.

I immediately ran down to the front desk. "My suitcase is missing! Someone has taken it!"

The clerk, who'd been filing receipts in a drawer, refused to look at me. "Were you out last night then?"

"Briefly." I blushed, wondering if everyone in town knew about my escapade. "But I locked my room. I took the key. I was only gone a short time. The door man saw me leave, but when I came back he wasn't on duty, and—"

"That poor coot Jim left us last night," the clerk said. "Asked for the week's paycheck. Seemed in a pucker. No telling where he's gone."

"But he wouldn't!"

The clerk looked into a drawer. His fingers tapped the top of the desk impatiently. "Goddamn him then. He's made off with the master key. I doubt yours is the last theft I'll hear about today."

Other than the train ticket money I'd sewn into the lining of my trunk, all the money I had was gone—everything William had given me. I fell back on the bed, sobbing. If Mama knew what I'd done, she would say it was the price I had to pay for behaving in such an immoral way.

I went to the basin to splash water on my face then picked up the reticule I had carried to the Opera House. I had sewn two gold coins into a secret pocket inside it. I could pay last week's bill for the hotel but would have to find a new, less expensive place to live on Monday or return in shame to Oshkosh.

Mr. Mooney told me of a cheap room in a boarding house near the assay office.

It was a terrible, run-down place, with wooden boxes instead of real chairs, and the washbasin rested on a carton. He and the boys helped me get a month's lease then left me to settle in with the few belongings I still had. For the next few days, I ate cheap ash-pone for breakfast and baked beans for lunch. I went to bed early so I could do without supper. If I couldn't sleep, I read headlines and notices in the old newspapers that covered the walls:

Civil War Hero General George A. Custer and His Battalion
    Destroyed to Last Man
National League of Baseball Founded
Girl Wanted: The subscriber will pay good wages for a girl to
    work in the house, who understands cooking
    in all its departments. Call immediately. John Organ

Mr. Mooney had reassured me I would have a job with him as long as I wanted, but I needed to earn a higher wage. I was not ready to go home with my life in such a shambles. Truth was, I needed a miracle. Father Bonduel had told me all the miracles Jesus had brought to pass: changing water into wine, healing a leper, calming a storm. Was I really such a sinner that He couldn't perform a miracle for me? I knew that my divorce from Harvey meant the Church would excommunicate me. But surely Jesus wouldn't leave my side?

Mr. and Mrs. Mooney invited me to accompany them to their church the next Sunday. I could no longer receive the Eucharist because of my divorce but listened carefully as the priest told the story of Jesus and Peter being asked to pay taxes for the Temple. Even when Peter was completely without hope, Jesus had offered reassurance. That very day, Peter caught a fish with a coin in its mouth, enough to pay the money he owed. If only such a miracle could happen for me!

We returned to the Mooneys for Sunday dinner. At the table, Mrs. Mooney handed me a platter piled high with slices of beef then nudged Cornell to pass the bowl of buttered potatoes. I was starving.

"Have you heard from your Mama lately?" The flames on two wax candles flickered between us.

"No, ma'am."

She frowned. "If you were my daughter, I'd want you home."

I looked down at my plate, embarrassed. I didn't know why Mama had stopped writing and could only imagine that the scandal of my divorce might have closed her heart to me.

After dinner, Mr. Mooney said he would read *The Adventures of Tom Sawyer* to Bertram and Cornell. So I followed Mrs. Mooney into the kitchen to clean up.

"You must ask for help, dear girl. This is too much for you to handle on your own." She lifted a blue plate from the sink and handed it to me to dry. "Jesus said, 'Ask, and it shall be given.' Do you still have your faith, child?"

Her question startled me. While my heart had been crying out for help, I realized I hadn't really spoken to Jesus, or seen Him in my dreams, for months. I was too certain He wouldn't answer. I was plagued with shame and doubt. I looked at Mrs. Mooney in her frilled apron and wondered if she had ever asked Jesus to make her poor sons whole in mind. And if so, how had she had come to terms with His absolute failure to do so?

Cleaning another plate, she said, "You must stop thinking you can handle this without God's help, Lizzie. Only Jesus can heal your woes."

She glanced over her shoulder toward the sitting room. I could see Mr. Mooney sitting there in a high-back chair, Bertram and Cornell cross-legged on the floor in front of him as though they were children. She shut the door and wiped her hands on her apron then motioned for me to follow her to a small desk. She pulled a book from a drawer and handed it to me.

"The mister doesn't know I have this, and I wouldn't be giving it to you if he were here. I can barely get him to accompany the boys and me to church on Sundays; I can only imagine what he would make of this." She fingered the gold embossed title: *Science and Health.*

"It's a new edition," she said proudly. "Oh, I know there are doubters. Including that Mark Twain my boys love so much! But I personally believe the Lord wrote this book through its author." She pushed the book into my hands. "Maybe it will do you good."

Later that night in my small room in the boarding house, I read what Mary Baker Eddy had to say about prayer. About how important it is not just to ask for what we want but also to be thankful for all that has already been given to us. I dropped to my knees on the hard wood floor, offering thanks to God. I thanked God for bringing the Mooneys into my life and before them, Arvilla Bunn. I thanked God for the immense love shown me by my parents when I was a little girl. I thanked God for revealing hints of his mysteries to me both in my dreams and below the ground in the Fourth of July and Matchless mines.

As I thought more about the feelings that came over me below ground, I realized that just like the miners did, I too might have to dig through rubble to reclaim my faith. I too had to step forward in darkness.

I heard a boarder down the hallway loudly hawk spit but kept murmuring my prayers, my head bowed. "Thank you for giving me a place to live," I whispered. "Thank you for giving me paying work." I stayed there on my knees for nearly an hour, until long after the street lights had been extinguished. That night my prayers to God continued in my dreams:

> *I have nothing to eat not a cent & no rent money God don't let me get hungry I have had very little to eat lately. Bless God forever.*

In the days that followed, I went down on my knees again and again to pray in that simple room. No miracle came, at least none that I could see. Two days before the next month's rent was due, I decided I would go to the train station to buy a ticket home to Oshkosh. I would return home a divorcée, a failure, and an embarrassment to my parents. But I had nowhere else to go.

The station was crowded with prospectors pouring into town to find work. I was angry that these men would easily find jobs at any number of mines in the area, simply because they were men, and chafed at the restrictions forced upon me because I was a woman.

"So where were you?" A voice boomed loudly through the station. "Why didn't you come to the Opera?"

My cheeks grew hot with anger as I turned to see Horace Tabor stride toward me.

"I have no idea what you mean, Mr. Tabor." My heart pounded in my chest.

And then he was there, standing just in front of me, smelling of lavender and spice. I tried to move past him, but he caught my arm.

"I picked up the ticket you left for me." I stared at a rail poster behind his shoulder, refusing to meet his eyes. "I went to my seat. You weren't there."

To my shock, he laughed. "The boy was supposed to send you to my box, not off into the hinterlands!"

A train pulled into the station, and I saw a man standing near the platform, waving frantically at Horace. "Someone is trying to get your attention," I said. "You'd best not miss your train."

"I didn't know where to find you." His face was serious; his eyes searched mine.

But I didn't believe him. I couldn't believe him.

The train whistle blew.

"I'm heading to Denver," he said suddenly. "Come with me."

It was my turn to laugh. "No!"

"Then tell me how I can find you when I get back?"

"All 'board! Denver and Rio Grande to Stray Horse Gulch, Canyon City, Denver! All aboard!"

I feared my knees might give out. "Go!" I urged him. "Your friend is getting on the train."

But he didn't budge. "Just tell me where to find you. Tell me, Lizzie."

I knew I shouldn't. But I was so weak, so hopeless. And the man in front of me was so strong and kind. He took my elbow, as if knowing I might faint. For the first time in weeks, I felt less dizzy; I felt as though the ground had stopped spinning beneath me, and I was home.

"Mooney's Assay office," I finally said.

"All aboard! Last call!"

He bent, and his lips grazed the back of my hand.

The next morning Mr. Mooney handed me a telegram from Denver.

> *I am entranced by your face, your figure, your eyes.*
> *May I call on you when I return to Leadville?*
> *Horace Tabor*

I crumpled the thin paper in my fist but instead of throwing it away, stuffed it deep into my pocket.

CHAPTER 18

A week later, Horace Tabor strode into the assay office.

"I'd like to take this lovely lady to tea," he said.

Poor Mr. Mooney simply shrugged, his cheeks turning a bright red. Tabor grabbed my bonnet from a hook by the front door. He was old enough to be my father. And married. Every logical thought in my head warned against befriending him. And yet, when I remembered the immense safety I'd felt when he lifted me into the bucket to descend into the Matchless, when I remembered his firm hand on my elbow at the train station, I couldn't say No. I took my bonnet from his hand, tied its ribbon under my chin, and taking a deep breath, stepped through the door he opened for me, out onto the street.

Shame instantly rushed upon me when someone called out a greeting to Horace. What if we ran into Mrs. Tabor? I had no large measure of ill will against her, and certainly no desire to break up someone else's marriage. But I was lonelier than I had ever been in my life. And this powerful man was expertly guiding me through the chaos of the street; his touch alone calmed my nerves. As long as I was with Horace Tabor, I was safe.

I don't know if he knew how anxious I was. But he kept up a steady monologue—about the new Union Station in Denver and the debate on women's voting rights they'd discussed at the state legislature meeting he'd attended. I was grateful just to listen.

When we reached the Opera House, he led me up the marble steps and through the front door. The lobby was empty.

"No show tonight." He steered me to the staircase I'd climbed before. This time, we passed the auditorium and continued up the set of smaller stairs I'd noticed. At their end, Horace opened a door onto the glass-walled catwalk I could see from my room at the Clarendon.

Heart pounding, I followed him across the catwalk and down a hallway until he stopped before a door marked Number 301. The suite was much larger and more elegant than the room I'd stayed in one floor down. Two red velvet loveseats stood near a marble-surround fireplace, and two flute glasses and a bottle of champagne sparkled on a table with sled runner legs

He'd known I would come.

I walked over to the bookcase that filled one wall, trying to calm myself by running a finger down the cloth spines: *Jezebel's Daughter* by Wilkie Collins, *Ayala's Angel* by Trollope, older titles by Dumas, deTocqueville, Poe.

Finally I ventured to speak. "Are these for display? Or have you read them?"

Chuckling, he came to stand behind me. "I've read most."

When I turned, he held out his arms, and I fell into them. He was so tall, my face pressed into the v of his black vest, and he bent down to untie the ribbon of my bonnet. Then he kissed me, firmly and sweetly, on my lips.

"I shouldn't be here," I whispered. "I shouldn't be here at all." But I made no move to leave.

My pulse raced. I could feel his warm sweet breath on my face, and his arms were strong around me. I wanted to surrender, and I did and let him carry me into the bedroom and drop me gently on the bed.

"No," I managed to say. "I can't," and yet I drowned on that bed, never wanting to leave its soft whiteness, never wanting to leave the man in his starched white shirt leaning down and further into me.

After we made love, he pulled away, a high flush on his cheeks.

"I'm sorry," he said.

He stood and dressed and left the room.

My head spun. How many women had he made love to on this bed? Was this what all the feelings I had toward him had led to? Had he slept with Augusta in this bed?

He came back to stand in the doorway. "My wife has never joined me here," he said as if reading my mind. "Our lives rarely cross."

I got out of bed quickly, turning my back to him so he would not see my nakedness, and dressed. Behind me, I heard him leave the doorway and then I heard the popping of a cork. When I walked out of the bedroom, I saw my bonnet still lay on the floor. He bent to retrieve it and placed it carefully on one of the loveseats.

"And despite evidence to the contrary," he said. "I am at heart a gentleman."

I felt nauseous; my hands shook.

"So please… will you appease an old man by at least sharing one glass of champagne with me before you go?"

I wanted to run out of the room and never see him again. He had done this so cavalierly, as though it meant nothing.

"Wait," he said, walking towards me. "Your hands." He took my trembling hands into his own large ones and looked deep into my eyes. "What's wrong, Lizzie?"

I couldn't speak, but he moved me gently toward the love seat and sat next to me.

"Have I hurt you in some way? I didn't mean to!" He wouldn't let go of my hands or gaze. "Augusta and I haven't shared a bed in six years. You must understand, surely."

But I didn't. I didn't understand the waves of feelings washing over me. I wanted his hands to always hold mine. And yet I feared being a fool, feared being wanton, feared I would be only one of many young women to share his bed.

"Are there others?" My voice cracked.

He bowed his head then again met my gaze. "There have been. Not for a good while though. And this is very different, Lizzie. Please believe me." He held a glass of champagne to my lips, and I almost swooned in its strong scent of orange peel, berries, flowers.

"Augusta and I live separate lives," he repeated.

I pointed to a photograph on the mantle. A boy, in a suit with a white bow tie and tall boots. "Your son?" I asked.

Once again, he looked down at the floor. "Yes, Maxcy. I love him dearly." He rose from the loveseat and walked over to the photo. "I must appear to be an awful human being," he said. "But I don't know what I will do."

The bubbles of champagne rolled like tiny pearls on my tongue.

We didn't kiss again that day. But we told each other our stories.

"You were very brave to risk the wrath of the Church by divorcing your husband," he said. "I have not found that courage."

A knock on the door interrupted us.

It was the desk clerk. His eyes widened when he saw me. "There's a man downstairs who's anxious to speak with you, sir," he said. "Something about an investment in Honduras. He is quite insistent, so I came to see what you would like me to do."

"Distract him with that fine rye you have. Old Westmoreland. I'll be down shortly."

"Yes, sir." The clerk left with a quick bow.

"I must go, too." I stood and put the bonnet on my head.

Horace pulled a silver key from his vest pocket. "For this suite. And also the door to the catwalk. In case you feel more comfortable avoiding the hotel lobby." He wrapped my fingers around the key before I could object and left the room.

From that day forward, Horace Tabor wooed me with handwritten letters and handkerchiefs, flowers and books, invitations to the Opera and elegant dinners in his suite. Within two months, he had moved me out of my room at the boarding house into a suite next to his at the Clarendon.

Did I question what I was doing? Constantly. I also fell deeply in love.

Each time I tried to stop seeing him, Horace renewed his efforts to keep me in his life. And the truth was, I had nowhere else to go. Even the Mooneys had grown distant, and though Tabor's name was never mentioned, I knew they disapproved of my seeing him. Naively, I reassured myself that I could love Horace and he love me, while he remained a husband to Augusta and father to Maxcy. But it wasn't long before this proved impossible.

Within a year, he had moved all his belongings out of the house he shared with Augusta. That summer, she filed for a property settlement, claiming Horace had deserted her, though she refused to grant him a divorce, and he still made public appearances with her and kept up the pretense of being a loving husband. He became cautious about not being seen with me in public, saying it could doom his political ambitions if word got out about us during his efforts to divorce Augusta.

At the end of one of our afternoon rendezvous, I watched as he struggled to cross the pointed ends of his tie.

"What a show there was at the Opera House last night!" he said.

I had spent the prior evening alone, doubled over with sorrow, picturing him seated next to Augusta in their private box. It made no difference that I knew he no longer loved his wife, that he no longer even lived with her. As far as the public was concerned, Horace and Augusta Tabor were still the first couple of Leadville.

"We used the largest set for the stage—'Light Fancy.' You remember the one?"

I'd seen the set with its green paneled walls and rose garlands when he'd taken me on a backstage tour.

"I remember." I remained on the bed, the white duvet pulled to my chin.

His eyes caught mine in the mirror. "I'll take you to the show next week. I promise."

I fingered the duvet, not wanting to reveal how much pain I was in.

"Lizzie," he said slowly. His tall form filled the oval standing mirror. Such a handsome man, so elegant in his fine clothes. Mama would love him, I thought irrationally.

"I haven't even told Augusta but I've just learned there is a vacant seat for Colorado in the Senate. Full-term. The legislature will meet soon to fill this seat, and I need to spend time in Denver to press the case that they choose me."

The news shook me, but I stayed silent as he kissed me good-bye and as always, returned to his life without me.

CHAPTER 19

Horace asked me to go with him to Denver, saying he would put me up at the Windsor Hotel so I could be close during the time the legislature was in session. I refused. Our relationship grew strained, and I did my best to pull my heart away from him. Though inevitably, whenever he returned to Leadville, I would agree to meet him at his suite at the Clarendon.

One afternoon, after we'd made love, I asked again if he would hire me to work at the Matchless mine. I had told myself that if he refused as he had before, I would return to Oshkosh.

He stood with his back to me, tapping the cardboard stiffener in his cigarette pack on the leather top of a lowboy. "I've spoken with a judge in Durango," he said.

"Why?"

"I'm going to divorce Augusta."

"What?" My stomach dropped.

"Judge there owes me a favor. The divorce will be final in 3 days."

My mind raced, scrambling to understand. I didn't even know if this was what I had wanted.

"Have you told Augusta?" I asked, holding my hand up as he walked toward me, keeping a distance between us. "Does she know what you've done?"

"Not yet." His arms hung straight at his sides, and I was relieved he did not step forward to touch me. "Her sister is ill. She's considering a trip to California to visit her. It seemed a bad time."

He turned to the lowboy and lifted the stop from a crystal decanter. "I didn't have papers served because I want to tell Augusta myself. To grant her some privacy and dignity, at least in the beginning. God only knows the newspapers will enjoy sensationalizing this."

I walked to him and reached for the pack of Marquis cigarettes, but he stopped me.

"I won't lose you, Lizzie." He held my face, insisting I meet his gaze. "I won't lose you, but I also don't want to lose the legislature's vote. Rumors are flying that Senator Teller is about to be made Secretary of the Interior. If that happens, we'll need someone to serve out the last months of his term as well. I want the other seat, the full-term one. But I need to honor the process. We need to be patient. I promise I will marry you as soon as the legislature makes their selection."

He bent down to kiss my neck. "I will take care of it," he whispered into my skin. "All of it, I promise."

He left for Denver the next day and within a week I received a note:

> *It is sweet my darling babe to write you but I do so want to see you it seems an age since I saw you last. What if we had never met? This world would have been a blank to me and I think it would have been cloudy to you. I love you to death and we will be so happy. Nothing shall mar our happiness for you are all my very own and I am yours from hair to toes and back again. My darling I do so feel rejoiced that you love me as you do, you do love me I know ... your loving boy.*
> *With Kisses*

Three weeks after Horace told Augusta what he had arranged in Durango, she grudgingly agreed to the divorce, though she put it on the court's record that "it was not willingly asked for." She received in settlement two houses, $300,000 in cash, and the legal right to keep the name Tabor. Horace and I received the torrent of ill will he had predicted.

The editor of the *Rocky Mountain News* charged "a bonanza king can purchase anything he wishes, even a divorce in four hours" and railed against "the Colorado magnate who threw his wife over for the embraces and smiles of a tawdry, painted courtesan."

I was humiliated, and there was more humiliation to come.

The state legislature showed their disapproval by giving Horace the shorter of the two Senate terms available, but he refused to let this snub derail his ambitions. He would be a Colorado Senator for thirty days to complete Senator Teller's term, he said, and I would be a Senator's wife. His excitement was contagious, and he insisted we begin planning a wedding to take place in Washington, DC.

Horace convinced me to write Mama and tell her the good news. I had been hesitant, afraid she wouldn't look kindly on me marrying a divorced man, let alone one who was nearly Papa's age. But I also knew that Mama would want to attend the lavish wedding that was being planned and that Horace would charm her out of any objections.

CHAPTER 20

September 24, 1882

Dear Mama,

I hope you will share my happiness in the news that a wonderful man named Horace Tabor has asked me to marry him. I know you will be pleased that Mr. Tabor is far more mature and financially responsible than Harvey was. In fact, the plans he has made for our wedding—which will take place in Washington, DC—astound me! I know you will appreciate them, too.

Do you remember the necklace given to General Sherman's daughter for her wedding? The one you showed me on the day of my confirmation? My husband-to-be has promised me a necklace just as grand! Can you imagine, Mama?

He has also arranged for an elegant wedding to be held at the Willard Hotel. I am beside myself with excitement… and quite unbelieving at times that after so many years of hardship such a wondrous thing has happened. I thought after leaving Harvey that I should never be happy again. But this man makes me very happy, Mama, and I know that in your heart that is all you want for me.

I will tell you more about my beloved later but I write this short note now inviting you and Papa to the wedding, which will take place on March 1 of next year. We will make all arrangements for your travel.

The Willard Hotel is where President Lincoln stayed before his inauguration! I have seen pictures of it, with towering marble columns and mosaic floors. There are even elevators and private baths.

I will write again soon and long to hug you and Papa, to hold you both physically close to my heart again.

Your loving daughter,

Lizzie

CHAPTER 21

We checked into the Willard Hotel the last week in February. It was a sprawling building on Pennsylvania Avenue, with a special Ladies' entrance on Fourteenth Street. The front desk was petal-shaped and made of yellow marble. Huge chandeliers hung in the lobby, white globes surrounded by female figures in bronze.

We sent invitations, bordered in silver, to now Secretary of the Interior Henry Teller, whose Senate term Horace had been asked to finish, members of the Cabinet, even President Arthur himself. I was surprised not to receive any responses but mostly forgot about that in my excitement at seeing Mama and Papa. They arrived two days before the wedding, and I was beside myself with joy. We spent hours in the hotel rooms, hugging and crying, talking and laughing. Mama raised her eyebrows when she first saw Horace at Union Station, and for a moment I was afraid she would say something impolite about his age. But he greeted her so graciously, and was such a gentleman, and once they were settled into the hotel, he further won her heart by giving her a beautiful dress he had purchased for her to wear. He gave Papa a silver tie pin and cuff links, which Papa admired with much fanfare.

On the eve of the wedding, after dining with my parents in the hotel restaurant, I sat with Horace in our room. I could see from the window the half-built shaft of a new monument being built to honor George Washington. When the street lamps turned on, I closed the heavy yellow drapes and was returning to my chair when there was a knock on the door. Horace set his cigar down in a monogrammed ashtray.

"I'll get it," I said. "It's probably Mama who's forgotten something."

But when I opened the door I saw a coachman in scarlet livery. He handed me an envelope with a silver border.

I kept my back to Horace as I opened the envelope. Inside was our invitation, torn in half. I stared at the ragged silver edges and the florid signature that had been added: Mrs. Henry M. Teller.

Horace came up behind me.

"Pay her no mind," he said and took the invitation from me and dropped it in the fire.

I stared down at my bare feet.

"Why would she do that?" I asked, my voice catching. "I don't even know her, Horace."

He rubbed his right sideburn. "Damn if I know, Lizzie. Teller himself is a good man—a staunch supporter of silver and, by all accounts, a man with a good heart."

"So why would his wife…?"

He put his hands on my shoulders. "I thought that coming to Washington would give us a fresh start, Lizzie. That people here would be more sophisticated. Less concerned with the affairs of an old man and his bride. It looks like I was wrong about that."

"Is it because of our ages, Horace? Our divorces?"

"I suspect both." He turned to walk into the bedroom and returned with a white box tied with a pale violet ribbon.

"I think we should ignore them, Lizzie. I won't have anyone ruin my happiness or yours. I'm not marrying either of the Tellers; I'm marrying you. And you make me happier than I have ever been in my life. So I think now is a good time to show you what I've found."

He opened the box to reveal an extravagant diamond necklace, its center stone larger than any I had ever seen.

"It's the Isabella diamond," he said, spinning me back to face him. "From the Queen of Spain."

"Oh my goodness! Horace!"

He fastened the necklace around my neck then led me to a mirror in the bedroom.

"Oh my, you shouldn't have done this. Not that I don't think it's beautiful. It is! But how on earth…?"

I knew the wedding gown we'd had made cost $7,000—I'd seen the receipt one day on his desk. When I found out, I'd been horrified, saying it was far too much money to spend on a dress I'd wear only once. But he countered all my objections with kisses and reassurances that it was his pleasure to buy me such beautiful things. I wanted to show the necklace to Mama, but Horace was standing so close to me, and the bed was right there, and we fell into it, all thoughts of Mrs. Teller's rudeness forgotten.

An hour before the wedding the next night, Horace dressed in a black tailcoat, white bow tie, black satin vest. I fastened his black onyx cufflinks.

"I told Father Chapelle I would meet him downstairs," he said. "And I don't want to see you in your gown before the ceremony. Bad luck. I've asked a maid to come help you—and of course. your mother will be here."

Mama had nearly fainted when I ran to her room that morning to show off the necklace. She insisted on being the one to put it around my neck once Hazel had fastened the rows of pearl buttons on the back of my gown.

"You look stunning!" Mama said. She had tears in her eyes. "I always knew you would wear fine jewels one day!"

We met Papa in the hallway, and Hazel lifted the long train of my gown as we made our way to the elevator and down to the three rooms we'd rented for the ceremony and dinner.

Three rows of white wooden chairs had been set up in the smallest room, each chair back tied with a lavender bow. My stomach sank when I saw how few chairs were filled, and all of those with men. It looked like Mrs. Teller wasn't the only wife who condemned the marriage of divorced Catholics and refused to attend.

I squeezed Mama's hand, and she clicked her tongue, shaking her head.

"Such rudeness," she finally said. "But it doesn't matter what other people think, Lizzie. This is your day. Enjoy it to the hilt."

So, stomach clenched, I stepped into the parlor, looking down at the thick green carpet and tightly clutching a small bouquet of lily and heliotrope.

When Horace cleared his throat, I looked up to see him standing next to the priest. I hadn't asked how he persuaded the Father to marry us. Behind them stood a huge bell fashioned from white delphinium and purple columbine, with a scarlet heart atop.

Keeping my eyes firmly on my beloved's, and reassured by the presence of Mama and Papa on either side of me, I walked past the rows of empty chairs. Towering white lilies rose from an amphora at the end of each row; I inhaled deeply.

The ceremony was short. We were doing something highly out of the ordinary by having the wedding in the evening and had decided to make our focus the reception and dinner to follow. After completing our vows, Horace and I walked back down the aisle without meeting the gaze of any of the dozen or so guests. I was grateful for this custom since I had no idea how I could even pretend to be polite to the men whose wives had refused to attend.

A long table had been set up in the center of another room, filled with multi-colored liquor bottles and silver platters of patés, smoked tongue, radish roses, stuffed eggs, a salmon in aspic. A string quartet played softly in a corner of the room. I determined to enjoy the rest of the evening as best I could. We would have wonderful food to eat, and I would dance with my new husband. And if appeasing my husband's fellow politicians was important to him, I would do my best to engage them in conversation.

A uniformed maid served champagne from a silver tray.

From the far side of the room, I heard someone offer an unenthusiastic toast, "To the bride and groom."

"Come on now," Papa cried. "That's no way to celebrate!"

I was afraid he might embarrass us—Mama said he had already had more than enough to drink from the flask he always carried now in an inside pocket. But just then, a distinguished-looking gentleman, surely more than six feet tall, appeared in the doorway. The waxed tips of his large, gray moustache reached to his chin. His cheeks were red, and his hair, blacker than his moustache, parted neatly on the right. It was President Chester Arthur.

"Oh my!" Mama said, one hand to her mouth.

"So glad you've come, Mr. President," Horace said. "You are just in time to meet my wonderful wife."

The President was sturdily built, even portly, but fastidiously dressed. He bowed and kissed my hand. He smelled like boiled beef, and I remembered Horace telling me the man had fallen ill with Bright's

Disease shortly after being elected President. He was a new widower as well.

"It's a great pleasure to meet you, Mrs. Tabor," he said. "You are truly a beautiful bride."

Mama came up beside us, dragging Papa by the hand. I introduced the President to my parents before he turned his eyes back to Horace.

"Congratulations to my Vermont cousin as well," he said, smiling.

"I didn't know you hailed from that fine state, sir," Horace said. "I'd heard upstate New York."

"Born in Fairfield, Senator Tabor," the President's thick side whiskers were streaked with gray. "And my mother Malvina, blessed be her memory, was born there as well. 'Course those facts don't stop my political enemies from arguing that I'm not a native-born citizen. There've been a slew of rumors I was born in Ireland or Canada, you know."

Horace laughed.

"And of course, back in Vermont, my preacher father would have taken me out back to the wood shed for being late to your wedding. Please accept my apologies."

Just then, two maids opened wide double doors into another room where a table had been decorated with huge four-leaf clovers made of roses, camellias, and violets—red, white, and blue. A dozen white candles burned in sparkling silver candelabras. A wreath of violets encircled each place setting, and more flowers draped over the sides of half a dozen silver ice buckets. Our names were written in violet ink on cream-colored cards bordered with silver. Horace was to sit to my right, the President to my left.

I stared at the dazzling array of silverware and crystal in front of me and winked at Mama sitting across from me. She looked so happy! I counted four forks, four knives, three spoons—all of varying sizes. And a fourth spoon lay horizontal above the plate. There were two wine glasses, a new champagne flute, a water goblet.

"Intimidating, isn't it?" the President asked as soon as we were seated. "I had to ask one of the White House servers to explain things to me before my first official dinner. I'll pass along what she told me."

"I would appreciate that!" Across the way, Mama's cheeks were red with pleasure.

A waiter brought a magnum of champagne and filled fresh glasses. President Arthur stood, and the conversation around the table immediately stopped.

"Ten years ago," he said, "I sat in this room listening to Henry Stanley enthrall a crowd of cynical Washingtonians with his adventures tracking down Dr. Livingstone in Africa. Tonight, though she's said few words to me yet, a young woman from a world nearly as foreign to me as Africa has already enthralled me."

Horace squeezed my hand under the table.

"As most of you know," the President continued, "my thoughts have lately been elsewhere. In fact, as even the gracious Senator Tabor may have guessed, one of the reasons I came tonight was to help push for passage of the Pendleton Act."

Several men at the table chuckled.

"Such expediency has become part of my nature, I'm afraid." He fingered the rim of his glass. "Of course, you, Senator Tabor, have your own causes—silver at the top of them. But pay close heed during your time here with us in Washington. Eastern financial interests have become increasingly vocal about their wish for a solid, gold-backed dollar."

Horace started to stand, but the President stopped him, saying, "However, in the presence of such loveliness, all such low talk must fall by the wayside. Gentlemen, if you will join me in a more appropriate toast—to Senator Tabor and the very beautiful Mrs. Tabor."

When it was clear no one else cared to add their good wishes, Horace stood. "Then let me lift a final toast as well. I will continue to place my bets both on Colorado silver and on beauty. In both respects, I consider myself a fortunate man indeed."

I don't think I'd ever felt more special in my life. I thanked both Horace and the President for their kind words then dipped a small spoon into the lemon sorbet that had been placed before me. We dined for more than two hours as course after course arrived: fresh oysters, paté de foie gras, quail with croutons, wild turkey stuffed with walnuts and brown rice. There were sixteen side dishes, including potatoes in clover blossom butter, tiny green peas, and always more oysters, both curried and steamed.

Champagne flowed freely, as did red and white wines from France. I kept an eye on Papa across the table, concerned that he might drink too much, but Mama was being careful, sometimes removing a glass from his hands with a smile.

"So what do you think of our nation's capital so far?" President Arthur asked me as a crusted pie of shallots and onions was served.

"I miss Colorado," I said. "I'm surprised that that's my answer, but it is what comes to mind. Please don't tell my parents!"

Two men at the end of the table were engaged in a heated conversation, their voices rising. The President nodded toward them. "That one on the right is angry I vetoed the Chinese Exclusion Act. To my mind, the Chinese have contributed a great deal to our economy On the railways and from what I hear in the Colorado mines as well."

"Yes."

"A ban on immigration is completely unreasonable," he said.

"What do you want to accomplish while you are President?" I asked. "I couldn't imagine having such power."

"It's not as much power as you might think, Mrs. Tabor. But if I had my druthers, I'd like to see us have a Navy. And I'd like that damn monument on the Mall finished before I leave office!" He laughed then grew serious. "Social justice is important to me, as is women's suffrage."

"I've been reading about Susan B. Anthony," I said. "The Press writes so admiringly of her. I would love to hear her speak one day."

He leaned back in his chair.

"'Woman wants bread, not the ballot,' yes? An ironic title indeed." He sighed. "But the only way women will achieve economic equality is through the vote, as Miss Anthony knows."

About ten, two servers rolled in a cart with a four-tiered cake, its top layer canopied with trails of chained violets.

The President pulled a watch from his pocket. "I'm afraid I must leave you to the rest of your celebrations," he said, standing. "I have thoroughly enjoyed spending time with your wife, Senator Tabor. She is as intelligent as she is beautiful, as I'm sure you know. That is a rare combination and one to value."

He bent to kiss my hand and before letting go of it said, "When you return to Colorado, will you return to good friends?"

I hesitated, afraid to tell the uncomfortable truth. "I doubt it," I answered. Horace had told me that when Augusta traveled to Denver, a group of society ladies always threw a party to welcome her. I didn't expect them to do any such thing for me.

"But you have your husband, and he is a very powerful man out West. I hope the future is kind to you both." He hesitated. "I would like to ask one favor of you before I go."

"Anything."

"May I have a bloom from your bridal bouquet to keep as a memory of you?"

I knew my cheeks must be beet-red. But I reached for the bouquet that rested near my plate and pulled out a single rose then stood on tiptoe to slip it into his buttonhole. He bent to kiss my cheek then, as I caught my breath, he turned to leave.

After dessert, the men retired to a smoking room for cigars. Horace insisted Mama and I join them. Mama begged off, saying she wanted to get Papa safely to bed before he passed out. I found myself a chair near Horace. The man on his other side reached for a glass of cognac without offering me one. "So, Tabor, the President said you are originally from the East. Is that correct?" he asked.

"Yes," Horace answered. "Vermont."

"Did you attend school up there?"

"No. I trained as a stonemason. I left home early to work in the quarries."

"I see." The man drained his glass and motioned for a waiter to bring another. "Yet somehow you made your way to Colorado, and to Leadville, and to vast riches."

Horace's eyes flashed.

But the man pressed on. "You've done quite well for yourself. I dare say the Treasury's decision to buy silver every month gives quite a boost to your fortune."

The man leaned closer into Horace; I could smell the butterscotch scent of cognac on his breath even from where I sat. "*Mr.* Tabor," he continued, "for you are just filling the last month of Senator Teller's term, yes? And then you will be gone from Washington and on your way back to Colorado and its mountains and its silver mines. And its multiple wives."

I gasped.

"You have managed to do what all men sometimes long to do. But being gentlemen, Mr. Tabor, we rarely do."

At this, I popped up from my chair and holding the train of my gown in my hands, positioned myself between the two men who towered over me. "How dare you!" I said.

Horace pulled me to his side, gripping my elbow tightly.

"Have you dined well tonight, sir?" he asked the man, his tone even and calm.

"Yes, I did, sir." The man lifted his glass as though asking for more but Horace raised his hand to stop the waiter from refilling it. The room had gone silent. The man cleared his throat and took a step toward the door then stopped.

"And I expect to dine well again here. Many times. The Willard is excellent at entertaining *guests*." He said the last word with disdain. "It's a shame you'll have so little time to enjoy our Eastern hospitality."

The tips of Horace's ears were bright red. "I believe it is time to call it a night."

There were muffled thanks as the other men quickly finished their drinks and readied themselves to leave. I didn't see any of them again during the entire month we stayed in Washington.

After Mama and Papa returned to Oshkosh, I mailed them a clipping from the *Washington Post*:

> *The bold originality of the methods and hour (8 p.m.) of celebrating his marriage and the splendor of its surroundings are exciting much comment, and none that is not favorable to the Senator's taste and independence.*

I did not send the write-up from the *New York Tribune* which was far less complimentary:

> *There is nothing... so picturesquely vulgar as this gorgeous hotel*
> *wedding of a pair... who were determined to have the éclat of*
> *being married ... in a senatorial capacity.*

Two days after the wedding, Father Chappelle refused to sign our marriage license when he learned we were both divorced, a fact Horace had somehow failed to tell him.

CHAPTER 22

On our return to Denver, we moved into the house Horace had had built for us. It stood at the corner of Sherman Avenue and 13th Street on three acres of rolling lawn. Six fountains ran clear water continuously, and a hundred peacocks roamed amidst life-size marble nudes of Psyche, Nimrod, and Diana and cast-iron sculptures shipped from Italy: two dogs, a deer, a white fox with green glass eyes. Two long driveways approached the house, but not a single neighbor walked or drove up in their carriage to welcome us.

Another house, as sprawling and extravagant as ours, stood across the street. On the day we moved in, I caught sight of a woman in an upstairs window there and thought of my first glimpse of Arvilla Bunn back in Dogwood. But unlike Arvilla, this neighbor never made an effort to befriend me. I understood gossip about the scandal of Horace's divorce and our marriage had preceded us.

About a month after we moved in, we sat in the drawing room after dinner.

"So did you notice anything different in the yard when you came home?" I asked. I was bored out of my mind staying in the house alone while he went to his office and had taken it upon myself to drape a large white sheet over the nude Psyche. I meant it as a joke, a sign of surrender to the matrons in my neighborhood who had made their prudish condemnation of me so clear.

He sighed. "Yes, I saw it. I'm not certain they will understand your sarcasm, Lizzie."

"I don't know what to do with myself, Horace. I can't stand wandering around this huge house with nothing to do. You've hired so much staff that there's no work left for me." We had a cook, two maids, a groundskeeper, and a chauffeur.

"You must find something appropriate, Lizzie. You don't need to earn money. Never again." He motioned for me to come sit on his lap. "I think it would be lovely to have some children to fill the rooms of this house. Don't you?"

"Yes, I do." Mama had already sent me a recipe to promote fertility she'd found in a magazine. Worcestershire sauce and ketchup with mace, nutmegs, clove, and ginger. "I can't get Cook to let me into the kitchen. Will you please tell her I'd like time alone there sometimes?"

"Of course. Remember, you are her employer, Lizzie. You must be firm." He shifted as though uncomfortable, so I stood and pulled up one of the other chairs to be close to him.

"A few of the men in the legislature want me to go up against those political yahoos in D.C.," he said.

I'd been surprised that his time in Washington had strengthened his political ambitions rather than dissuading them.

"The Republican Party needs me," he said.

"They need your money."

"That too."

I picked up a music box automaton from a side table near me. A painted enamel cardinal sat on a perch inside a brass cage. When I turned the lever, the bird began to turn, flap its wings, and open and shut its beak. Warbles and trills filled the room.

"I've tried to make friends with the staff," I said. "It's just not working."

"You need something to occupy yourself."

What I really wanted to do was move back to Leadville. To be up in the clouds, close to the mountains, close to the mines I still longed to explore.

"I won't lie to you, Lizzie. The months ahead will be busy ones. I've made new investments—the Vulture Mine in Arizona is one of them. I'll be travelling. I need you to run the household in my absence."

"This isn't what I wanted, Horace."

He looked so hurt.

"I don't mean that all of this"—I gestured at the room around me, with its turquoise-and-white flocked wallpaper and tapestry carpet, the velvet-covered sofas and embroidered footstools—"isn't beautiful. It is, Horace. It's wonderful! But ..." I didn't know how to explain what I felt. That no matter what extravagant furnishings we had, they would never be enough. I wanted him. I wanted his love. I had once been the lucky object of his obsessive wooing. Now, he was concentrated on wooing his Republican colleagues.

"We need a child, Lizzie. I want a child."

I did, too. I fingered the bars of the cage and turned the lever again, leaning to touch Horace's cheek. I ran my finger down his thick sideburn, and leaned in even closer to give him a kiss. "We'll have a child."

At night, I dreamt of mines: rust-colored pilings, an ore wagon ready to roll downhill, a bucket falling down a bottomless shaft. When I asked Horace about the Matchless, he reassured me that he would take me back to Leadville that summer to visit.

One evening, Horace arrived home looking more excited than I had seen him in months. I had not been able to get pregnant, despite Mama's recipe. I still enjoyed making love with Horace, but there was a new urgency in both of us.

"I have good news!" he said, walking into the front hall and lifting me up to twirl me round and round on the marble floor.

"The great Miss Bernhardt has agreed to perform at the Opera House!" One of Horace's projects had been to build an Opera House in Denver, just as he had done in Leadville. It would open in June. "We'll have her to the house for a party. Surely our neighbors will join us for such an occasion!"

I was dizzy when he set me back down on my feet but excited at the possibility of something to plan. "A party would be wonderful!" I said. "It's just what we need. And Sarah Bernhardt! I read that she left Paris early this year to tour America."

"Yes, indeed. And Denver will now be one of her stops."

"I also read that she sleeps in a coffin! To prepare herself for tragic roles."

He laughed. "I'm afraid we won't be able to offer her that kind of accommodation."

"No, I suppose not! But to have her here at the house—that would be lovely. I'll start planning the menu now. When will she come?"

"In four weeks. Plenty of time to prepare."

So we wrote up a guest list that included all of Denver's social elite, and I worked with Cook, a woman named Madeline who insisted on wearing a man's chef uniform: crisply starched blue-and-white herringbone trousers and a double-breasted white coat with two front layers of cloth to protect against spills and fires. Its cuffs were split so they could be used as potholders.

Our kitchen was huge, with a ten-plate cast iron gas stove, an open fireplace in rose-colored marble, a rectangular butcher block table, and 12-foot ceilings. There were rows of green glass Ball preserving jars, shelves lined with colorful Italian pottery, and two Hepplewhite cabinets with tapered legs and decorative inlays. The pantry was filled with brightly labeled canned foods—tomatoes, corn, peas—and Pillsbury flour, soda crackers, Heinz ketchup, cookbooks, copper molds and more.

The weeks before the party, I oversaw the entire staff as they cleaned, scrubbed, and polished. The rugs were cleaned with a brand new Bissell vacuum. I'd follow behind the maids, plumping pillows, turning down the curled corners of Oriental rugs, sitting down on couches or chairs I hadn't tried before.

I had a seamstress make a pretty dress of celadon green satin, with a cream-colored sash.

"You look gorgeous!" Horace said the night of the party. He pulled a small sack from his pocket and emptied it into his hand. Pearls piled high on his palm.

"Oh, Horace, no. I don't need more jewelry, really. I have so much…"

His smile faded, and I knew I had once again hurt his feelings. I turned quickly to let him fasten the double strand necklace around my neck and followed him to the mirror to admire its beauty.

"Now let me go make certain everything is set in the kitchen," I said. Madeline and three extra cooks had spent the week preparing miniature meat pies and bullock's heart, butternut squash soup, Beef Wellington, beet greens and potatoes, and sweet milk buns.

Promptly at ten, after the performance ended, Horace brought the actress to our home. She stood no taller than I, about five feet tall. And her hair was as fiery red as the newspapermen reported. As soon as she walked in, she pushed a bouquet of roses into my hands.

"Here, *ma chère*. I get more than enough of these. And they will look lovely in your home, *oui?*"

I handed the flowers to one of our maids, who stood quietly behind us. "Thank you, Miss Bernhardt. They're lovely. Nancy, will you put them in water in a vase for us?"

The actress removed her hat, which was decorated with long purple feathers.

"Such a beautiful hat and gown!" I said. Her dress was also purple, with a large bustle and very low décolletage. I noticed that fine blue lines were painted on the actress's skin.

She caught me staring. "Oh, *merde*, I forgot to remove my paint! It's to make the skin more translucent."

"It's fine," I said quickly. "You are just as beautiful as I expected. More so!"

I was so excited to see this famous woman. I wanted to remember every detail so I could write about the evening in a letter to Mama.

The three of us went to the front parlor, and Miss Bernhardt chose a chair near a lamp.

Horace had arranged for absinthe, and a maid rolled in a large fountain of hand-blown glass, with three glasses and slotted silver spoons.

"For our lovely guest from France," Horace said. He placed a sugar cube on one of the spoons and balanced it on top of a glass which held an inch of green liquor.

"You make me feel as though I am at home, in Paris. *La fée verte!*"

Horace held the glass under ice water streaming from the fountain. It ran over the sugar cube, and the drink grew cloudy.

"*La louche,*" she said, smiling.

A perfume of herbs filled my nose.

"Anise and fennel," Horace said.

"I did not expect such culture here in the Wild West, Mr. Tabor."

"We had the pleasure of Oscar Wilde's presence at my other Opera House, in Leadville. Here's how he described the drink to me: 'After the first glass, you see things as you wish they were. After the second, you see things as they are not. Finally, you see things as they really are, and that is the most horrible thing in the world.'"

The actress instructed us to take a deep breath to clear my head before taking the first sip.

"You mustn't fear it," she said, noticing my hesitation. "At home, the drink is quite the rage. Many drink it first thing in the morning and last thing at night. Your mind will be clear and relaxed. And you will experience no hangover in the morning!"

I took a taste, surprised by its strong taste of licorice and herbs.

"If it is too bitter for you," she said quickly, "add a little sugar."

I sipped slowly as the actress began to tell us about her recent meeting with the inventor Thomas Edison, to whom we owed the electric lamps that now lit Denver's streets.

"I was at his home in New Jersey earlier this year," she said. "I did a private reading for him and several of his friends. A reading of *Phèdre* by Jean Racine. Mr. Edison recorded my reading onto a wax cylinder." She finished the last drop of her drink. Horace offered to make her another, but she declined. "A fascinating device," she continued.

I was eager to hear more, I could listen to her lovely voice forever, but just then the doorbell rang, and I was pulled away to meet guests I really had little desire to meet.

The first to arrive were Governor and Mrs. Routt. For the next fifteen minutes, Horace and I welcomed each arrival as the actress held court in the parlor.

"My dear, you look lovely," Mr. Dirby, our neighbor across the street said as he and his wife arrived. Without speaking, Mrs. Dirby handed me her limerick gloves and disappeared into the other room.

But Horace kept hold of Dirby's hand. "Dirby, old man, it's good to finally see you in our home. Even a Gold Populist like yourself." Horace laughed, but our neighbor did not. "You must come more often," Horace said. "The walk between our houses is much less than the distance between our politics." He slapped Dirby on the back and motioned him in to the parlor.

At eleven, Nancy announced that dinner was served.

I led our twelve guests into the large dining room. A four-tiered crystal chandelier gleamed with candlelight. Each silver serving plate and utensil had been burnished to a high shine.

As we ate the delicious meal, Miss Bernhardt entertained us all with stories.

"Last month I introduced Nikola Tesla, the great inventor, to Swami Vivekananda. The swami had come to see me when I performed in *The Buddha's Concubine* in New York. You know he recently received a standing ovation after his speech at the Chicago World's Fair!

"I try to see all the interesting people I can whenever I travel to America," she said. "I was fascinated to learn that both the Swami and Mr. Tesla believe everything in the world is made of ether."

Mr. Dirby raised his eyebrows.

"Tell us more," I said quickly. "You are fortunate to meet such interesting people. I've read about Tesla. He appears to be a true genius, one whose work will have a large impact on our futures."

"I agree, Mrs. Tabor," she said.

"Call me Lizzie, please."

"Nikola told me that he believes one day we will be able to send messages and pictures long distance, without any wires. *C'est la magie!*"

To my dismay, Mr. Dirby changed the topic to the growing conflict between France and China. The men who had sat silently at the table while we spoke of science and spirituality now talked loudly. Miss Bernhardt was far less interested in talking politics and war, as I was. Perhaps it was the absinthe we'd drunk earlier, and the glasses of wine served throughout dinner. But I decided to turn the conversational tide.

"I read about your exhibition at the Salon," I said as soon as I found a brief opening.

She gave me a radiant smile. "Yes," she said, "my sculptures. I had the immense good fortune to study with Mathieu Meusnier and Emilio Franchesci. Do you know their work?"

"No."

"The Paris Salon has been quite gracious in letting me show my art. There have been exhibitions in London, New York, and Philadelphia as well."

"I must ask you, Miss Bernhardt," Mrs. Dirby said, "about your beauty routine. Your skin is flawless."

Mr. Dirby frowned at his wife and patted her on the hand. "Really, dear."

Mrs. Dirby looked down at her lap.

"I am interested as well, Miss Bernhardt," I said quickly. I couldn't stand to see that man be so condescending toward his wife, even if she was no friend of mine.

The actress laughed. "It is one of my favorite topics! There is a Doctor Caissarato in Paris. He is my *magie*! I owe it all to him."

Mrs. Dirby removed her hand from under her husband's. "Oh, do tell! I would love to know what the latest beauty advice is from this Parisian doctor!"

Sarah Bernhardt refused a piece of the cake Nancy was placing in front of her. "One of the good doctor's secrets is diet," she said. "That and exercise and bathing.

"He recommends few sweets, less coffee and tea. Plenty of pure water, cool but not iced. And, of course, a bath every day. In stimulating herbs like dried rosemary. Or milk. Much better than the soap one buys though I have agreed to do an advertisement for Pear's!"

I smiled, remembering the soap Arvilla had given me that second night in Dogwood. How could I ever have imagined then that I would one day be sitting with the greatest actress in the world, in a home so much grander than that cabin. It stunned me.

When Horace suggested the men retire to the smoking room for cigars, the women went back to the parlor and listened for nearly an hour to the actress's tales of her travels. About one in the morning, the men joined us, and Nancy served a final round of French brandy.

Miss Bernhardt shook each guest's hand as they left.

"I'll get the driver to take you back to your hotel," Horace said.

The great actress and I were left alone in the front hall.

"Are you tired?" I asked.

"Oh my, no! Back home, this is the beginning of our evening. My life is lived at night!"

"It's been lovely having you here," I said. I truly meant this.

"Yes, some day you will come to Paris, and we will talk further. I can tell you are a *femme intelligente*. A woman who searches, *comme moi*."

I heard the landau pull up in front of the house.

"*Mon cher* Dr. C. says he wants me to be as beautiful as God meant me to be when He first thought of me." She lifted her small shoulders and let them drop. "But *Dieu, divinité*. Must it always be a man? I love men dearly! But *la divinité* is something else entirely!"

I wanted to tell her about an article on Vedantic literature I'd read in a recent issue of the *Theosophist* but Horace was at the door. Nancy appeared with Miss Bernhardt's cape and hat, which the actress set on her head at a dizzying angle. She embraced me and kissed both my cheeks.

"I wish you would stay longer," I said.

"Ah, no. You will visit me in Paris one day. We will walk the Tuileries, and I will take you for one of Dr. C's milk baths. And we will talk more about this elusive *Dieu* we search for. My good doctor believes; I do not, but I search."

As I watched Horace walk her to the landau, I realized this was the first interesting conversation I'd had since moving to Denver and that it had taken a famous French actress to articulate my deep longing.

CHAPTER 23

December 1883
Denver, Colorado

Dearest Mama,

I write with news that I hope will bring you much joy!

I am finally with child.

Horace assures me that when the baby is old enough, we will travel to Oshkosh to see you all and to introduce you to the newest member of our family. My beloved husband works hard but continues to give me the moon and sun and stars to make me happy.

Until the Hoped-for Day, I remain Your Loving Daughter,

Lizzie

CHAPTER 24

I gave birth to Lily in the gigantic, elaborately carved walnut bed Horace had purchased for us. It had taken eight men to carry the bed into the house and up the marble stairs to our room. The sheets on that bed billowed around me like clouds, and sweat ran down my forehead, cheeks, and neck. I could hear Horace pacing outside the door as the face of the midwife hovered above me like a shimmering opal.

This good woman held my hand tightly as I arched off the mattress, screaming. I had seen Mama give birth several times, but nothing had prepared me for the pain I felt.

I had somehow known the baby would be a girl, and I bought dozens of lace gowns for her, which I folded and re-folded as though they were altar cloths. I bought and polished a silver rattle, baby bowl, and spoon and stored these along with the gowns in a special trunk. At night, lying in bed, I caressed my swollen belly and traced the veins crisscrossing my breasts like veins of silver running through rock.

But that night, once the pains started, all romantic fantasies flew away, and I gave in to my body. The early hours were easy, a soreness low on my back, nothing more. After about ten hours of labor pains, the contractions became sharp and stabbing. It was excruciating to lie in bed, so I stood and leaned against a wall through each contraction, the midwife on one side of me, supporting me. I was finally so exhausted I had to lie down, despite the discomfort. Still, the contractions were almost impossible to bear. It felt as though my body were splitting apart.

Somehow I made it through the next hours. Horace kept wanting to come in to comfort me, but each word he spoke pulled me out of the safe place my mind had escaped to, far away from my body, and I begged him to be quiet.

I have never felt such tiredness.

I began to vomit. "I can't do this!" I screamed and vomited again. My whole body shook.

And then, I felt one more huge contraction and, kneeling by the bed, began to push the baby out. For nearly thirty minutes I pushed. I felt a sharp tear when the head crowned, but the stinging lasted only a second. I looked down and saw a tangled cord. The midwife reached down to untangle it. The bulk of the baby remained inside me, kicking frantically.

I smiled and cooed to her, despite the pain. Once the cord was untangled, I gave one more push and the midwife pulled my baby out of me. Fluid gushed between my legs, and my belly collapsed. The midwife lifted me onto the bed and placed my daughter in my arms.

Within the week, Horace had a hundred silver medallions struck and delivered to the most prominent citizens in Denver to announce the birth.

We named this miracle, this new heart of my heart, Elizabeth Bonduel Lily Tabor. Elizabeth after my Mama, Bonduel after the priest who had confirmed me, and Lily so she would have a name that was all her own.

One afternoon, *Harper's Bazaar* sent a man named Thomas Nast to draw our baby's portrait. Mr. Nast was a staunch anti-Catholic, and many of his cartoons depicted Irishmen in an unflattering light. I was not looking forward to his visit, but Horace insisted I make certain the maids dusted, polished, washed, and scrubbed every item in every room of the house. And Mr. Nast made certain I knew as soon as he entered our door that this was *not* the kind of assignment he usually took from *Harper's*. His real interest lay in politics and the affairs of the nation but still, he said, "Money must be made if one didn't marry into it."

I wanted to send the man packing but kept my mouth shut because Horace had made it clear how important this opportunity was to him. Lily rested in my lap for nearly an hour as Nast drew. When her portrait finally appeared on the magazine's cover, I saw he had added a window hung with juniper and ivy vines to frame us. But the accompanying article made my blood boil.

"Fifty lace robes!" its author exclaimed. "A tiny jeweled necklace worth $15,000 around her neck!"

"They don't even see us as people!" I complained to Horace that night.

I was going to write a letter to the editor saying that, in fact, Lily's favorite doll was a simple cloth Miss Poppet sewn by Mama and shipped from Oshkosh.

"Not a good idea," he said. "It would seem very ungracious. Let the readers enjoy what they want to enjoy."

"But I feel invisible," I said. "All people know of us comes from the money they see us spend."

"I see more of you than that."

We lay on monogrammed sheets in the grand bed Lily had been born in. I looked around the room: silver boxes shone in a curio cabinet, a silver-backed mirror and brush lay atop my dressing table. The doors of my armoire were closed, but I knew there were thirty elegant gowns inside; two dozen pairs of shoes; feathered hats and beaded purses. Horace showered me with gifts. At first I loved this; later, I longed for something more from him.

"Will you come home earlier this week?" I ran my fingers across his chest; the hairs there were gray but he was still a handsome man.

He covered my hand with his own. "I'll try. I've brought in a new accountant and promised I'd show him the ropes this week. Once he can handle bookkeeping for all our investments, I should be free to focus on other things. You'd like to see more of me?"

I snuggled into his warm body. "Yes. Much more."

"But I thought you and Lily were having a grand time here in the house without me." He kissed the top of my head.

"We are. I love Lily. But I love you as well. And we don't have much time together anymore. Just the two of us."

It was true. When Horace wasn't working in his office or I wasn't caring for the baby, we often spent our time with his political colleagues. I had little interest in their discussions and would usually excuse myself to go to bed while the men stayed up late talking. I missed the days when Horace wooed me so insistently. I knew he still loved me, and our daughter, dearly. And I loved him. But even with his love, and my beautiful new baby girl, and a magnificent villa filled with all the material possessions one could ever want,

I still felt a longing inside me. It was the longing that had electrified me as I waited for Communion as a child, the longing I had felt in the bowels of the Fourth of July and the Matchless. A longing for an answer to a mystery. And so far, neither a loving marriage, motherhood, nor money seemed to have satisfied it.

Horace continued to shower me with jewelry and Lily with toys as she grew: a talking doll from France that said "Maman" when its left hand was raised to shoulder level and "Papa" when its right hand was raised. A 16-room dollhouse complete with brass beds, lace window treatments, porcelain candy boxes and place settings for twelve, colorful food, and a working water pump.

And, five years later, I was pregnant again. My second daughter arrived during a storm. Lightning flashed outside my window a second before her head crowned.

When one of Horace's friends, a rising young politician named William Jennings Bryan, visited us, he said the baby's laughter sounded like the chime of silver dollars.

"That's it!" Horace said as we sat in the drawing room drinking cognac. The gift Bryan had brought for the baby—a blue linen slip dress—lay on my lap.

"I think we shall take this daughter's birth as a good omen for free silver, William!" Horace tapped his foot on the carpet. "We've got the farmers and the miners with us. Now all we need do is convince the Republican Party that lies east of the Mississippi!"

From the little I'd been able to understand from Horace, the Silverites like him and Bryan favored the free coinage of silver and the use of both silver and gold as U.S. currency. It was quite complicated, and Horace usually deflected any questions I raised. But I gathered that those who were against free silver—the railroad owners, the bankers, the businessmen—feared it would raise prices. While farmers and miners would be more than happy to see prices raised for their crops and ore yields. My husband and his fellow Colorado Republicans were eager to have the government buy more silver.

And so, our second baby girl was named Rosemary Echo Silver Dollar.

A year after Silver Dollar's birth, the Sherman Silver Purchase Act was passed, increasing the government's monthly silver purchase by half and doubling Horace's fortune. He said he would be worth $30 million, an unheard of sum, even for him, within a year.

But he continued to work long hours and travelled often, always returning with expensive gifts: chiming clocks with Paris movements, bronze and crystal waterfall chandeliers. I had to be very strict with the girls to keep them from accidentally breaking the pretty things that covered every surface. Lily was a quiet toddler and usually played alone, amusing herself, while I took care of the new baby. She spent hours cradling that simple rag doll Mama had sent her, ignoring both the expensive toys that filled her room and her baby sister. Silver was colicky, and I slept little those first difficult months. When I did, I dreamt.

I was blessed by our Divine Savior with a wonderful dream &
two others Our darlings Tabor and Silver were with me in the
garden of our home on Sherman & the trees had big white fluffy
feather-like flowers on them I said get us a few of the flowers
Papa

CHAPTER 25

The summer Silver turned three, I woke one Sunday morning surprised to find the other side of our bed empty. I threw on a peignoir Horace had brought me from Paris and slipped my feet into a pair of satin mules. I went down the hall to peek into the girls' bedrooms; both were still sound asleep.

I found Horace downstairs in the library, seated in a high-back chintz chair. Piles of papers covered the carpet at his feet. An oil lamp of cranberry milk glass burned brightly on a side table to his right, casting a warm light on his now-gray head of hair, which was bent over even more papers in his lap.

When he heard me enter, he looked up without smiling.

I walked over to him and started to lift the papers from his lap. To my surprise, he stopped my hand. I caught a glimpse of his bold signature on several pages and the names of investments that were only vaguely familiar to me: the Vulture mine in Arizona, the Santa Edwiges in Mexico. Two sheets of paper fell to the floor, and I bent down quickly to get them. One mentioned the 15th Street Theatre, which had burned down in June.

"What is this? What's going on, Horace?"

He pulled the papers from my hand then put the full stack of them next to the lamp. "Nothing important, Lizzie." He patted his lap. "Come here now—there's room for you now."

I refused to sit.

"Lizzie, it's nothing. I'd taken out a loan to help finish construction of the new Post Office. I used the theatre as my collateral. Then, when it burned down, the bank reminded me of my promissory note. It's standard procedure. I'll take care of the payments this week."

"What about all of these?" I touched some of the papers still on the floor with the toe of my shoe. "Are these our investments, Horace? Is everything all right with them?"

He turned to gaze out the bay window. The sky to the east had lightened.

I heard noises from above. "Mama?" It was Lily, who must have run into our bedroom. "Mama, where are you?"

"Down here, sweetheart. I'll be right up," I said then more quietly to Horace, "Is there anything I should know? Anything at all you want to tell me?"

He smiled half-heartedly and stood.

"If there's a problem, I want to help," I said.

I could hear Lily's bare feet on the carpeted steps. "Mama, I'm coming down."

Horace reached to hug me and for a moment, I rested my head on his velvet dressing gown. He whispered into my hair, "I can handle it."

There was a noise behind me, and I turned to see Lily standing in the doorway, her long blond hair tousled from sleep.

"I couldn't find you, Mama," Lily said

I heard Silver begin crying in her room upstairs. "Let me go get your sister," I said quickly.

"And have Cook bring my coffee!" Horace had swooped Lily into his arms and was spinning her around. Behind him, the sky had turned pink.

It was much later that afternoon when I passed by the library and noticed a piece of paper caught under a leg of the chair where Horace had been sitting. It was from our lawyer, Lewis Rockwell. The letter began innocently enough, saying that a minister in Denver had objected to Horace presenting plays at the Opera House on the Sabbath. But in the fifth paragraph down, Mr. Rockwell mentioned a lien on the Tabor Block and another on the Grand Opera block.

I asked Horace about it that night.

"When did this happen? Why did you mortgage those buildings?"

"It's paper," he said. "Nothing more. Rockwell's helping me start a new company, and I'll put all our holdings under that. This was old business."

He reached to touch my waist, but I pulled back.

"If I need to, I'll borrow more money," he said. "Believe me, silver mining isn't done for yet. And those fools who say our gold reserves are being undermined don't know what they're talking about."

The next morning, after Horace left for work, I decided that the girls and I would go see the new ice cream parlor that had just opened. It was a block from Horace's office, and I hoped we could make a surprise visit to him. I dressed the girls in matching gingham, and Lily wore a new pair of leather boots with pearl buttons.

The heat was unbearable. All that week the temperature had been close to 100 degrees. I asked the driver to take us right to the parlor, and he helped unload Silver's wicker stroller. Brigham's Ice Cream Parlor and Fudge Shoppe was charming, with a tin ceiling, dark red wallpaper, and large mirrors on its walls. I asked a waiter to seat us at a wooden settee and table near a side window.

Before I'd even removed my bonnet, Silver climbed out of her stroller and up on to the bench next to her sister.

"What are they doing, Mama?" Lily asked. "What are all those people doing?"

I turned to look.

A large crowd had gathered across 16th street, in front of the three-story building that housed the Columbia Savings & Loan Association. Traffic there was completely blocked. I saw our phaeton driver sitting impatiently, waiting to turn the corner but unable to move. The driver of a delivery wagon stood up and shook his fist.

I positioned myself to block the girls' view. "It's all right," I said quickly. "Let's see what we want to order, shall we?"

The waiter handed us three tall red-and-white menus.

"Just give us a minute, please. Look, girls, let's see what you'd like."

Muffled shouts could be heard through the window behind me.

"It's quite a commotion out there," the young waiter said. He wore a long white apron and the wispy beginnings of a mustache.

I scanned the menu quickly, knowing the sooner I got the girls their treats, the sooner we could go home. If we hurried, we might even be able to catch our driver before he got through the blocked traffic.

I handed the menus back to the waiter. "Three slices of Neapolitan ice cream, please."

"But I want a jelly whip," Lily said.

The waiter was staring over my head.

"Three slices of Neapolitan, please," I said more firmly.

"Yes, ma'am," he said and, menus in hand, walked to open the casement window onto the street. Shouts and curses rushed inside. "Just for a minute, so's I can tell what's happening."

I heard angry voices:

"What the hell are we supposed to do now?"

"And what about my mortgage?"

Lily was up on her knees on the bench. "There's Papa! Look, there's Papa standing on the steps next to that man!"

I couldn't even turn to look. "No, dearest, I'm sure it's not Papa."

The voices grew louder and angrier.

"It's President Cleveland's fault."

"And Governor Waite's."

Lily started biting her fingers, and I pulled her hand to stop her.

"Please, young man," I said. "Please shut the window for us. And bring the ice cream."

I didn't want the girls to know how frightened I was. I reached into my purse and found a coin. "Look," I said, handing it to the waiter, "would you watch the girls just for a minute. My husband—I think I see my husband and…"

The young man nodded yes, his eyes wide.

"I'll be right back," I said to Lily and Silver. "This will be very quick. But if it's Papa he'll want to know we're here. Maybe I can get him to come join us before the ice cream is served. Wouldn't that be nice?"

"Yes!" they cried. "Bring Papa!"

Forgetting my bonnet, I rushed out the door and turned the corner onto 16th Street. I pushed my way up front so I could see the man in a burgundy frock coat who stood at the top of the marble steps into the bank. And Lily had been right: Horace stood with his back to me, clearly focused on the man speaking.

"It's rumors. Nothing more than rumors, folks. People trying to rile you up. The bank's not closing. Your money is safe. And I suspect folks back in Washington will do everything they can to keep it that way."

"How do we know we can trust you, Oliver?" This from somewhere behind me.

The man in the frock coat shrugged. "You have to trust me, and the politicians back in Washington."

Angry laughter. A man pushed in front of me, and then another. I couldn't reach Horace so I made my way back to the girls. I was glad we had the ice cream to entertain them, because I didn't have a clue how to answer any questions Lily might ask.

Next day, the headline in the *Rocky Mountain News* read:

Shoulder to Shoulder, Men,
While the War Against Colorado Continues

I read every word of the article. It seemed the battle between those who backed silver and those who backed gold had intensified, and the chances for more legislation to boost silver prices were slim. Colorado's economy was reeling.

CHAPTER 26

Less than a year later, Horace came home early one day. As usual, he carried his black leather valise with nickel locks and a folded-up newspaper under one arm. I met him at the door and took the valise from him, setting it on the marble floor before standing on tip-toe to kiss his lips. When he didn't respond, I reached for his hand, hoping he'd put the newspaper down on the low entry hall table. But he wouldn't release it.

He shook his head slightly and moved past me into the front parlor.

We'd recently had new wallpaper hung—a pattern with meandering foliage atop a grid of flowers in green, ochre, and blue colors. There was a small burled walnut sideboard that served as a liquor cabinet, and Horace lifted its top to reveal a blue glass decanter set. Still clutching the newspaper under his arm, he lifted the stopper and poured a drink.

"Would you like one, Lizzie?" he asked over his shoulder.

"All right." I didn't often drink.

He poured two glasses, handed me one, then sat in his favorite rocking chair.

I stood in front of him, holding my glass. Finally I couldn't bear the silence any longer.

"What's happened, Horace?"

He pulled the newspaper from under his arm, unfolded it, and held it so I could see its screaming headline:

Wall Street Topsy-Turvy, The Famous 'Street'
Passes Another Eventful Black Friday

He gave a half-hearted shrug then leaned forward, elbows on his knees. "It's complicated. I've seen it coming. We all have. And none of us knew how to stop it."

I felt dizzy and closed my eyes. As I struggled to understand, I saw strange shapes, visions: of hundreds of rail cars toppling off wooden tracks, shiny silver coins pouring down as if in a waterfall into a deep hole in the earth.

Until that day, whenever I raised questions about stock market upheavals I saw mentioned in the news, he had reassured me quickly and thoroughly. He and I and the girls would always, always be fine, he'd said, sweeping his arms to indicate the grand house we lived in. As long as the government kept buying silver, we were solvent. I believed him because there was no reason not to. Nor was there any reason for me, at least, to worry about whether or not the government would keep buying silver. That was for Horace and his colleagues to handle; it wasn't women's work. Even without anyone saying those words to me, I had been taught that. Financial matters were a man's domain; I didn't even consider myself smart enough to fully understand them. So I hid my head in the sand and assumed all would be fine.

Now I realized how naïve I had been.

Horace patted his leg and motioned for me to sit on his lap, which I did. He wrapped me in his arms and whispered in my ear that really, it would be all right. This was a bump in the road, nothing that would harm us. His reassurances sounded hollow, but I didn't press him, not wanting to worry him any further.

All that summer, he and I continued the pretense that all was well. We even imported two ponies from Scotland's Shetland Isles for the girls. They were silver dapple, with flaxen mane and tail. The stable manager built a pony ring, and I'd sit for hours watching the girls ride. When they weren't riding, they were reading books or playing, and I was busy with them, always. I had no time to worry about the stock market.

The only change I saw in our lives was when Cook asked if she could come in an hour later in the morning. When I asked why, she explained that the trams had cut their service schedules; people simply didn't have the money to pay their fares any more.

Horace had always had several newspapers delivered to the house— the *New York Times* as well as the *Rocky Mountain News*. I read what little I could when I found time.

On August 8, President Cleveland called a special session of Congress because of the financial panic that had occurred, calling it "an alarming and extraordinary business situation, involving the welfare of all our people." During this session he called for the repeal of the Sherman Silver Purchase Act. Almost immediately, the price of silver plunged from more than $1 an ounce to half that. Ten Denver banks closed in three days, several with our money in their accounts.

As much as I might have wanted to pretend otherwise, I knew that Colorado's glory days of silver mining were over, and that the life of extraordinary wealth Horace and I had taken for granted was gone.

I knew that most people in Denver would assume I would leave Horace once he was no longer rich. And it's true I could have run away with the girls to find another gentleman to care for us. I was only in my thirties, and men still eyed me in the streets.

But I had no intention of leaving Horace. Instead, I went to work, standing side by side with the staff as we wrapped translucent china and sparkling silverware, brass lamps and crystal chandeliers, linens and bedclothes, first in newsprint then in boxes marked to go to auction houses and put up for sale. We sold the necklace Horace had bought me for our wedding, and creditors came to haul away most of our furniture. The Opera House in Leadville was sold, but Horace tried desperately to hold on to the one in Denver, even writing a pleading letter to a Senator, asking him to persuade the state Supreme Court to block its purchase. The Senator refused.

I began keeping coins in a ginger jar, remembering Arvilla's admonition to have my own secret savings. I altered my expensive gowns into dresses for the girls. My plan, which I knew Horace shared, though we didn't speak of it, was to save enough money for us to somehow afford a small cabin in Leadville, where we could live the rest of our lives raising our girls and doing what we loved best, mining.

On our last day in the villa, I watched the stable manager—the only one of our staff to remain—help Horace carry our personal suitcases, including a basket of framed photographs and the dome-topped trunk I'd brought with me from Oshkosh, out of the house.

I stood across the street, in front of the Dirbys' house, holding the girls' hands. The landau, soon to be sold, waited to take us to a small cottage in West Denver, something Horace had found for us to rent for the short term.

As Horace crossed the street, a man approached from our right.

"Stratton," Horace said and reached out both hands in greeting.

The man was quite well-dressed, with a diamond stick pin in his tie.

"Good to see you, Horace," he said and took Horace into a bear hug in his arms.

When the men parted, Horace introduced us. "This is Winfield Stratton. Winfield, my wife Elizabeth."

The man tipped his pecan-colored hat to me, smiling broadly. "Pleasure to meet you, ma'am," he said. "Soon as I heard today was the day you were going to be out on the street, as it were, I knew I had to hightail it over here."

I looked to Horace for explanation, but Stratton spoke over him.

"I'll have you know, Mrs. Tabor, that your husband is the finest man on God's earth. Bar none."

"I know he is, Mr. Stratton," I said. "Girls, don't forget your manners."

Stratton responded graciously to Lily's and Silver's brief curtseys; then, throwing an arm over my husband's shoulder, said, "Horace lent me a dollar years ago when I was broke. Never forgot it. Now I get to repay the favor."

"I'm glad you've done well, Winfield," Horace said. Then looking at me, he explained, "Our friend here is rich as Croesus from his investments in Cripple Creek."

"Yes, ma'am," Stratton said. "When I heard of Horace's troubles, I knew I had to help. So," he continued. "Tell me what you need."

And right there on the street, as I clutched my daughters' hands, Horace told him about a gold mine in Boulder he wanted to develop. The mine was called the Eclipse and if he could invest in it, Horace said, his voice more enthusiastic than I'd heard it in weeks, he could use whatever profit he pulled from it to re-open the Matchless, which, he assured Stratton, would once again yield riches as soon as the government came to its senses about the value of silver.

Stratton threw his head back and laughed.

"Your husband and I made our riches on opposite sides of the fence," he said. "I'm a gold man myself, and that's what I found in Cripple Creek. Made millions there, just like your husband did with silver.

"Right now, at least, gold's the winner," he said good-naturedly. "No telling how long that will last."

Horace shrugged, but Stratton caught him by the arm.

"Look," he said. "Your tale is my tale. But for the grace of God—and our fine President—it could just as well be me on the sidewalk, kicked out of my home."

He leaned in toward Horace, who later told me that the man had said something rude about the possibility of my leaving. Like Horace, Stratton had divorced his older wife and married a young beauty and was wary that she would leave him if he ever lost his fortune.

I saw Horace nod once and glance over toward me and the girls. And then I watched Winfield Stratton pull a check from Wells Fargo Co. Bank from the pocket of his linen suit, as well as a black fountain pen with gold filigree. The check he gave us was for $15,000, and Horace wrote him a note, also standing there on the street, promising to repay it as quickly as he could.

We moved into the cottage on Tenth Street in West Denver. It was a single-story, two bedroom house, with a narrow front porch and white railing. We rented it for $30 a week.

I dove into work there in the same manner I had done at the cabin in Dogwood. But I did it without the help of Arvilla Bunn. I thought of Arvilla often those days; we had completely lost touch after my marriage to Horace. I would have loved to talk with her and have her no-nonsense wisdom to help me cope with my girls, whose behavior took a sharp turn for the worse after Horace's fortune disappeared. The cottage was far less primitive than the cabin in Dogwood had been, but the girls took every opportunity to criticize it, and me.

Each morning Horace dressed in one of his few remaining suits and walked downtown as though his business investments still required over-seeing. Sometimes he'd sit all day in the lounge at the Brown Palace Hotel, where he hoped to run into former fellow legislators or business colleagues. I understood it was far easier for him to forget his drastic fall in life by sitting in the elegant hotel rather than in our new home.

Lily had just turned ten, and occasionally I managed to persuade her to help me run laundry through the mangle to wring out water before hanging clothes out to dry, or to iron her dresses with the Coleman iron I bought from the new Sears Roebuck catalog. We no longer had the luxury of any staff to do these chores and, quite honestly, I felt grateful to have the tasks this time around—they helped keep my mind off other things.

But whenever Lily would finally agree to help, she did so grudgingly, complaining endlessly about the loss of clothes, carriages, ponies. I never once saw her cry, though. Silver, on the other hand, was prone to crying spells. Only fairy tales comforted her. I read Cinderella, Snow White, and The Girl with No Hands to her over and over at night until she fell asleep, sweaty dark hair plastered against her pale forehead and neck.

The girls had to share a bedroom for the first time in their lives. I'd saved two simple iron twin beds from one of the guest rooms at the villa. And I'd managed to salvage some of their toys: a dollhouse Horace had had made for them, a wicker doll carriage with parasol and tinned wheels. Lily spent hours with the Miss Poppet doll Mama had sent her, pushing it in this carriage, up and down the sidewalk. Sometimes I stood on the porch, watching her. I'd see her leaning down into the carriage, talking to the cloth doll in its red-and-white checked dress and yellow yarn braids.

The girls were due to start at a new school that September. I bought a sewing machine, a copy of the Singer 12, from the Sears catalog for just nine dollars, then found Butterick patterns and flowered cotton prints and strip'd dimity at B. Black & Sons in downtown Denver. I sat for hours at this machine, my foot on the black wrought iron treadle, after the girls had gone to sleep.

On the morning of their first day, I presented them each with a new dress: a blue-and-cream plaid for Lily, and a red check for Silver. I'd made special eggs for breakfast, adding the chopped whites and yolks of hard boiled eggs to a creamy sauce of broth and mushrooms.

It had always been a favorite of both girls, but that morning, they refused to come out of their room when I called them. Horace was already at the table, still in his pajamas, reading the newspaper and drinking a large cup of coffee.

I heard Silver cry out, "Mama told me I could wear the black stockings today! Mama said I could!"

I hurried to their room, where I found them wrestling on one of the beds. Black wool hose were pulled halfway up Silver's legs. Lily straddled her, trying to pull them off.

"Stop this!" I said sharply. "Lily, look in your dresser for another pair."

"But they have holes in them!" she said. "I won't wear stockings with holes in them!"

"Bring me a pair anyway," I said, running to fetch my sewing basket. Over my shoulder, I added, "Silver, those are going to bunch up around your boots, but if you don't care, neither do I."

I heard a shriek from Silver.

"She pinched my arm!"

"Get off your sister, Lily. Right this instant! Go down and eat your breakfast with Papa."

I quickly darned the hole in the only other pair of black stockings we had and pushed them onto Lily's lap. Her eggs sat uneaten before her.

"Put these on now and finish your food."

"I don't want it."

"I don't either, Mama," Silver whined.

Horace held the newspaper up in front of him, ignoring the girls' protests.

"You've got to eat something."

Lily stood and pulled the stockings on, then her ankle boots. The dress I'd ironed so carefully was already wrinkled.

"Do you have your books?" I asked. The girls nodded.

"Then get your lunch pails and let's go. We're already late."

"Mama, look!" Silver pointed at the paper that still shielded Horace.

I saw a drawing of an incredible palace with towers and turrets

"What's that, Mama?" Lily poked the newsprint.

Horace laid the paper down on the table so we could all see.

"It's an Ice Carnival they're going to hold in Leadville come winter," he said. "That's the Ice Palace."

"Can we go, Papa?" Silver tugged on his sleeve, her stockings already bunching up between the hem of her skirt and her boots. "Can we go?"

"Get your coat, Lily," I said.

"It's too small. I don't want to wear it."

I pointed at the shelf clock with a picture of a heron on it. It was almost 9 o'clock.

Lily stomped her foot but went to get her coat. I made her go back to get Silver's as well. Finally they were ready.

"I want to go to the Ice Carnival," Silver said.

Horace stood and lifted her in his arms but put her down quickly. He had aged so much in the last year, was thinner and frailer than I had ever seen him.

"We'll take you, Honeymaid," he said. "Now go to school like your Mama wants you to!"

"We're going to get laughed at," Lily said. "I know it."

"Just be quiet! I don't care how they look at us and neither should you!" Silver said.

I pushed them out the door, and we set out to walk the few blocks to their new school.

Horace was still reading the paper when I came back.

"I think we should go," he said.

"Where?" I was looking at the girls' uneaten plates of eggs, wondering how not to waste them.

"The Ice Carnival," he said. "Listen to this: 'It must be everything or nothing,' the committee had said. 'Leadville has never yet done anything by halves. The greatest, the strongest, the most substantial mining camp in the country cannot advertise to the world a Crystal Carnival that will be second to other similar entertainments. This must be unique; this must be majestic and unrivaled.'"

A trip to Leadville sounded wonderful.

"I'll see if someone would loan us a room at the Clarendon," Horace said. "There are still folks who owe me favors there."

He left to dress, and I read the article while I waited for him.

Leadville's population had fallen dramatically in the last two years, dropping from 40,000 to 14,000 people. The Matchless itself had closed, though Horace was still trying to keep it out of the hands of our creditors. A group of townspeople had come up with a plan to create an amazing tourist attraction, something no one had ever seen before, to bring visitors and much-needed money into what was quickly becoming a ghost town.

The Ice Palace was to be built on five acres, with 90 foot octagonal towers and turrets, a promenade, skating rink, ballroom and more. It would open January 1 of the new year.

I'd just finished reading when Horace came back into the kitchen. He put his hands on my shoulders and leaned down to kiss the top of my head. Tapping the newspaper, he said, "This will be our family Christmas present. I'll make it happen." He reached into his suit pocket and brought out two shiny silver dollars, which he pressed into my hand. "And we should have something special for dinner tonight. To boost the girls' spirits. Get a round steak and potatoes. Make a raisin pie. We can afford to eat well occasionally!"

He turned to leave for work, the elbows of his jacket shiny and threadbare.

CHAPTER 27

On New Year's Day, 1896, the four of us stood on top of Capitol Hill, between 7th and 8th Streets, near a gigantic ice statue of Lady Leadville. Her outstretched arm pointed back toward the Ice Palace, which looked like an image from one of my dreams: both substantial and flickering, both real and not. The statue held in her left hand a scroll embossed with the number $200,000,000—the amount of money the mines in the area had once yielded.

"How on earth did they build this?" I reached for Horace's gloved hand. We'd all dressed warmly; the temperature was in the low twenties. I'd knitted matching caps, gloves, and knee caps for the girls.

"I want to go in now!" Silver cried. "Can we stay all day, Papa?" She tugged at his old gray overcoat.

"We'll stay as long as you like," Horace said. He looked happier than I'd seen him in weeks. The owner of the Clarendon had given us a free room for three nights. He said he could be generous because the hotel was booked solid for January. Even the three railroads that now served Leadville offered discounted prices for the trip from Denver.

"It's like a fairy tale," Silver said.

Horace looked at me over the girls' heads. "There's an entire structure inside what you see of the ice, built of wood and metal. I heard two hundred and fifty men worked day and night to build this. Once the inner structure was up, they set trimmed ice blocks on top of it. Five thousand tons of ice.

"But how does it stay together?" I asked.

"They sprayed the blocks of ice with boiling water so they would freeze together. It's an amazing feat of engineering."

"Papa, Papa, we want to go inside!" Silver whined.

"First, the parade." Horace led us into the crowd.

I saw glimpses of bright clothing under peoples' coats; the newspapers had encouraged people to wear special costumes for the opening day festival. I'd worn flannel knickers under my skirts and a long winter coat. Even so, I stamped my boots on the snow to try to keep warm and held the girls close.

A trumpet blared; cymbals crashed. A group of maybe two dozen men marched from around the back of the Ice Palace, dressed in dark shirts, leather breeches, neck kerchiefs, and gray slouch hats with badges. Their brass instruments gleamed in the sun. Two men in front carried a banner that read "The Cowboy Band of Dodge City, Kansas." The Grand Marshall gave a short speech, then announced that he would be taking the first ride down the toboggan run to start the day's festivities.

"Oh, we must do that, too, Papa!" Silver said. She seemed so much more excited than Lily, who stood quietly by my side.

We followed Horace to buy our tickets: 50 cents for us and 25 cents for the girls. An exorbitant amount—enough for six pounds of butter. Horace handed me a flyer he'd been given with our tickets. There were time and date listings for special activities: a state skating championship, competitions for best costume and best impersonation of the President, a Wheelman's Day for bicyclists, a Shriner's Day, "Colored People" day in late February.

But neither my daughters nor the crowd pressing behind us wanted to wait for me to read. I stuffed the flyer into my pocket, grabbed both girls' hands and, keeping my eye on Horace's broad back, followed him into the main hall. A huge black locomotive, its side emblazoned with the letters *Denver & Rio Grande RR*, filled the room, which was lined with translucent walls of ice that sparkled with hundreds of electric lights.

"Look, Mama, look!" Ripping her hand from mine, Silver ran past the train car to the side wall. We caught up with her in front of an exhibit of stuffed animals: a black bear standing on its hind feet, its teeth bared and claws raised. A coyote with glass eyes and leather nose. A striped skunk, red fox, a bobcat.

"They're so life-like," I said to Horace, and he nodded, pulling me to follow the girls on to the next glassed-in displays. I was jostled by people on all sides as we admired life-size statues of a prospector standing beside a gentle-eyed burro and a miner driving his drill into solid rock. I grew dizzy. It had been too long since I'd gone down into the sweet mysteries of a mine. I decided that once Horace and I were in bed that night, after the girls were asleep, I would ask if we could make a special trip out to the Matchless tomorrow. I longed to see it, even covered in snow.

When we stopped in front of a statue of a gentleman in a high silk hat, Lily made a face. "He has a diamond stick pin like Papa used to have!" she said, more loudly than I would have wished.

I leaned down, putting a finger to my lips. "Ssshhh. You'll make Papa feel bad," I said but she frowned and shook her head.

Luckily, Horace hadn't heard, and I pulled him quickly past the exhibit.

"Look there!" He was pointing up to ice stalactites that hung from the ceiling.

Silver pulled on my hand. "Let's go skating," she said. "Over there! See, where those people are going. Can we go, Papa? Please?"

Horace pulled her in close to him but she squirmed free and ran toward a grand staircase to the left, with Lily following close behind her.

"Wait!" My voice was lost among the deafening noise echoing off the walls. Children ran everywhere—girls in fitted coats with shoulder capes, boys in kneepants and wool jackets, caps perched jauntily on their heads.

When we caught up with the girls, Horace was out of breath. "Don't do that again!" he said. "We stay together as a family."

The indoor ice skating rink on the mezzanine was surrounded by tall pillars of ice, each with a gas lamp encased inside it. Red, yellow, and green lights flashed from the corners of the room, meeting in an explosion of color in the middle of the rink.

Even Lily smiled, and I realized how long it had been since I'd seen either girl look so happy.

"Go with Papa to find skates that will fit you both," I said. I'd taught the girls to skate as soon as they were able and told them stories about the winters I'd spent on Lake Winnebago and the beautiful green velvet skating dress Mama had sewn for me.

When they returned carrying two pairs of wood and leather skates,

Horace and I helped them put them on and watched as they ventured onto the ice, Silver of course in front with Lily following gingerly behind.

"Let's get ourselves something to eat. I saw a small restaurant where we can watch the girls," Horace said.

We sat on a velvet sofa in front of an oval table. Beautiful red roses, fruits and vegetables, even rainbow trout were frozen in blocks of ice on the wall behind us.

The waiter brought us our menus and after looking at the prices, I quickly said I wasn't hungry. "It's very expensive. We can eat later; I brought some food for the hotel."

Horace looked crestfallen.

"Hot chocolate then?" the waiter asked.

"Yes, please," I said. "Two hot chocolates will be fine."

The waiter brought a silver pot, and Horace and I watched as he poured the thick drink into two china cups decorated with roses. At first we sat in silence, trying to catch sight of the girls among the skaters.

"There they are!" I said. "Near the far wall. Lily's holding on to the railing for dear life, I'm afraid." I swirled my drink with a swizzle stick. "I miss this town."

Horace nodded but didn't answer. His face was so pale, and the circles under his eyes dark.

"Do you think we could go out to the Matchless tomorrow? I'd love to show the girls. Do you realize they've never seen the place their Papa made his fortune?"

"Yes, well, they might not be so happy since that fortune is now gone."

I hadn't meant to make him feel bad. I wouldn't bring up the mine again during our stay.

A voice boomed from a loudspeaker: "Skating rink will close in ten minutes. Hockey game due to start promptly at 11."

We finished our chocolates then hurried to meet the girls and find seats before the Leadville hockey club skated out from a door off to the side. They wore maroon sweaters and stockings with bright white knickerbockers. Their rivals were a team from Denver.

We sat with the girls between us and when the game ended, stood to cheer the victory of our Leadville boys.

"I'm hungry," Lily said. "There's a man selling bags of popcorn over there. Can we get some?"

"It's up to your mother," Horace said. "She may want you to have a real lunch, you know."

"It's all right. One bag."

We spent the next hours exploring the rest of the grounds: game rooms, a carousel, a theatre with a puppet show. When the puppet show ended, I said I thought we ought to return to the hotel. "It's getting dark outside."

"No!" Silver said. "We haven't done the toboggan yet. And Papa promised!"

"No, he didn't," Lily said. Purplish circles hung under her eyes. "I don't want to go on the toboggan. It looked much too high and scary. And I'm very hungry. I want to go back to the hotel."

I was tired, too, and perfectly happy to leave. We'd covered acres of ground. Even as I stood there, figuring out how I could get Silver to leave without throwing a tantrum, the exterior of the ice palace was suddenly outlined with thousands of lights.

"Come on," Horace said quietly. Whispering in my ear, he added, "God forbid they realize their father is an old man."

I started to object, saying he had nothing to prove to me or our daughters, but he had already lifted Silver and set out toward the toboggan run.

I caught Lily's hand. "We'll do this, then go."

She pulled her knitted cap low over her ears.

"I'm cold," she said, refusing to look at me.

"So am I. Remember how we used to sled on the hill behind the house in Denver?" As soon as the words left my mouth, I wished I could take them back.

"Of course, I remember," Lily said petulantly. "I remember everything about that house, and I miss all of it every day."

"Hurry up! Don't lose us," Horace said. "And no sad faces, Miss Lily Bonnet. I want to see smiles all around. It's the New Year! For Leadville and for us."

Multi-colored search lights streaked the black sky and snow-topped mountains. People stood in two lines waiting for the toboggan slide. Steps made of sawed-off logs led to a platform where two young men in white sweaters, knickers, and wool caps were seating people. Ahead of them two chutes, built on top of tall wooden poles, curved into the distant darkness.

"I don't know why these lines wouldn't move quickly," Horace said. "But you and Lily stand in this one, and Silver and I will wait over here."

A toboggan rushed down one of the chutes, spraying snow, travelling maybe a mile a minute. I couldn't see its passengers but heard their screams and shouts.

Lily stood biting her fingernails.

"We don't have to do this if you'd rather not," I said, not sure even I was up for such a wild ride.

She crossed her arms and stamped her boots on the ground. I looked over to find Horace and Silver, to suggest we try to do the ride the next day, but they'd already moved several feet ahead of us.

The sky was black and clear; whatever stars it held were hidden by the electric lights and the brightness cast up from the snow.

A player from the hockey game stood in front of us, his arm around a pretty young woman in a dark red coat.

"Only one way to stop a toboggan," I heard him say. "And that's to run it into a snow-bank."

The girl smiled and pulled his arm closer around her waist.

A second toboggan rushed down the parallel run, again shooting sprays of snow and howls of delight and terror. I looked up to where people were climbing onto the runnerless sleds. It looked like they were fitting four people on each one.

I searched again for Horace and Silver, but they had already reached the platform. I'd assumed we would meet at the top but somehow, their line had moved faster. Horace looked down at me, his hands cupped around his mouth, but I couldn't make out what he was trying to tell me.

"They're going without us."

"It's all right, Lily. Shall we just go to the bottom and meet them there?"

But the steps below us were packed with people. There was no way we could get back down.

So we kept climbing, surely more than a hundred steps.

When we reached the platform, the hockey player pulled his girl up behind him.

"Put us in the front!" he shouted to one of the boys in white.

One of the toboggans re-appeared, creaking and emptied of its downhill passengers. Four slats crossed its base, and a rope for steering was tied to its curved front.

Suddenly Lily's hand was pulled from mine.

"Lily!" I shouted, but the hockey player and the girl had somehow pushed us apart. I took a step back, looking for Lily. A boy who'd been behind us in line rushed to try to sit behind the girl in the red coat.

"Wait a minute!" The young man in white shouted at the boy then pointed at me. "You! Climb in!"

"No, I've got to find my daughter! She was right here…"

"You'll find her at the bottom, ma'am! Can't stop now. There's another toboggan coming up right behind this one. Somebody's gonna get hurt if you don't climb in fast."

He grabbed me and literally forced me to sit down. "Stop it!" I said. "I won't leave my daughter." But he had already turned to push the boy onto the seat next to me. I caught a glimpse of Lily standing on the platform with another group of people.

"Lily!" I cried. But she didn't hear me. She looked frightened. I tried to stand up but the boy pulled me back down.

"She'll be fine," he said. "This is my third ride tonight. You'll get her down below."

I tried again to climb out of the toboggan.

"Too late for that. Sit down. She'll be in the sled right behind us." He turned to hold the rope that ran along each side. "You're gonna get your head knocked off if you don't sit down right now, lady!"

There was a whirring noise, and I fell back down on the seat as the sled began a short climb uphill.

"Hold the rope," the boy shouted.

The toboggan plunged down. Cold air slapped my face, and snow and the lights of the Ice Palace and Lady Leadville sped past beneath us. When we hit a curve, the boy's weight fell on me. The ride was terrifying but thankfully short. We skidded to a jarring halt, and the hockey player in front of me was already standing, yelling, "Again!" but his girl was frowning, shaking her head no, as she let him help her stand.

The boy next to me jumped up as well.

"Better get out fast, lady! That's going to head back up top any second now!"

I took his hand to climb out to the narrow platform at the base of the run and waited for the next toboggan to race down the chute. But there was no sign of my daughter. I ran down from the platform and into the crowd. Despite the lights, it was impossible to see peoples' faces, though I ran up close to many, hoping for some sign of Lily, Horace, Silver. I was out of breath and claustrophobic in the crowds of people in their big, dark winter coats.

"Watch it there! Watch where you're going!" A woman drew two girls close to her side, frowning up at her husband as I brushed past them. Part of a long brown scarf hit my cheek as another woman whipped it around her neck then stuffed her hands back into a fur muff. I saw a walking stick with a crystal knob; a little boy of maybe two in a green velvet jacket and pleated skirt; a man juggling plates; a row of food stands selling hot chocolate, popcorn, candies. But no sign of any member of my family. I was running through a crowd of people, searching for someone I loved, just as I had when I was twelve. This time in ice, not fire.

No sparks flew around my head now, no smoke burned my eyes. What I saw instead was like something from one of my dreams or visions: swirling dark capes that turned into the webbed wings of bats, streaks of light exposing the white skulls of those I passed.

My boots skidded on a patch of ice. I fell to my knees and grabbed at a man's longcoat to help me stand. He looked down at me and smiled, then pulled a silver flask from his coat pocket, handing it down to me, but I pushed away from him as quickly as I could and ran on.

I don't know how long I pushed my way frantically through that nightmarish crowd. I remember crying out their names until I was hoarse: Lily. Silver. Horace.

I could not bear to lose anyone else I loved.

And then finally, the crowd parted, and Lily ran towards me, with Horace and Silver right behind her. Fireworks lit the black sky, filling it with gold carnations and silver streaks of light.

CHAPTER 28

One spring afternoon, Lily sat at the kitchen table solving arithmetic problems: how many cords of wood a Missouri steamboat would burn in 43 days, how many hogsheads of molasses a grocer had bought. Silver had a health alphabet to practice, and she repeated its first lines to me several times:

> As soon as you are up shake blanket and sheet;
> Better be without shoes than sit with wet feet;
> Children, if healthy, are active not still;
> Damp beds and damp clothes will both make you ill.

Horace's old friend Winfield Stratton had arranged to have him named Postmaster of Denver. Working in the very building Horace had paid to have constructed, he was now reduced to sorting and handling mail, checking its contents to make sure nothing was over- or under-charged, inventorying the property, writing reports for the postmaster general, and lifting boxes that were far too heavy for a 69-year-old man.

He usually didn't get home until just before dinnertime, so I was immediately worried that day when I heard a double set of footsteps on our small front porch. When I opened the door, I saw Horace, his face ghostly white, leaning for support on one of the young postal clerks. Horace clutched his stomach with both hands and groaned as we helped him into bed.

I immediately went to the doublebox phone on the wall and rang up the doctor, pressing my lips close to the brass mouthpiece so the girls wouldn't hear the concern in my voice.

Dr. Mahoney arrived within the hour, carrying his overstuffed cowhide medicine bag. He had delivered both our girls and had reassured me during our call that, knowing our reduced circumstances, he would not charge us for the house call. I trusted him implicitly.

Lifting the rubber and silver stethoscope that hung around his neck, he leaned down toward Horace to position the chestpiece. He moved this from place to place on Horace's chest and stomach, his eyes squinting in concentration. Next he gestured for me to bring the bag, which he'd dropped at the foot of the bed. Opening it, he picked through its contents. I caught sight of a giant hypodermic syringe, an ear trumpet, a small kit of scalpels, and a small sewing kit. Finally he pulled out a large head mirror on a leather strap which he positioned around his forehead. Its circular mirror had a small hole in its center, and he positioned this directly over his right eye.

Horace was unable to sit up, so the doctor again bent down over him.

"Turn on that lamp," he instructed me.

I watched as the light bounced off the mirror and up into Horace's eyes, nasal passages, and mouth.

"What do you think it is, Doctor?" I asked.

Instead of answering me, he carefully removed the mirror from his head, stood, and dropped it unceremoniously back into his bag.

I looked to Horace to see if he could give me more of a clue as to his discomfort. His eyes were closed, and his forehead glistened with sweat.

The doctor cleared his throat and reached to pat my shoulder. I was vastly relieved when I saw him smile.

"Nothing to worry about, Mrs. Tabor," he said. "Your husband will be fine in a day or two."

"But what is it? What's come over him?"

"Nothing more than dysentery, ma'am," he said, snapping shut the cowhide bag.

"So what do we do?" I asked. "How can I make him more comfortable?"

"Make up some warm lye-water. Soak his feet in it. Do you have castor oil on hand? Spirits of turpentine? If not, I'll leave you what I have. Tonight, mix up some warm milk and molasses. Dissolve a teaspoonful of fruit in it. Can you remember all this or should I write it down?"

"I'll remember." I heard a noise out in the hall and turned to see Silver Dollar crouching by the door, listening.

"I see somebody wants her Father to be well!" the doctor said. "But neither of you two ladies should fret another moment about this. Ring me in a few days and let me know how he's doing."

"Are you certain?" I asked. "He seems to be in such pain, and he's never one to complain."

"I'm certain. It's nothing more than old-fashioned stomach pain. All you can do is wait it out."

"I want to sit with Papa," Silver said.

"Only if you sit quietly. And just for a moment. Let me see the doctor out and I'll be right back."

"Your husband is a good man," the doctor said to me as we stood in the kitchen. "Get him on his feet and back to work."

Lily still sat hunched over her homework at the kitchen table. "What's wrong with Papa?" she asked without looking up.

"Doctor Mahoney said it's just stomach pain. It will be all right."

"One of my teachers at school had stomach pains," she said. "It turns out she had appendicitis."

The doctor laughed.

"She had to have surgery," Lily said quietly.

"Oh, I don't think it's that, dear girl," the doctor said, reaching for the door knob. "And if it is appendicitis, the current fad for surgery is nothing more than that. A fad. There's no need to operate, especially on a man your father's age.

"Look," he said, turning to me. "Even if it is appendicitis, a recent study said over 90 percent of all cases recover without any operation. Your husband is far more likely to die under the knife than not. So keep him hydrated, give him the medicines I've suggested, and ring me if things look worse."

I found lye under the sink, mixed up a batch in water, and soaked some strips of torn flannel in it. When I went back upstairs to give Horace his first dose of castor oil, I found Silver lying on the bed next to him. With her help, I managed to get the medicine past his dry lips then wrapped his feet in the warm flannel. He tried to smile but it was obvious he was still in pain. I kissed his forehead and sat quietly on the side of the bed until his eyes closed and his breathing grew more regular.

It had grown dark outside the windows. "I need to fix something for dinner for you and Lily. Let's go downstairs. Papa's sleeping now."

I peeked in on Horace several times in between feeding the girls and getting them ready for bed. His stomach looked bloated, but other than that he seemed to be resting peacefully. But when I woke him to give him the milk and molasses, he vomited. I cleaned him and the bed up the best I could and spent the rest of the night lying next to him. His fever persisted, but I was thankful when he fell asleep again. When the sun rose, I woke the girls and asked them to get themselves ready for school.

"Is Papa going to be all right?" Silver asked.

"Yes," I said, thinking I would call the doctor as soon as they had left the house.

When I told the doctor that Horace had vomited during the night, he laughed and said, "That's fine. Good to get whatever poison is in his system out of him. Keep feeding him the castor oil."

I stayed in our room with him all day, wiping his brow and whispering to him how much I loved him.

Occasionally, he woke and tried to speak to me though his mouth was so dry, despite the water I kept pressing to his lips. Mostly he lay still with his eyes closed. I was relieved when the doctor stopped by that afternoon. But after taking no more than a quick look, he said, "Let's give it one more day. Both the fever and the pain should break by then."

But that didn't happen. The doctor returned the next day and the next, and seemed at a loss as to what to do. I did my best to keep the girls out of the room and never had Horace out of my sight for more than five minutes at a time. I lay on the bed or sat in the chair close to him, praying to a Sacred Heart of Jesus card I had propped up on the night table beside him.

One morning, I heard Horace speak.

"I want to see a priest."

I was thrilled to hear his lovely, deep voice, sounding just as it had when he first wooed me all those years ago in Leadville. At first I felt the same sense of wonderful calm reassurance his voice had always brought me. But then the words he'd said sunk in.

I don't know how I managed to do it, but somehow I found the strength to ring up the nearby parish. I asked for Father Marist, whom I had seen on several occasions, though he continued to refuse to allow me to take communion there.

For some reason, the good Father agreed to visit us, to offer the sacrament of reconciliation and give absolution.

After the priest left, Horace motioned me to sit on the bed beside him. He kissed my hand with his parched lips. His skin was so pale, and his fingertips were blue.

My beloved husband spoke to me then of several things that will remain between him, me, and the God I know was present in that room. He spoke to me of Lily and Silver, of how important it was that they get good educations and grow up to take care of their mother. He encouraged me to remarry should I so desire. And finally, he said, "I have one last promise I want you to make to me, dear Lizzie."

"Anything." My voice cracked. My face felt frozen in its effort to not betray the despair that was roiling around inside me.

"I know that what you most love after me and the girls is the Matchless Mine. I want you to take the last money Winfield gave me, hire more men. Start operations at the mine again."

I shook my head no. I couldn't imagine doing anything if I were to lose Horace. "Promise me, Lizzie." He gripped my hand tightly.

"I, I don't know how I could…"

"You can. The Matchless can make millions again. You and the girls need to be taken care of, and that mine is your best hope. There's nothing else I can leave you."

And so I promised him but begged him not to leave me. "I need you, Horace," I said, over and over again.

Hours passed until we heard the girls come in from school, heard their shoes as they ran up the stairs. I quickly wiped the tears from my face before they entered the room holding hands, their eyes big as saucers.

"It's all right," Horace said, managing a smile. "You don't have to be afraid."

Silver ran over to him first, jumping up on the bed beside him.

"Be careful, sweetheart," I said. "Be careful not to hurt Papa."

Horace wrapped her in one arm and pulled her close to him, whispering in her ear. Her black curls bobbed up and down, and when he'd finished, she slid off the bed and motioned solemnly for Lily.

"Papa wants to tell you something, Lily," she said. And Lily went and stood by the side of the bed, her hands clasped in front of her. Tears welled in her eyes.

"What's wrong, Papa?" she whispered.

"Nothing's wrong, sweetheart. Papa is old and tired and wants to sleep." He reached to take one of Lily's hands in his own. "But before I sleep I want to make sure you know how much I love you. And your sister. And your beautiful mother."

Lily nodded, unable to answer.

I held her by the shoulder until I saw that Horace's eyes had closed. His chest moved gently up and down.

"Ssshhh…" I said to Silver before she could speak. And then quietly to both of them, "I want you to go now. Just for a bit. There is soup downstairs you can heat for your dinner."

The next morning I woke when the first rays of the sun came through the window. In our small kitchen, I found the remains of the girls' dinner preparations from the night before and, on top of Lily's school notebook on the table, a folded piece of paper and an envelope addressed to my sister in Wisconsin.

I opened the folded paper and read:

Dear Aunt,

Papa is very ill. He lies in his bed all day every day. Mama sits with him constantly. She gives him baths in the bed. She tries to feed him but he will take no food.

Sometimes I see Mama make the sign of the cross. Sometimes I see her sit with her head bowed and her eyes closed. Sometimes I hear her pray.

So we are putting Papa's fate in God's hands. Will you also please pray for Papa?

Your loving niece,

Lily

I put the letter back into its envelope and said nothing of it to Lily. Once the girls had left for school again, I went back to sit by my beloved. Surely my prayers to Jesus would be heard. Surely Jesus would not take my sweet and lovely Horace from me now. I watched each rise and fall of his great chest, studied every hair on his head and the beautiful lines of a face I knew so well.

At some point, his eyes opened. "I cannot see a thing," he said.

His breathing slowed. I left the chair and returned to the bed to lie beside him, wrapping my arms around his great, strong form, pressing my body into his as I had done so many, many times. Even beneath his pajamas, he felt cold.

I kissed his forehead and his lips, kissed them again, then leaned forward to try to pour all the love that was in my heart into him in one last effort to save him.

But his breath grew noisy. There was a terrible, ominous rattling sound, which then stopped completely. I could not move but lay with my true love for hours as his body stiffened and the long hours of the rest of my life began.

CHAPTER 29

Things I Put in Safe at Jesuits House

Dec 31 1899

Papa's Watch Fob given him when he Built Opera House by Citizens of Denver

Honeymaid's Silver beads given by her Page

Lily's gold chain diamond & gold military badge gold & diamond heart-all on chain

Another plain gold military badge

1 gold diaper pin

1 gold 7 diamond diaper pin

1 paper of fine seed pearls given by Uncle Pete

1 choice yellow topaz given by Andrew

1 silver dollar with Silver's picture inside of it – for Silver given by Boyd Shelton

2 choice pieces of blue turquoise given to Mama from Papa

3 settings for Isabel diamond all gold

2 gold sets of chains each set has 3 diamonds in them

1 diamond christmasy ring Stone cost 100.00 dollars

Lily's gold beads given her by Mrs. Page

1 small moss agate

1 head of Christ cameo

1 white head of a woman pink flowers in her hair

CHAPTER 30

In the weeks and months after Horace died, I somehow managed to move the girls and me back to Leadville, despite their protestations that the cabin was too cold, too small, too far from anything they knew and loved. The Mooneys were kind enough to offer us a place to stay for a week while I prepared the cabin at the Matchless Mine to be our home.

When I woke that first morning in the Mooneys' bed, I felt as though someone had literally pierced me through the heart. I was constantly filled with longing for what was gone. I wanted Horace's arms around me; I wanted the life I had led when my family was whole. I felt completely hollow inside, completely without hope for any kind of future, and yet I had to go through the motions. For this, I was grateful. Without my girls, I might well have died myself. But I somehow managed to push myself out of the bed, to dress, to help my daughters begin another day of their young lives.

"We will go up to the Matchless today," I said as I brushed Silver's black hair. As always, I prayed that they would not hear the deep catch in my voice or recognize the great sorrow in my eyes.

When Lily objected to my plan, I had to steel my insides. Everything felt as though we were in a play, written for someone else, performed for strangers. I had no desire for my daughters to know how completely broken their Mama was; I had no desire for the kind Mooneys to know how vulnerable and frightened I felt. I vowed to myself that I would be strong. I knew that Horace would have wanted that. And so I sat at the table and ate breakfast; I chatted with Mr. Mooney about the assaying shop and with Mrs. Mooney about how much Leadville had changed and how much she missed Bertram and Cornell who now lived in their own small place in town. I was grateful that neither one of them mentioned anything about my former wealth; they welcomed me as warmly as they had when I first arrived in town, penniless then as well as now.

"We'll be home after lunch," I said, even while I wondered if I would still be here in this world come lunchtime, if my body, face, and voice could keep pretending that long.

But Mrs. Mooney gave us lunches to take—"You'll want a picnic, while the weather is still warm"—and this quick thinking thankfully turned Lily's sour mood.

"Yes, Mama, a picnic!" Suddenly she was smiling and spinning on tiptoe, and I wanted to feel even some small joy deep inside my heart. I could not, but smiled as though I did.

The girls were both my blessing and my curse. My reason to stay and my obstacle to leaving life. Those first days after Horace's death, I longed to join him in dark oblivion. But the girls needed breakfast and lunch and their hair combed and their dresses washed, and I had to stay behind and fill my role as their mother. My most important job now, I knew, was to keep them from falling into the terrible, overwhelming grief that had taken hold of me.

And so, together, we set out for Fryer's Hill. I wore a pearl gray dress, with pearl buttons. It was one of Horace's favorites. When I put it on that morning, I remembered his hands on my waist, sliding down the fabric. His hands had made me solid, his hands had tied me to this earth. The lust I'd felt for Harvey was another matter completely—it had catapulted me out of childhood and awoken me to the pleasures of the flesh. But Horace, my Horace, had been my one true love. And now he was gone, never to return but in my dreams.

Most people in Leadville believed that my hopes for returning the Matchless Mine to its former glory were baseless. All the other claims up on Fryer's Hill had long been abandoned, completely tapped out. But Horace had urged me to do my best to keep the Matchless going, promising me it would make millions again. Whether I believed him or not didn't matter. I had made a vow to him that I would never break.

I hadn't laid eyes on the mine in years. But once I saw the sunwashed vertical planks of the main cabin and the nearby headframe tilted to the left, my heart quickened for the first time since Horace's death. Without stopping to remove my gray gloves, I took hold of the dusty crank on the hoist and began to push. Nothing budged.

I jumped up and came down for one last thrust on the crank. Like ice cracking, the hoist began to creak then turn, its rope and bucket lowering a few feet into the mine's shadows.

"Look what you did, Mama!" Silver said.

When I turned to face her, I noticed for the first time the beauty I'd been oblivious to before. A painter's palette of color burst behind her: deep maroon tallgrass and bright small blossoms of purple, orange, and yellow. And to my right, I saw a band of elk; one of the elegant creatures raised its head and wailed like a bugle that had long been silent.

I took in a deep breath, inhaling the life I realized was still around me, life I had failed to notice in the months since Horace's death. It wasn't that my grief was gone. But even with grief lodged forever in my heart, I saw that the beautiful yellow aspen still quaked, the lodge pole pines still rose majestically toward the sky.

"Mama!" Lily said. "You've got dirt all over your face." She scowled. "And I'm not working in this dirty place! I wore my best jumper!"

I walked over and put my hand on her shoulder. "Come on then, both of you," I said. "Let's go look inside the cabin, see what shape it's in. We came up here just to see the Matchless again. Papa wanted us to."

I pulled off one glove and rubbed the back of Lily's neck. Still, she hunched her shoulders like an exasperated cat and refused to look at me.

I headed to the door of the main cabin.

"I want to come, too, Mama!" Silver ran quickly to join me, her sister standing back. "I'd live here with you."

"What on earth are you talking about, Silver?" Lily asked petulantly. "No one's going to live here."

Silver glanced guiltily at me.

"It's all right, darling," I said quickly to Lily. "No one has made any decisions. I thought maybe we would stay here in Leadville for a month or two. And while the Mooneys are so nice, and so gracious to take us into their home, I don't think we can impose on them more than a week or so."

Lily's face turned red with anger. "But what about school? School starts in a month. We have to go back to Denver at least by then."

I bit my lip. "I know. But there are schools here…" I hadn't made up my mind to stay in Leadville until that morning. I *needed* to stay there. For me. For Horace. For hope.

Lily dug a small trench in the dirt with the toe of her boot. "I don't know anyone in Leadville. I want to stay in school in Denver with the people I know. And I won't live in such a run-down place. Otherwise…" she looked up at me defiantly. "Otherwise, I'm going to go to Wisconsin. Aunt Cordelia already invited me."

My skin grew cold, despite the warm air. I knew that my sister and Lily had been exchanging letters since Horace's death, and I knew that I had been a shell of myself. Lily had needed someone to talk to and had found that someone in my oldest sister.

"Nonsense," I managed to stay. "Aunt Cordelia loves you dearly, I know. But you are not moving to Wisconsin. Not now, not ever. Silver and I and you are all we've got now. We're family, and family sticks together."

Lily muttered something I couldn't hear.

"I'll stay with you, Mama," Silver said, wrapping her arms around my waist. "I love it here in the mountains. Will you let me ride a horse? If I work at the mine with you, will you buy me some new boots?"

I gave up trying to catch Lily's eye. "Of course you can ride a horse," I said to Silver. "But you're too young to work at the mine."

"A baby ten-year-old," Lily said meanly.

"Not a baby, Lily. Just not old enough to go down into the mine. It can be dangerous down there. I was far older than both of you when I first worked at the Fourth of July." I was remembering how excited I was every day I worked alongside Tommy Birdsall and the men, how focused I'd been on the work at hand. There was nothing else in my life that had ever felt so compelling to me. When I was working in the mine, I felt like I was doing what I had been put here on earth to do.

I stepped across the narrow threshold of the door to the cabin. Its thin slat would have to be replaced.

Silver skipped across the single room's bare floorboards, touching the brown paper that covered the cabin's unplastered walls, opening the metal door on an old Excelsior stove.

Through the door I watched Lily finally trudge toward us, stomping purposefully on a batch of silvery lupine.

She came inside and sniffed loudly. "There is no way I will live here," she said. "I won't do it."

"Oh my!" I laughed, though I didn't feel like laughing. "If you look any angrier, that paper on the walls might burst into flames!"

She glared at me.

I started to say, "We'll get nice beds…" then realized I had no idea where they would fit. How *we* would fit. But somehow I had to make it work.

"What are you going to do, Mama? Pray about it?" Lily asked.

"Lily!" Silver said. "You shouldn't talk to Mama that way."

"God never listens," Lily continued. "He let Papa die, even though I specifically asked Him not to. I asked Aunt Cordelia to pray. I know you prayed. Constantly. Sometimes I couldn't fall asleep at night because I kept hearing your prayers. But Papa died anyway. God didn't listen. God never listens."

She stood there, staring at me, shaking her head back and forth.

"I don't know what to say," I said. I didn't know what to tell her. I didn't know how to admit that yes, sometimes I had doubts, too. Many times. And yet, I wanted to make her believe. I knew in my own life that I simply couldn't continue without some measure of faith. How would my beloved daughters live their lives without faith? The loss of Horace was only the first of many they would experience. I knew that but they didn't.

"It's good you don't know what to say, Mama, because you aren't going to convince me of any of your silly beliefs. You've always been a silly woman. Writing down your stupid dreams. Reading stupid books about spirits and life after death and angels. And now you've got this stupid idea that we'll somehow get rich again thanks to the Matchless Mine."

My eyes burned with tears, but I had to let her have her say. Silver had positioned herself in front of me, as though she were protecting me from bullets instead of words.

"None of it's real, Mama. Dreams aren't real! We needed Papa, and Papa is gone. You're an old woman, all alone except for me and Silver. And how much help can we be to you? You need a husband, not two girls."

"Stop it, Lily!" Silver cried out. "Mama's still beautiful. If she wants to marry again, she can. You know that."

"She won't ever marry anybody like Papa. We won't ever have somebody as good as Papa to take care of us again," Lily said.

I reached out to steady myself on the card table in the middle of the room and watched as Lily stormed outside.

I wiped my eyes on my sleeve then followed her, pulling Silver behind me. Lily had already raced far ahead of us down Fryer Hill. Her hair, white-blond like my own but so much longer, streamed out behind her. I knew she would find her way to the Mooneys in time for dinner. I knew we would eat a good meal at the Mooneys' and lie in comfortable beds. And I knew I would be awake all night picturing the headframe and bucket that would one day take me back down into the quiet mysteries of the Matchless, wondering for the thousandth time if dreams really could come true, if Horace's promise to me was something I could count on even without his warm, strong body at my side.

CHAPTER 31

Instead of moving the girls into the shack at the mine, I found us rooms to rent at 303 Harrison Avenue for the rest of that summer. I sent a wire to Tommy Birdsall, who agreed to join me in Leadville as soon as he could.

I began writing letters to creditors and investors, finding out everything I could about the current status of the mine and the possibilities of finding new ore there.

"Before Horace died," Tommy told me one day as we sat at my table in the kitchen, "he had men sink a shaft, Number 5, to explore the northern part of the claim. They found ore in a nearby drift."

"That's good, yes?"

He shook his head. "Not great. Not bonanza grade. It ran maybe ten to thirty ounces of silver per ton."

I stood to go to the window and looked out on the street. "Still, it's a sign. Something is there worth finding, isn't it, Tommy?"

"To tell you the truth, I'm not sure, ma'am."

"I told you not to call me that." I turned to face him.

"Lizzie." He stood and joined me at the window.

I stepped back, turned again to look at the busy street outside. "I know there are problems. I know it won't be easy. But we've got to try. Horace wanted me to."

"Did you know Mr. Tabor had transferred ownership of the Matchless to two capital companies?" Tommy asked.

"To defer our creditors."

"Well, it didn't completely work. There are still outstanding debts. You've got to satisfy those before starting any kind of operations. Otherwise, you're setting yourself up for far worse problems down the road."

"What can we do?"

"For now, we sell the mine. A sheriff's sale if we have to. I know a fellow named Herman Powell who's interested. You could make maybe

$25,000, use that to pay off the outstanding debt. Then figure out a way to buy it back."

"And how in the world do I do that?"

His gray eyes met mine. "Don't know. But I can't in good conscience send any of my men down in that mine until you clear up your debts, Lizzie. I won't do that to them."

I ran through the list of things I'd put in storage: a gold watch fob, a diamond pin. Not nearly enough. "Then I've got to get another investor," I said. "I promised Horace."

He reached for my hand, but I shook my head.

"Maybe you should consider going back to Wisconsin, Lizzie," he said gently. "Take the girls, go home to your family. Or come with me back to Kansas."

"No."

"Why not?"

"I promised Horace." My heart beat in my chest. "And I need you to help me here, Tommy. Please."

"I'll do what I can, but none of this will be easy."

"I know," I said, then went back to poring over financial records and wracking my brain for ways to get the mine operating again. I knew Tommy was offering me love, but I could not imagine anyone other than Horace ever capturing my heart again.

"Did Mama get over her fever?" I asked Lily that night as the girls got ready for bed. Most of the news I got from Oshkosh now came from my daughter, who was in frequent correspondence with both Mama and Cordelia. I didn't like feeling jealous of Lily. But ever since Horace had died, I had felt increasingly like an outsider even in my own family. Mama's letters to me were rare, and when she did write, she mostly questioned how on earth all of Horace's fortune had disappeared.

Lily spent most of her time in her room, alone, and kept a stack of letters from Oshkosh under her bed. It was hard for me not to open them when they arrived but so far I had managed to respect my daughter's privacy. I told myself I should be happy she had a relationship with my Wisconsin roots and did my best to sound interested and not bitter when I had to ask her for news I would much rather have heard first-hand.

She stood now, brushing her blond hair in front of a small oval mirror that hung on the wall.

"Did Mama get over her fever?" I asked again.

She shrugged. "I think so."

"Mama," Silver said as she climbed into bed. "Mrs. Mooney lent me a book. *The Wonderful Wizard of Oz.*"

I moved to tuck her under the covers. At ten, she still permitted me a good night kiss. But fifteen-year-old Lily was turning into someone I barely knew. And my standing in her eyes had gone terribly downhill since Horace's death. If she had managed to adjust somewhat to the loss of Horace's wealth, she seemed to want to blame me now for all the losses she'd suffered—not just money but her father as well.

"Lily," I said, hesitantly. "When you write Mama back, why don't you see if she and Cordelia will come visit us here in Leadville? Wouldn't that be nice?"

She turned to face me with a huge smile on her face, the first I'd seen in months.

"Oh yes, Mama, can I? That would be wonderful! I'd love to have Aunt Cordelia and Grand-mama here!"

"I'll show them how good a rider I am!" Silver said. She'd not spent much time at all with my family, only one visit to Oshkosh in all her years. "Can they take the train?"

"We'll see. I hope so. I would love to have them visit. I'll see if we can get a room at the Clarendon hotel for a few nights." I knew that Mama still had some of the money Horace and I had sent them. He had bought her and Papa a beautiful house shortly after Silver was born, and he'd helped them invest in some of his other properties. I didn't know exactly how much they had, but if she didn't suggest paying for the hotel herself, I would sell one of the girls' diamond diaper pins and rent them a room. It would be lovely to have them with us, I thought. Their visit would entertain the girls and hopefully, bring us all closer.

Mama and Cordelia refused to visit us in Leadville but said they would like to meet in Denver. It was easier to reach by train, Mama explained, and she thought there would be more things to do with the girls in the city. Mama booked two rooms for her and Cordelia and said that Lily and Silver were welcome to stay with them. I managed to scrape enough money together to get a small room for myself. We stayed busy every day, visiting the new Museum of Science and Nature, walking past the old house on Sherman Avenue, taking afternoon tea at the Brown Palace. We went twice to visit Horace's grave at Prospect Hill Cemetery.

"Do you remember giving me this, Mama?" I pulled her crucifix from behind the collar of my dress. The week had passed quickly, without any chance to speak to Mama privately about my hopes of re-investing in the Matchless Mine. Now we stood on the platform waiting for the train that would return them to Oshkosh.

"Of course I do." She had her hand on Lily's shoulder. "So much has happened." She looked down at her shoes, shook her head, and I felt the sharp jab of all I had done to disappoint her.

"I wish you had come to Leadville," I said. "To see the mine. I really think we can make a go of it. Tommy Birdsall says that with an investment, he can get operations up and running by next spring."

"I want to come visit you in Wisconsin," Lily interrupted. She wore a blue sailor dress with a large matching bow in her hair—a gift from Mama. Silver had been given a new dress as well but still wore the riding breeches she'd had on the day before when Mama took the girls to a stable near our hotel. Lily turned to me. "Can I go with them back to Wisconsin now?" she asked.

"Of course not!" I felt my cheeks flush.

"You will definitely come visit me in Wisconsin, sweetheart," Mama said. "You must meet your other cousins." She looked at me. "You should come home now, too, Lizzie. It's time to come home."

"I can't. I promised Horace."

"Don't be foolish. Of course you can. If you don't have enough for a ticket, I'll buy them for you. Three tickets for you and the girls. Come back to Oshkosh."

"I can't," I said quietly.

I heard the train pulling into the station, watched smoke spiraling above the large black locomotive.

She shook her head. "Foolishness. You and your Papa."

We hugged and said our goodbyes, and I returned to Leadville with the girls. One month later, two envelopes arrived, one addressed to Lily and one to me. I opened mine first and found a check for $20,000— enough to buy back the mine from the temporary owner Tommy had found. I looked at the envelope addressed to Lily a long time, my eyes poring over my Mama's beautiful, curling script. Finally, I steamed it open. Inside was a one-way ticket to Oshkosh.

Lily left us that September, and when Silver and I saw her off at the train station I had nothing to give her but my tears.

I had the most horrible dream. I was in the house on Algoma Street. There were several green rooms. And my mother, P.D. and Cordelia and Papa had taken my children away from me and made the children not care for me anymore and that set me wild. I thought I would die of grief and anger and I told mother I would kill her and kill P.D. and Cordelia for robbing me of my children. And they all looked at me calm and defiant. It was a terrible dream. Then Silver came she sat on the floor and all her hair was the color of the goldfish and her eyes looked strange. The whites of her eyes were yellow, she looked terrible and she talked with some man, my heart was broken.

CHAPTER 32

Dearest Mama,

I would give anything if you—and the Church—would finally forgive me. I did not plan to be a sinner; I do not see myself as one. I wanted love, nothing more. And I cannot believe that you or Jesus would truly have wished me to stay with a man who betrayed our marriage vows so blatantly. Or not to marry a man who saw the moon and sun and stars in my eyes and gave me the moon and sun and stars to make me happy.

There are many days now I wish I had never married Harvey, never left your loving arms, never come to Colorado. I thought I was marrying a good man, one who would love me forever. When William gave us the gift of a share in the mine, I thought I could fulfill my dream of helping you and Papa start over, too.

Instead, I disappointed you.

I know a part of your heart has left me, Mama. I know the Catholic Church has given up on me. I would give anything not to have gone against its teachings. And again, I had no intent to. My guilt weighs heavily on my heart.

I know you have not made peace with my decisions but am glad you accepted the money Horace sent you years ago. And I greatly appreciate your returning some of it to me now. I am grateful, too, in a more sorrowful way, that you have taken my first born into your bosom.

I still talk to you in my heart every day, and I still hear your voice in my ear.

I keep those letters you first mailed me when we lived in Dogwood, before Harvey's terrible fall. I keep them tied with a ribbon in a secret drawer. Sometimes, I take the letters out and hold them to my nose, trying desperately to recapture your scent, your touch, your love. I read them and hear your voice through your written words on the page. I recall your immense faith and the immense love you once felt for me.

Those two things cover all the miles and years that now lie between us.

Your still-loving daughter,

Lizzie

CHAPTER 33

After Lily left for Oshkosh, Silver and I moved out of the rooms on Harrison Avenue and into the larger shack at the Matchless. I enrolled her in school, and she did well, particularly in her Literature and Writing classes. A man I met in town came out regularly to give her riding lessons. Tommy hired some miners to help get the mine operating again. I spent my days working alongside them and my evenings in the cabin, reading my books and helping Silver with her schoolwork.

Tommy was a good second father to her and would sometimes stay for dinner with us after his day of working at the mine.

I met a second investor in 1914, a Mr. James R. Mullen. His wife had just died, and this was our bond. Though my loss of Horace was older, it still felt as raw as though I had lost him yesterday.

Mr. Mullen was a devout Catholic; we met at church in town. For some reason unknown to me, the parish in Leadville agreed to let me take the Eucharist. I felt immensely grateful for this gift.

I visited Mr. Mullen to provide companionship in his new loneliness and to ease my own. I had no intention of marrying him, though he proposed six months after we'd met. My skin was still soft, my eyes clear. I could have had any man I wanted; people often told me this. But I didn't want any of them. I had had two great loves in my life. The loss of each had damaged my heart; I simply could not see opening it up to any new grief of that sort again. Besides, my heart could never pull itself away from Horace.

I was straightforward about this with Mr. Mullen from the beginning. He honored my loyalty to Horace and honored my desire to fulfill Horace's dying wish to bring the Matchless back to life. Over the next years, he gave me ten generous checks in all, at two- and three-year intervals.

At first, Lily was a garrulous correspondent, writing long letters to me and Silver about how much she loved the city with its elevated street railways and electric trolleys and loved being "Aunty" to Cordelia's children and spending time with my Mama, reading or doing needlework. Then a letter arrived bearing news that she had married her cousin Jack Last, a manufacturer ten years her senior. Nine months later, a second letter announced the birth of their child, a girl they had not yet named. I read the letter at least a dozen times and dreamt that night:

> *I dreamed of being with Lily my lovely darling child & my dead sister … she said Lily's legs are the most wonderful & beautiful legs in the world but they are not about brain and then she said something about twins & Lily. I am worried about this dream for to dream of (my sister) has always meant sorrow to me, & this is the 3 times lately I have dreamed of Lily's legs. Lily had the greatest brain & she is the smartest and best child in this world.*

CHAPTER 34

O ne day Silver was asked to read a song she had written at a presentation by the former President Roosevelt to the Colorado Livestock Association. She had dedicated the song to her father.

She and I would travel together to Denver for the occasion. I took money from the tea canister to buy her a black blouse with dark and light gray striped sleeves. She already owned a black cloche hat with velvet trim and a gray skirt that fit nicely around her trim waist. In my trunk I found a single strand of pearls and fastened them around her neck.

For days before the event she rehearsed her song standing before a full-length mirror in our room. I watched her carefully, anticipating this great honor as much as she did. Since Lily had left us, all my hopes were now pinned on Silver Dollar, my Honeymaid.

A parade gathered to welcome the ex-President to Denver that day. A dozen bands played a dozen different songs, thousands of people lined 17th street, and bunting hung from the façade of every building. Troops from Fort Logan and the state National Guard rode past where Silver and I had been seated near the stage set up in front of the Brown Palace Hotel. There were Spanish war veterans, a division of the Rough Riders in their khaki uniforms. Cowboys in blue suits, blue scarves, and khaki trousers galloped up and down the parade line, letting loose with loud whistles and yodels.

The crowd greeted President Roosevelt with loud cheers. He wore a short black coat over his suit, with a long watch chain draped across his massive chest. Peering through glass-and-silver spectacles, he spoke first about catching bear in Colorado then about his commitment to preserving our country's irreplaceable natural resources. He spoke about financial panic and warned against extravagance, monopolies, and law-breaking corporations. The crowd stood throughout his speech and burst into loud applause several times.

I felt enlivened. No matter that I wouldn't dine with Roosevelt personally, as I might have done in earlier days. It was enough to be in the crowd before him and hear his noble thoughts.

The Denver mayor approached the President to pin a medal on his left lapel. Silver Dollar sat on the edge of her seat next to me, her papers rolled tightly in her hand.

Finally, the mayor glanced our way. Then, turning to Roosevelt, he said, "In addition to this medal honoring your presentation today, we have another special gift for you."

He motioned Silver up to the stage.

My daughter looked so like Horace with her high cheekbones and dark hair. But her voice was low and tender as she read the words she had written. It was over too quickly, of course, like everything. The president of the Colorado Livestock Association gestured to Roosevelt to follow him off to the side where a black car waited, and Silver was left alone on the stage. She took one last look out at the emptying audience, and I saw a flush of disappointment wash over her face as she realized her moment of glory had passed.

I hurried up to meet her.

"You did beautifully, sweetheart. Like a true actress. As emotive as Miss Bernhardt was years ago!"

Silver looked at me, skeptical.

"One day I'm getting out of here, too," she said. "I won't live my life like a nobody. I'm going to be a famous writer. You'll see, Mama."

That night I dreamt that my own Mama was frying a large platter of beefsteak and President Roosevelt was seated at our table. But the white tablecloth there was soiled and mussed. Still, the President kissed me or I him and as he swung me around I saw that my beloved Tabor was there.

But of course when I awoke, he was not.

A few weeks later, Silver announced that she had taken a job at the *Denver Times*. I helped her find a small apartment she could afford on her salary of twelve dollars a week and moved her few belongings out of the shack in Leadville.

She worked at the *Times* for six months then abruptly quit to write the novel she had always wanted to write. Thinking she could do her writing better elsewhere, she moved to Chicago. Like her sister, Silver wrote me regularly at first:

> *I've rented a room on Wentworth Avenue. A bit shabby but it will do. I bought many ten-cent notebooks. I write every day, far into the night. I found a sweet young woman living in this same boarding house who is a typist. The girl is impressed that I am a writer and has agreed to type my book after her regular office hours.*

When she failed to find a publisher for her book, I paid for *Star of Blood* to be printed. It was a short book, less than a hundred pages, bound in stiff gray paper with red type for the title. I wept when I read its final pages:

> *The heroine of this Bowery romance, Artie Dallas, now lies in an unmarked grave in pauper's field, with only gray rocks to mark her resting place and only weeds to decorate it. No friends visit her lowly grave, but perhaps occasionally a wild bird hovers over the lonely spot, chanting a carol whose plaintive notes ascend into the infinite realms above and invocate, "Be merciful to her, for she knew not what she did."*

Other readers' reactions to the book were less sympathetic. The printer had assumed our Tabor name would help sell copies, but *Star of Blood* disappeared like a stone thrown into a dark pond.

Then, like Lily's had before, Silver's letters abruptly stopped.

CHAPTER 35

Long after Silver had left me, I stood in the open door of the cabin, one hand shielding my eyes from the brilliant sun. I inhaled deeply of the long wished-for scents of spring: the rich, loamy tang of earth, that inimitable perfume of new beginnings.

Beneath my ankle-length white gown, my bare feet shone old-woman white, and my toes had gnarled into their own odd sculptures.

The sounds of morning entered my ears the way a lover's voice might have many years ago: now high, now low, now distant, now near. I caught the ringing trill of rock wrens, the churring of western bluebirds, the unearthly song of a hermit thrust. And high among the Douglas firs and aspens, the high-pitched call of a golden-crowned kinglet.

I stretched my arms above my head, slowly, gratefully. Arthritis had taken hold in both my shoulders and my knees, and sorrow had a permanent residence in my heart but, in that clear promise of a warm spring Sunday, I felt almost as limber, almost as hopeful as a girl of twenty.

I left the door open all day to let fresh air waft through the small room. I was reading the McCourt family Bible mid-afternoon when I looked up to see my neighbor Sue Bonnie standing in the doorway in her familiar red-and-black tartan flannel shirt and dungarees. The shirt's sleeves were rolled to the elbows. Sue carried something in her arms, swaddled in a white tea towel.

At first, I mistook the bundle for a baby. Might Lily have traveled all the way from Chicago, bringing my granddaughter to surprise me?

My mind so often tricked me. I had not seen either Lily or Silver for years.

"You can reminisce all your life after I've gone, Mrs. Tabor, but now it's time for bread and tea," Sue Bonnie called from the open doorway. She was fifteen years younger than me, and her use of Mrs. pleased us both. "I've got a fresh-baked loaf of anadama bread. Look at this beauty," she said and held the offering out in front of her.

Fragrant steam rose as Sue unwound the towel. She put the rich, dense loaf on a wooden cutting board near the sink. It was a lovely dark gold, with three long marks stretching across the top where Sue had vented the dough with a sharp knife.

I put the Bible and thoughts of my long-absent daughters aside and stood to boil a pot of water for tea. Sue rustled through the drawers and cabinets, pulling out two knives and two teaspoons, two cups and two thin saucers decorated with closed red rosebuds, a block of butter, and a Mason jar of blackberry preserves I had put up last August. Our shoulders gently touched in the small kitchen area.

After setting the table as carefully as if she were serving at the finest hotel, Sue set the bread down.

"Nothing's better, nor brings more comfort, than a warm loaf of bread," she said.

I measured a rounded teaspoon of chamomile leaves into each cup then covered the leaves with boiling water.

Sue whispered a short grace, thanking the Lord for all the blessings laid out before us then, smiling broadly, lifted a long serrated knife she'd removed from a block near the stove and cut the first slice.

She offered it to me, but I waited until Sue had cut herself a piece of the bread. We were silent as we spread butter and preserves that were as fresh-tasting as if the blackberries had been picked that morning.

That first wonderful, warm bite of bread, tasting of corn and molasses and comfort, reminded me of Mama's fresh bread, baked weekly in the house on Algoma Street. I took a second bite, chewing slowly.

"Any news from family this week, Mrs. Tabor?" Sue asked the same question every week, and every week my response was the same.

"No, not this week." My fingers trembled slightly on the edge of the saucer.

She reached a hand over to cover mine. "The past must not impress itself on the day. Look where we two fortunate women live now! In the valley of God's splendor!"

I tried to smile.

"Remember when Silver read her poem to the President, Mrs. Tabor? You must have been the proudest mother in Colorado that day."

I could feel my eyelids grow heavy. I knew she came to look after me, an old woman living alone, but her mention of my girls always made me heavy-hearted.

"I envy your life, Mrs. Tabor. Hard as it's been." Sue drank the last of her tea but shook her head no when I stood, partly to rouse myself and partly to offer to boil more hot water.

"See, I never went to school past third grade." I'd heard this tale many times before but didn't want to be rude. Other than Mr. Zaitz in town, and an occasional visit from Tommy, Sue was the only other human being who deigned to speak to me. I'd become the eccentric old woman of Fryer Hill, and people I used to know crossed the street when I made my few trips into town.

So I listened.

Sue scratched her elbow through her flannel shirt. "The things you've told me—those peacocks in the yard and marble statues, the opera houses, Sarah Bernhardt—are from a world different than mine."

I sighed and walked to the door.

"I came here to Leadville with my beau, Fossett Cramer," Sue continued behind me. "We came all the way from New Haven, Connecticut. I was fourteen years old when I got pregnant with Fossett's child. Our parents kicked us both out of our homes, so we decided to head west and see if we could make something of our lives."

The words ran together like the chorus of a lullaby, and when I could stand no longer, I made my way to the rocker where I could sit, close my eyes, and pretend to listen. I knew Sue would wash the few dishes and put them away if I fell asleep in the chair.

Sue shifted her own chair to face me. Each time the story she told was slightly different. Each time I wondered if Sue were repeating the story for my sake or her own, trying to make sense of the senseless.

"I lost my baby on that trip west. No need to tell you the details again." In one version, the baby had died of colic; in another, it fell out of a kayak in raging whitewater.

"But Fossett and I made it to Colorado, and he got work at one of the mines for a while until he got his stupid right leg cut off when an ore wagon let loose and ran down the hill and over him.

"Like I said, I'd only gotten to third grade in school"—once she'd said fourth grade, once fifth. *Does it matter?* I thought. *There are so many versions of our stories*—"so I didn't have much to offer in the way of a job and needed money like you don't know." I lifted my eyelids to see Sue blush, as though she were a child who'd said something foolish in front of the grown-ups.

"So I became a prostitute," she continued matter-of-factly. "I'm proud to say I worked with the best in the business. Poor Fossett said he didn't mind, said he truly appreciated my going out and doing that kind of low work for us and loved me for it no matter what, but I know it broke his heart. He died a year after I started."

She suddenly slapped her hand on the table, and I bolted upright in the rocker. "Don't rightly know which one of us had it worse, do you? Or better?" She laughed heartily and started to move the saucers and cups to the sink. "Ain't nothin' you can do about any of it now, though. Right, Mrs. Tabor?"

Closing my eyes again, I whispered that yes, she was right, the past was past and should not impinge on the present moment, though it often did.

I then slept for what seemed only a moment, but when I woke Sue was gone.

I stood up to go to the door again, half-expecting to see Lily and Silver burst through, drop their bookbags on the table, and kiss me, before running out to ride burros at Jim Stackhau's until dinnertime.

CHAPTER 36

March 1935
Leadville, Colorado

This L-shaped cabin has been my home for nearly 35 years now. Its walls are close. I see the two calendars from Zaitz's on the far wall. There's a small square table with one leg shorter than the others. Two white wooden chairs and a rocker. My dome-topped trunk stands sentinel at the foot of the bed, and a pine dovetailed blanket box sits lonely in the corner. More trunks pile against the eastern wall. I've taped newspapers on the wall near a cloudy mirror:

Unemployment Still 20.1%
Nuremberg Laws Passed
New Board Game Monopoly Released

Their headlines freeze time like losses freeze a heart.

It is only now, when I am an old woman, that I understand how every loss has been a preparation for the next. I didn't lose my family that long-ago day at the Ice Carnival, but I lost each of my beloveds in the years that followed—years that have hurtled by as rapidly as that toboggan ran down its chute, aiming steadily toward a final stop against a rigid wall of snow.

Today, I am surrounded by snow and feeling weak. Doc Symonds warns I've developed chronic mountain sickness after living in Leadville for so long. Sometimes I feel the next breath may not come. My ears ring and dizziness floods my head. And my calloused old feet are so numb, rubbing them is like touching a corpse.

It's been two days since I walked up Fryer Hill at the start of this storm with my few groceries. And there is still no sign of the boy from Zaitz's grocery or even of Sue Bonnie. I'm rationing my food carefully, hoping that somehow, someone will find a way through the snow that has continued to fall.

I slept poorly last night and woke with a cramp in my leg. I rub liniment oil on it, then move a chair over by the dome-topped trunk. This is the trunk Mama helped me pack when I followed Harvey and William to Colorado. I often see Mama's spirit here with me in the cabin, and I remember how it felt when she held me as a child and remember her breath against my cheek, the horse-mint scent of it; her silver crucifix swinging above me. Christ's eyes open and arms extended wide. The cloud of soap and lilac powder that rose from her breasts. I lift the lid of the trunk, remove its upper tray, and set it beside me on the floor. The tray is filled with scores of papers on which I've written down my dreams and visions—on advertisements, Western Union telegram forms. Below it are some of my most precious possessions: a Belgian lace baby cap that belonged to Silver, Horace's porcelain shaving mug, a faded copy of Harper's Magazine, *with my Lily on its cover.*

Suddenly restless, I stand to check the logs in the wood stove. I open the door with its curlicue letters: Chief National Excelsior Stove & Manufacturing Company, Quincy, Illinois. After banking the fire, I set the iron kettle on the burner.

Whenever will that boy get here with groceries? I've seen how he and his friends point when I walk through town to get food or coal, or when I walk into a hotel to warm my feet and write letters. The boys point at the newsprint in my boots, the burlap wrapped around my feet. From under the hood of the bonnet that shades my face, I see them. I hear their childish giggles.

But I pray he will come soon.

I am running out of firewood. There is some in a lean-to ten yards from the cabin, but its door is blocked by man-high drifts of snow.

Once the boy comes, I will give him two letters I wrote last night to mail to my daughters. One to Lily in Wisconsin and one to Silver Dollar, my Honeymaid, in Chicago.

I've had many visions of my girls and others, enough experiences of the mysterious to make me believe. As a child, I believed the promises of my parish priest that Jesus and angels stood always at my side. Since that start in the garden of childhood, I made my way, sometimes strong in faith and sometimes dark in doubt. I've read so much about spirituality, metaphysics, and New Thought, a new movement pioneered by New Englander Ralph Waldo Emerson.

Of course, poor Mama would weep to hear me speak such sacrilege.

Writings like Emerson's threaten the strict, priest-led, and ritual-bound Catholicism in which she raised me.

But I believe, even if the metaphysical world is one I cannot always see behind the bed, the table, rocker, wood stove and stacked trunks, the solid things that fill this room. It is a world Mr. Zaitz's son and the folks who frequent his store don't readily acknowledge, as far as I can tell. But, to me, it has become the underpinning of all.

Everything I see now is an embodiment of God. Sometimes the very word makes me uncomfortable. But those astounding mountains that rise outside my windows, their peaks frosted in snow, their valleys such ready, welcoming nests for clouds—these are truly God made into form.

When the windows finally turn black with night, I stand to remove my clothes. The khaki shirt and men's work pants, similar except in size to what I wore when I first worked at the Fourth of July, drop to the floor. I retrieve them then hang them carefully on a hook to the right of my bed.

I pull red flannel pajamas over my head. Their fabric has worn thin, and the buttons are discolored and cracked. I brush my teeth at a small basin next to the stove, using a mixture of honey and pulverized charcoal.

Then I climb into my bed, with its iron headpiece in the shape of an egg.

Once under the gray blanket, I move anxiously and brush my arms and legs against the coarse sheet as if it were a human hand.

A fierce wind blows outside. I had thought Sue Bonnie would have climbed the hill on snow shoes to check on me, but she has not, and as I lie in bed I wonder if it is because of the falling-out we had about my Silver on her last visit.

My heart was broken about Silver and the low crowd she was with in Chicago and all so terrible & I was walking passed the church on Poplar and 7th Streets & after I had knelt down on the sidewalk in front of the church this lovely bright thing blew down from the air above me & landed close to the church touching the church on my left I picked it up & it looked so bright to me in my worried condition I hope it means that all this will change & things will be bright for me and that Silver will recover from Edd Browns hypnotism he has cast over her God help her.

Someone, I'm not sure if it was Sue Bonnie or someone else, once sent me a newspaper article that said my sweet Silver had died. Scalded to death in a bathtub in a seedy boarding house in Chicago. I know this is not true; my Honeymaid is safe in a convent there; I could not have it otherwise.

There are so many things one can believe.

I remember saying morning and bedtime prayers as a child, kneeling without pain on floorboards white as a hound's tooth, in the house on Algoma Street. Praying the Angelus those hard early days in Dogwood and Central City until Harvey shamed it out of me. Bowing before a picture of the Sacred Heart the last hours of my beloved Horace Tabor's life.

I still believe Horace's promise that there was a fortune to be made here at the mine. It's where I most clearly felt the deep, rich magic that runs through Earth's veins, where I most craved the work of digging down.

Come spring, we will shore up the No. 6 shaft and pump the water out of the lower levels before the tunnels flood with any thaw.

I saw in a vision myself down the No. 6 shaft in a drift—244 level—and I saw the most wonderful strike of rich lead ore and another strike close together of zinc.

I know that Mama would at least be pleased that, living alone, I have all the time in the world for prayer and contemplation. I have even begun to pray to a saint the Church has just recently canonized: Rita of Cascia, the patron saint of mourning women.

Blessed Saint Rita
Wonderful St Rita
God Jesus made us a Loan on the Matchless Mine in
Leadville all its great wealth will be used for charity and for
the glory of our Savior.
Mrs. H. A. W. Tabor

Like Saint Rita, I have been married, been a mother. I have lost my husband, lost my children. I have been rejected by the Church that was once my childhood sanctuary.

But also like Rita, I persevered, and at long last dedicated my life to God. There was not much I could do, a woman alone, a woman grieving, but I gave my life, my spirit, my dreams to God.

O there never was such a divinely beautiful bird but we all knew it was St. Rita's Bee. We were so sad for fear we had lost it but it would not stay but a few minutes from Silver. It always came right back to Silver and went first on the screen of the door which opened on a vine-covered porch and then the Bee went on outside of the window and Silver and Mother brought it in and I held its beautiful head by the back of its neck. Silver put the lovely Bee in the cage and the sticks for it to perch on were not round so I said we will get round sticks for the cage at once and she and me all were so happy and happy because St. Rita's Bee would not leave Silver and Mother and me. Wonderful beauty – can not be described and it was all airy and graceful and Heavenly, Heavenly.

I must rewrite this on best paper for children.

No longer my baby Lily nor Silver Dollar, my Honeymaid. No longer our sweet little girls who climbed into bed with their Mama and Papa and flung their laughter, sweeter than the ring of all the coins in the world, through the rooms of a house, through the rooms of my heart.

I dream today of being in a house. On a big sofa sit Lily and Silver. Lily was about 7 years old and Silver about 2 years old or less. She was sitting close to the right-hand arm of the sofa and Lily was close to her. Silver wanted Lily, who was caring for her and loving her, to put some pink silk ravellings around her neck for a chain. Lily held the ravelling in her finger, she would not put them on Silver's neck for fear it would hurt Silver. I said that is right, don't, then went out in the hall and sat down on the floor and cried because Silver was not as she used to be before she left the cabin.

In my above dream of Lily and Silver it seems so lovely to see Lily with Silver for when she was about 7 years old she would be with Silver every minute and Lily would always say "Silver is my baby. God sent her to me. She is my baby, she is my live doll." And she would hold her and hug her tight, oh how they loved each other so.

In the afternoon of the fifth day of the storm, I hear two knocks come, loud and plain.

I stand, slide back the heavy lock. Snow piles high outside. The lean-to tips dangerously from the weight of snow on its roof. White swirls before my eyes, as though I live in a snow globe that has just been shaken.

No one stands before me in the doorway.

I close my eyes, ask myself if I really did hear a knock, and know, Yes, yes, I did, and then I open my eyes, or maybe I don't, and I see Mr. Pearsall at my door, the butcher from Oshkosh, carrying that big slab of raw beef away from his burning shop. The beef is marbled red and white, and it drips blood.

"He says it belongs to us, Mama," I say out loud, frightened.

The blustery wind lashes my face. Snowflakes stick to my cheeks and eyelashes as though they will mask me in white.

Eyes close; eyes open.

No one is there.

Under my unmade bed are half a dozen boxes filled with papers. More dreams I have written down in my own hand. I bend on my knees in front of these pages, oblivious now to pain. I grab one box and carry it to the table.

There is something important here I must save. Something important I must tell.

But I am tired, and my head falls down on top of the box.

I dream.

"What if you don't come for me?" I ask out loud when I awaken.

What if the connection I have longed for so deeply, for so long, is never realized?

The wood stove sighs; ashes settle. Wind forces its way in through holes in the chinking, tears in the roof.

"Mama, I'm cold."

I've lost track of time but the steel-colored sky says twilight. I push the box of dreams away from me and stand, dizzy.

My tongue is thick and dry as sandpaper; it sticks to the roof of my mouth. I've already eaten most of what food I had: only one egg remains and a single slice of salt beef.

I blink, take a step forward, and look around to get my bearings. The day has flown by without leaving traces of its passing, except... that vision of Mr. Pearsall, the butcher, at my door, holding raw beef.

An empty cup still sits on the table, that brown crack rippling down its side.

The dizziness increases, and I close my eyes and swiftly drop to the floor. My muscles are weak, and, despite the day's sleep, I remain weary. I kneel for several minutes catching my breath, waiting for my body to feel solid again. When the worst of the lightheaded-ness has passed, I crawl to the bed and use its thin mattress to help me stand again.

I swallow and take deep breaths. Then I walk slowly and carefully toward the stove and lean against it for support as I bend to stir the ashes inside. Through the window I see only gray; snow and sky bleed together. The mountain ranges I know are there are completely hidden from sight, as are the trees that thickly speckle them.

I walk to the table to get the cracked cup, bring it back to the stove, and fill it with more sage leaves and what may be the last of my hot water. I bow my head to bathe in its small circle of steam. I've seen sage dance in the wind, know how it smells different in the spring and different at sundown. The smell of it now is sweet and reminds me I am home. Its wrinkled gray-green leaves will soothe me.

After a number of losses, one grows to expect them. Then it is not as though they lose their power but more as though they become part of the fabric of the day, of the hour, of the minute. Life seems made of loss and the will to move through it. I don't know how I would have survived if I had not believed in something—in God, in Jesus, in something other than this imperfect world.

If I had not turned to Mystery.

I look at the calendars hanging on the wall. I think it is Tuesday, but the days and hours blend together now as though time has lost its markings. Even the clock on the shelf above the stove has stopped.

That night at the villa in Denver, Sarah Bernhardt introduced me to the writings of Swami Vivekananda. The Swami said, "Time and space are in you; you are not in time and space." I understand now what he meant.

She was so different than I expected her to be. Small like me. Sad like me. Strong like me. I read of her death in 1923 and before that, of the amputation of her right leg. She'd been performing in South America and hurt her knee jumping off a balcony. Gangrene set in. She wrote me a thank-you note after the party, postmarked from New York City. She encouraged me to keep reading for spiritual knowledge, even though she gruffly claimed she had found no God to satisfy her but acting. She wrote, "No matter what, bet against all odds."

I read that a priest took her confession on her death bed.

I breathe in deeply, exhale. It is there, in that fraction of time between the breaths, that the illusions of time and loss disappear.

I would like to always rest inside that space.

CHAPTER 37

I wake hours later in my bed, not knowing how I got there or how long I've slept, remembering the snow fritters we made when I was a child in Oshkosh. Mama would let us bring bowlfuls of snow into the kitchen, where she had already mixed salt, milk, and flour into a thick batter. Each child could add a cup of clean, new-fallen snow to the batter. Fat already sizzled in the black iron skillet, and Mama would drop the batter in with a spoon. We'd eat the fritters with sugar and lemon juice.

I roll onto my side, having no desire to get out of bed. Stuck to the wall beside my head is a list of remedies for arthritis: pokeberry wine, black cohosh tea, borage oil. I remember how Papa suffered from arthritis, how Mama wrapped his knees in red flannel and gave him tea.

Finally I force myself to stand, open the door, and bring in another large cup of snow. I find an old rag, dip it in the snow, fold it, and place it on my right shoulder.

I am more afraid than I have ever been in my life.

"This is my body. This is my blood," Jesus said.

How long can a body last without food and only snow water to drink? How long can a person last without faith?

Outside, the wind wails.

I feel on the table for the last matchbook. Its cover is yellow and black. I tear off a match and use it to light the nub of beeswax candle that remains then move slowly, stiffly, toward the Excelsior stove. Inside, the last log has burned to ashes.

I will need to get back into bed, stay under the covers for warmth.

I turn and stare at the bed where I've spent I don't know how many hours these past days. I want so much to see my Horace waiting there for me, his arms outstretched.

If I look long enough, imagine his presence clearly enough, will he come back to me? Will they all hold me again in their warm arms? My daughters, my husband, my parents?

I had just got in bed for the night—I could not sleep, in a moment I knew our Tabor was close to me on my right, my husband Mr. H.A.W. Tabor who died on April 10-1899— he had his arms around my shoulders, his left arm around my shoulder in the back and his right arm across the front of my shoulders holding me tight his face was close to my face and his mustache long and beautiful as it was moved over my face. I could feel its hairs on my face and his breath only his same warm sweet breath with that same odor that only his breath had pleasing and sweet no one had that same breath, and his mustache on my face he held his arms around my shoulders the same way all the time, his presence showed health strength youth and a purified condition and state, he was so well and clear and his actions showed how loved and appreciated our love for him and the life and way I had lived and protected his name since he went home to live with Jesus Christ his Saviour. Still holding me around the shoulders his face close to mine his mustache always moved over my face and his breathing on my face, I knew God had sent our Tabor to me. So I spoke out very loud, thus—

In the name of Jesus is this Tabor?

In the name of Jesus is this Tabor?

In the name of Jesus Christ Who was Crucified and Died on the Cross for us—is this Tabor?...then I was certain it was Tabor—then I asked Tabor in a loud voice thus—Will our child Silver soon come back to me? Quickly Tabor in a strong clear voice—"Yes"—then in a moment he said "Keep awake" in his own natural firm kind voice—he still held his arms around my shoulders and breathed on my face his mustache moving on my face,—Where my Spine meets my head a strong current made my head bend down on my neck on my right where Tabor stood holding me and my neck in the back pained and then Tabor our Tabor went to God… I got out of bed at once—and my legs from my knees down seemed weak as if I must cross them to walk—this feeling was gone soon. Our Tabor only spoke twice as I have written above.

The gray blankets, the sheets—surely they move now as Horace turns to face me?

I walk over and press both palms to the blankets and the pillow again and again, but there is nothing to be seen or felt there, not in any tangible way.

When the mortician finally came that day in Denver, he had to pry me from Horace's side.

Hold on to the Matchless, my Sweet Lizzie, Horace said. Or perhaps it was the wind stroking the leaves outside or blowing through the hollow in my heart.

I see nothing in the empty, friendless bed. The blessing of a vision of his body beneath the blanket is gone. He is not under the eye-tricking heaps of pillows, sheets, and blankets. Or he is. Or he is not.

I crawl under the blankets, curl into a fetal shape for warmth.

I drift in and out of sleep. In a dream, the grocery boy delivers cartons and cartons of food: yellow boxes of Bisquick, fresh milk, fresh eggs, butter in pale yellow blocks, delicacies I don't remember ordering—a meringue with whipped cream and fruit, peach melba, Mars Bars candy. Blueberries, grapefruits, and tangerines. Colored squash and peppers, whole chickens, and turkeys.

Sleeping and waking, I dream of food.

I dream and dream and dream, though the line between waking and sleeping, dream and vision, has blurred.

I dreamed Mama Silver & I think Lily & Cordelia and some more were standing talking to me their backs were to the opening of our house & I was facing the opening & I was looking out on a very light wide path leading from our house. It had light colored & lacy looking trees on either side of this path, I said O look look see some one coming &

218 THE SILVER BARON'S WIFE

they turned & we saw Our dear Savior Jesus clad in a light
robe of pale lavender walking up the path towards us all
and something around the top of his head as the crown of
thorns were but I could not see what it was His arms were
extended full length over His beautiful Head His arms &
hands straight up high pointing to Heaven & we all looked
at Him coming & I thought it meant some one was going
to die O it was the most beautiful I ever saw He was slight
and very tall.

I get out of bed again, walk to the calendar hanging on its wooden screw: March 7, 1935.

I remember that earlier I woke and turned in bed to see Silver's tiny fingers and sweet brown hair mussed under the covers. Such comfort I felt knowing her body lay next to mine.

I see what I think is Mama sitting on top of a chest; I look again—it is only a stack of newspapers.

But things begin to move in the flickering candlelight: the crack on my teacup becomes a snake ready to slither off the enamel and onto the red laminate top of the table. The hawk on the lock of my trunk is poised for flight; its feathers quiver.

These things move, right in front of me. The world is animated in a new way: everything moves easily, as though vibrating in a clear soup in which I also swim.

Every place I look, the things that are in this room are alive. From the corner of my eye, I see the pillow on my bed. Its shape has a profile. It talks with a sheet in a conversation I cannot hear.

I do hear something, though. It is as though there is music playing in my right ear. Musical ear syndrome, Doc Symonds said; it can come with age. This music changes tone and mood often, like a radio. Now almost everyone has a radio in their home, with programs running 24 hours a day. It is thanks to that genius Nicholas Tesla, who says he has invented an electrical generator that will not need fuel, harnessed by cosmic rays.

What other unimaginable magic will the future bring? What magic can it bring that I and others have not already glimpsed?

Sometimes I catch a sliver of popular song: "Blue Moon" or "She's a Lady from Manhattan," but the words before and after these are hidden. I know there are voices singing just below my hearing, a radio with its inexplicable waves that we cannot see with the naked eye. But they are there.

Doc Symonds said they would heal, these oddities of sight and sound. But more and more, things take on new perspectives. There are dark flashes like small worms inside my eyes.

Last night I dreamt of silver. A vast expanse of the ore domed the sky over Leadville, clouds hung transparent against it. To dream of silver represents the ability to reflect God's light, Sue Bonnie once told me.

I lie down on the floor, too tired to make it to the bed.

There is no doubt that Fryer Hill is completely impassable now.

I smell the sweet horse-mint scent of my Mama's breath, the lilac powder dusted between her breasts. In my pocket, the silver nugget, which I roll between my fingers before crossing my hands over my heart, making certain the cross rests solidly beneath my fingers, as I lie waiting, remembering, waiting.

I dreamt of something I wanted to find. I tried and tried and failed or, perhaps, what I searched for was never missing.

I breathe in all that I have lived: all sights, sounds, touches, tastes.

I breathe out love for everyone I have ever known and even for those mysteries I longed to understand but could not.

I am ready to return below the earth. I am neither wife nor mother. Not daughter, not friend. I am neither wealthy nor poor, young nor old, sated nor starving.

I picture my pickaxe first breaking through the surface of the dirt wall at the Fourth of July. I have done the work I had to do.

This flesh, these bones will be dirt, and I will become one with the earth, one with the veins of rich ore running through this murky world.

What I sought, I am.

Slipping down, slipping deep, I weave and reweave my story, returning to its perfect source.

DONNA BAIER STEIN is the author of *Sympathetic People* (Iowa Fiction Award Finalist and 2015 IndieBook Awards Finalist) and *Sometimes You Sense the Difference* (Finishing Line Press Poetry Chapbook). Her work has appeared in *Virginia Quarterly Review, Prairie Schooner, Puerto del Sol, New York Quarterly, Writer's Digest*, and elsewhere. She was a founding Poetry Editor at *Bellevue Literary Review* and now publishes *Tiferet Journal*. She has received prizes from the Allen Ginsberg Awards, a Bread Loaf Scholarship, a PEN/New England Discovery Award, a Johns Hopkins Writing Seminars Fellowship, a grant from the New Jersey Council for the Arts, three Pushcart nominations and more. www.donnabaierstein.com.

ACKNOWLEDGEMENTS

I first learned about Baby Doe Tabor on a family vacation to Colorado when I was seven years old. Even to my young eyes, her story included fascinating contradictions: family and solitude, poverty and wealth, materialism and spirituality. What most interested me were the thousands of scraps of paper on which she had written down her dreams.

As I researched her story and tried to portray my version of this complex woman, many people came forward to help.

I owe thanks first and foremost, to my publishers Walter Cummins and Thomas E. Kennedy of Serving House Books and to Elizabeth Berg, whose patience and support have been unwavering.

Sincere thanks also to my Two Bridges Writing Group and the Third Floor Group, to Ronna Wineberg, Jude Rittenhouse, Diane Bonavist, Lance Mushung, Liz Rosenberg, Lynn Biederstadt, Jane Cavolina, Michelle Cameron, Stephanie Cowell, Beverly Swerdling, Hilma Wolitzer, Barbara Shapiro, Jan Brogan, Floyd Kemske, Jessica Treadway, Jill McCorkle, and Elizabeth Cox who nominated an earlier version of this book for a PEN/New England Discovery Award.

I am grateful to Judy Nolte Temple, author of *Baby Doe Tabor: The Madwoman in the Cabin*, a superb nonfiction book about Baby Doe Tabor and to the Denver Public Library for access to their historic records and images, especially Ms. Coi E. Drummond-Gehrig, Digital Image Collection Administrator and Melissa Van Otterloo, Photo Research & Permissions Librarian at the Stephen H. Hart Library & Research Center of the History Colorado Center in Denver. And to Allen Mohr for his patient and excellent work on the cover design.

Friends and family know how long Baby Doe Tabor's story has obsessed me. I thank my fantastic, wonderful children, Jon and Sarah, for their continuous love and support. And I thank my incredible parents, Dorothy and Martin Baier, for those early family vacations to Colorado and for the love they so generously and consistently have shared.

AFTERWORD

The Silver Baron's Wife is a work of fiction based on the life of Elizabeth McCourt Doe Tabor, known to many as Baby Doe Tabor. While key milestones in this novel are true to historical records, I have taken great liberty in imagining scenes, conversations, and thoughts.

I found the following books helpful in my initial research: *The Legend of Baby Doe* by John Burke; *Baby Doe Tabor: The Madwoman in the Cabin* by Judy Nolte Temple; *Silver Dollar: The Story of the Tabors* by David Karsner; *Leadville: Colorado's Magic City* by Edward Blair; *Leadville: A Miner's Epic* by Stephen M. Voynick; *So Much to Be Done: Women Settlers on the Mining and Ranching Frontier* edited by Ruth B. Moynihan, Stuart Armitage, and Christiane Fischer Dichamp; *Bordellos of Blair Street* by Allan G. Bird; *Keeping Hearth and Home in Old Colorado* compiled and edited by Carol Padgett, Ph.D.; *Tales of Early Leadville* by Rene Coquoz; *Tabor's Matchless Mine and Lusty Leadville, Augusta Tabor: Her Side of the Scandal*, and *Silver Queen: The Fabulous Story of Baby Doe Tabor* by Caroline Bancroft; *A Century of Medicine in Leadville, Colorado 1860-1966*; *The Leadville Story* by Rene L. Coquoz; *Horace Tabor: His Life and Legend* by Duane A. Smith; *Silver Dollar Tabor: The Leaf in the Storm* by Evelyn E. Livingston Furman; *Mining, Mayhem and other Carbonate Excitements* by Roger Pretti; and *The Ballad of Baby Doe*, an American opera by Douglas Moore.

I am also grateful for email correspondence and videos from David Wright of the Golden Burro Cafe & Lounge and Historical Colorado Video Productions of Leadville, and additional correspondence with Judge Neil Reynolds who explained to me that contrary to what is most commonly understood, Baby Doe did not freeze or starve to death. Her death certificate lists "Acute Myocarditis."

I have taken some liberty with the historical writings about Baby Doe Tabor, but hope I have added to our understanding of her as more than a scandalous mistress and more than a wealthy wife.

CPSIA information can be obtained
at www.ICGtesting.com
Printed in the USA
LVOW08s1504100117

520452LV00006B/1114/P

9 780997 101065